*in*

*Vanilla Ice Cream*

# Chopped Green Chillies

## in

# Vanilla Ice Cream

SAM MUKHERJEE

Rupa & Co

Published 2011 by
**Rupa Publications India Pvt. Ltd.**
7/16, Ansari Road, Daryaganj,
New Delhi 110 002

*Sales Centres:*

Allahabad Bengaluru Chennai
Hyderabad Jaipur Kathmandu
Kolkata Mumbai

Typeset in
Sunshine Graphics
Delhi-110 032

Printed in India by
Nutech Photolithographers
B-240, Okhla Industrial Area, Phase-I,
New Delhi 110 020

Dear Geeta, Dear Jay
&
Dearest Kyle David —
 Enjoy my musings!
 (Uncle) Lots of love,
  Sam
  May 29,
   2011

*To my wife, Savita*
*for inspiring me to fly*

# Contents

# Acknowledgements

*Chopped Green Chillies in Vanilla Ice Cream* was written at the behest of my most loved and trusted sounding board, my wife, Savita. Thank you for inspiring me to fly.

The novel found its distinguished home soon after the birth of our son, Rohin. So thanks, dude, you brought me luck!

*For their selfless love I shall forever cherish:*
Souresh Basu, Sudip Majumder, Baishali Dutt, Kalisankar Adhikari and Arvind Singhal. You provide the opening salvo for any venture I undertake.

*For their priceless affection I am indebted to:*
Supro Mukherjea and Lenie Scoffie, Lila and Arun Mehta, Arati Banerjee, Prasanta and Sushanta Banerjee, Lina Guha Roy, Pete and Sophia Bhattacharya, Mita and Chandra Sekhar Sircar, Emily Paul, Eric Chen and Jin Tang, Joydeep Kumar Roy, Ananda Shankar Ghose, Suddhasatta Basu, Roopa and Steve Schonwetter, Siddhartha Ghosh, Susmita Sen Roy, Uttam Chakrabarti, Anjana Banerjee, Surajit and Sumana Mukherjee, Ranajit Mukherjee, Biswajit Mukherjee, Bhaskar Ghosh, Pradip and Conchita Sarbadhikari, Indranil Ghosh, Srinjoy Sen, Sushobhan Mukherjee. And Ramesh Ramachandran, Sibaprasad Mukherjee, Ravi Kalra and their beautiful families.

*For their incorrigible bias I am ever grateful to:*

My doting mother-in-law, Kailash Singhal, Harish Chandra Gupta, Mohan Kapila, Malti Kapila, Subhankar Mukhopadhyay, Victor Kalyan Ghoshe, Suman Guha,  Pronoto Seal, Shruti Singhal, Saibal Mitra.


*For their infectious enthusiasm  in my work I thank:*

Suresh Jaura of Globalom Media, Shalini and Anu Rastogi, Ait, Sushma and Santosh Rungta, Vinod Agarwal, Darrell Pinto, Reshmi Das, Colli Christante, Dean Burns, Stephen Clarke, Ray Mooney, Lyn Shiells, John Mortimore, Max Robinson.

Special thanks to Eleanor Jackson, Literary Agent at Markson Thoma in New York whose words of encouragement made all the difference.

A very special note of thanks to my Editor, Himani Pande and the rest of the team at Rupa for their blessed eyes.

In the company of my friends from Gariahat Road, I never knew a dull day growing up. I feel lucky to have shared so many exciting moments of my life with you.

And above all, I thank my parents, Milly and Sunit Kumar Mukherjee for their unconditional love and blessings.

# CHAPTER ONE

# Lottery

$W$hen Tanmoy and Chitrani Bose rented a modest flat on Raja Basanta Roy Road in South Kolkata a week after their wedding, they thought of it as temporary housing. Little did they know that this would be their home for nearly two decades.

Raja Basanta Roy Road was a middle-class neighbourhood in the Lake Market area. Large trees formed a natural canopy in the scorching summer heat. Stray dogs and exhausted rickshaw pullers indulged in afternoon siestas comfortably under the shade of their leafy branches. There were two tube wells that drew fresh, cold water from the bowels of the earth to quench the thirst of the weary. An old cobbler sat on a small stool on the footpath surrounded by a small heap of cheap shoes. He hammered away all day long to feed his large family in a nearby village. A tailor occupying a makeshift nook served the entire neighbourhood for all chores, big and small. The street had an eclectic mix of houses. Some reflected the fading lights of the old aristocracy, while others had slipped into utter disrepair. Several humble new entrants vied for their rightful place in their midst. The Bose's flat was a part of the three-storeyed structure that resembled a ghost house in a horror movie. Its exterior had not seen paint in recent times and inside, it was equally baseborn.

I knew no other home for my parents brought me here from the Ramakrishna Mission Seva Pratisthan hospital, where I was born. We inhabited the second floor of the dilapidated structure. There were three large rooms and their walls were last whitewashed for my homecoming. The living room had floor seating for we could not afford a dining table with matching chairs. Baba always sat on an old cane easy chair that belonged to his grandfather. There was a second-hand sofa with pale orange upholstery and two chairs that did not match in size, colour or design. But they came in handy when more people were entertained. A shocking pink washbasin placed in one corner constantly glared at us. We did not mind the intrusion, for the washbasin of the toilet was fractured since the beginning of time. If the plastic tap was turned on by a momentary lapse of memory, the rivulet would not take long to transform the toilet into a reluctant reservoir. A new one would be too expensive. The toilet had a malfunctioning flush. The Indian-style commode, with cold cement footrests and a hole at the centre, had to be cleansed using a bucket of water, after every use. Each of the two bedrooms had beds with rock-hard mattresses and body pillows at the centre of the bed. The heavy steel almirahs in each bedroom that housed all our precious junk were often locked but their keys generally hung from their keyholes.

My father, Tanmoy Bose, was a clerk with the government of West Bengal. That was his first and only job. Honesty was his chief ornament because of which he had not progressed financially. It did not bother him, for our humble ends were met without much difficulty. My mother, Chitrani, was a housewife. She had completed high school and just entered college when her parents struck her matrimonial alliance with the modest but respectable

Bose family. At their introduction, Tanmoy Bose had expected to meet a demure Bengali lady but found a bubbly, spirited young woman in Chitrani. He made the smartest move of his life. He blurted out the life-altering 'Y' word in a trance even before he finished his cup of tea heavily laced with buffalo milk and sugar. Chitrani found his eagerness quite amusing but approved of his quiet, earnest demeanor. She could not play coy and when relatives stared at her for a reaction, she simply said 'Yes' and made my father the happiest man in the world.

Tanmoy and Chitrani Bose liked each other the first time they met. But they fell in love without much delay. My brother Mukul was born fifteen months after the nuptials and I joined the family three years later. Baba conferred my brother's name but when it was my turn, Ma insisted on a portmanteau word that would indicate without any doubt that Chitrani and Tanmoy fused to give birth to their little boy, Chinmoy.

Baba affectionately called my mother 'Rani' and she lived up to her royal moniker around the house. Although she was far from it in riches, she revelled in the attention generously bestowed upon her by her doting husband. In turn, she had a term of endearment for him: Tanmoybabu. It was not usual for housewives of her generation to bring their husbands' names to their lips. If they were absent from the room, they called out to their husbands with the aid of standard phrases acquired from their mothers, 'Are you there?' 'Can you hear me?' or other worthy equivalents. If the husbands were visible, their attention could be attracted by a simple, 'Listen,' or simply by starting the conversation. Without fail, men knew that they were being spoken to and would respond accordingly.

Ma believed in saving for the future and managed to save out of my father's paltry monthly salary to buy a house for us someday. She was convinced that my arrival was a harbinger of prosperity. An astrologer had planted the idea in her head when my father's horoscope was matched with hers to invoke celestial blessings for their matrimonial alliance. A confident prediction made in a dingy, ill-lit room by an astrologer who claimed to see the future of a life that was yet to be conceived gave me a special position in the Bose household even before I arrived. Baba nursed no such belief but meekly accepted Ma's conviction to appease her. Mukul believed that I would be more loved by our parents and was indifferent about me from the start. It must have been hard for him to be enthusiastic about my presence.

I loved Raja Basanta Roy Road and attended a local school. Tuition fees were reasonable and Baba appreciated the lack of interest on the part of the school administrators to insist on their students dressing in expensive shoes and uniform. All my friends were from the neighbourhood and lived within 300 metres of our beautiful ghost house. I could walk into any of our neighbour's homes and watch local football on their black and white TVs, usually covered by a hideous blue anti-glare screen. I was borderline overweight but my agility in sports fended taunts for the physical imperfection. I did not wear glasses and no one could call me names for that. Although I attended a Vernacular school, my English language scores were respectable. I believed that I would remain in my beautiful Raja Basanta Roy Road forever and ever. All my friends would never leave the neighbourhood. We would play and have fun for the rest of our lives.

Things were going according to plan until one day Baba made an unusual discovery that changed our lives. It was a cold Saturday morning in December. My final Grade VIII exams were over. School was closed for winter vacation and I was making the most of it. I played cricket during the day, football in the afternoon and badminton formed the evening staple. What more could Oliver ask for?

I had stepped out to play a game of cricket that morning. The venue was Vivekananda Park, which doubled as a popular haunt for young sportsmen during the day and amorous lovers when the sun went down. The field was moist and slippery from the accumulated dew. The pungent yet sweet smell of the earth could wake up the laziest boy who had been dragged to the field by over zealous cricketer friends.

The game had gone exceptionally well for us. We had won against our archrival, Dover Road. It was a high adrenaline match won by a razor thin margin of three runs. I ran into the house ready to recount the events of the morning to my parents. After all, my exploits at the match had been many. But as I stepped in, an eerie calm gripped me.

Baba was sitting with *Aajker Khabar*, a respected Bengali language daily in his hand, a filterless Charminar cigarette dangling from his tar-darkened lips. A massive frown had created such deep crevasses on his forehead that one could actually dive into them. Ma, the queen of garrulity looked as if she had been anaesthetised. Mukul was sitting with his back so straight that I thought he was in meditation. What had happened in my absence? Whatever it was, it must have been horrible. The Bose household had slumped into a strange calm. I could bear no more. 'Ma?'

'Shh,' came her response.

Most unusual. Ma would be the first one to blurt out the facts, be they calamitous or rapturous.

'Mukul?' I tried to tap the yogi. Mukul glared at me as if I had disrupted a solemn funeral meeting. No luck. What choice did I have? It had to be Baba. 'Baba?' Baba did not hear me, or so I thought, for he did not budge. What was going on? A relative must have died. Who? It had to be a grandparent. Which one? They were all old. Should I guess? What if I guessed the wrong one? That would be worse. I mustered some courage and spoke loud and clear this time, 'Baba? Can you hear me?'

'You are only two feet away from me, Chinmoy,' Baba stated the obvious.

Thank God. At least he was responding. 'Why is everyone so quiet?'

'You are talking. We are quiet.'

That was rude and uncharacteristic. He was obviously under unusual stress. I let it pass. 'Everyone is behaving strangely,' I pointed out my observation.

'You're right,' Baba agreed.

Thanks. That was very helpful. I looked at Ma. She began to cooperate, 'Something has happened, Chinmoy.'

'I can see that, Ma. What is it?'

Ma coughed a couple of times. Then in a voice trembling with apprehension she said, 'We think Baba may have won a lottery.'

'That's great news,' I was instantly relieved, 'So why does everyone look as if something bad has happened?'

'He may not have won it. What could be more terrible?' the ever cynical Mukul replied.

'What do you mean?' I countered.

Baba shifted in his seat and looked directly at me, 'Come here. Let me show you something.'

Great! There was some real progress after all. I walked across to his easy chair, semi- broken and so dangerously low that a stranger walking in could mistake it for peculiar ethnic floor seating. I was certain it would not survive the few more days left in the year.

Baba opened the newspaper wide so that I could have a better look. He whisked out a Griha Laxmi lottery ticket from the oversized, ink-stained chest pocket of his unimpressive half sleeved shirt. The once crumpled ticket now displayed signs of new respect. Careful hands had ironed out the creases. It contained several numbers at the bottom. 'Match the numbers,' Baba ordered and pointed to a spot in the newspaper with his nicotine stained index finger.

I got down to work. 'A61-A61, X05-X05.' Good. 'P09-P09, R25-R25.' So far so good. 'V12-V12.' Everything looked all right to me. 'T81-T81.' Wow! 'This is a perfect match!'

'I think so, too.' Ma interjected.

'Me too,' Mukul emerged from hibernation.

'No doubt about it,' I added. Then the obvious struck me. What was the amount in question? I looked again. This seemed unbelievable! 200,000 Rupees! That was absurd. I could feel sweat beads appearing on the tip of my nose. 'Two lakh rupees! That's a lot of money!'

Baba smiled, now that the realisation of its improbability had finally dawned upon me, 'Exactly.'

'But the numbers match,' I did not cow down.

'That's what bothers me,' commented Baba.

'Well if the numbers match, it means that we have won. Simple.'

Baba was annoyed, 'Do you know how many misprints the newspaper has everyday?'

'But only the other day you said that *Aajker Khabar* never makes a spelling mistake,' I was enthusiastic.

'Spelling error, perhaps not, but what about a misprint?' Baba said feebly.

Ma spoke to me, eyes wide, to drive home the point, 'You must keep this to yourself.'

'Why? This is such great news. The entire neighbourhood must know.'

'I knew this idiot would ruin everything,' Mukul wrestled with the handle of his chair. Ma looked nervous, 'If it turns out to be false, everyone will laugh at us.' She had a point. Anand, Manas, Sanjoy, Raju or Somnath would never ridicule me. But I couldn't be so sure of their parents. I would keep quiet if that gave some comfort to my mother. 'Okay,' I shrugged.

'Good boy,' Ma looked relieved.

'How will we know if these are the right numbers?' I asked.

'We can't until Monday. And Monday is two days away,' Ma said convincingly.

Mukul had already calculated the number of hours, 'Exactly 36.50 hours from now.' 'How so?' Ma demanded to know.

'It's simple maths, Ma,' he tried to show off. 'It's 11:30 a.m now on Saturday. So 11:30 a.m on Sunday is 24 hours from now. Add another 12 hours to reach 11:30 p.m. That makes it 36 hours. Then add half an hour to reach twelve midnight and it's Monday. 36.50 hours.'

Baba was irritated with Mukul's logic. 'I can't step out at midnight to verify if these are the right numbers. So add at least another eight hours to the 36.50 and the waiting period goes up to 44.50 or more hours from now.' He had a valid point. Mukul was quiet. His pride was hurt. Baba turned towards me, 'Can you keep a secret?' His inquiry was so sincere that I almost hugged him, 'You can trust me with your life.' This was my chance to contribute.

'My life is this ticket and the numbers printed on them,' he pointed towards the paper elixir and his eyes pleaded with me to be on his side.

'I won't tell anyone,' I said boldly.

Baba smiled for the first time that morning, 'That's my son,' he exclaimed proudly. Mukul was a lesser risk than me for he had no real friends. But to be on the safe side, Baba and Ma must have already extracted a similar promise from him.

The next 44.50 hours of my life were unforgettable. Not to obstruct any planetary alignment that may lead the family into good fortune, Baba and Ma refused to step out of the house until Monday. Mukul joined them in this superstitious endeavor. I had to prove my solidarity with my distressed family and forced myself to stay indoors to make them feel better.

When Somnath and Raju came calling in the afternoon for a routine round of football and yelled for me from the street below, Ma stuck her neck out of the living room window like a crane searching for fish in the swift current of a turbulent river. She arched her slender neck at an impossible angle and told the boys that I was down with fever and would have to miss the afternoon game. They looked surprised. Raju mumbled to Somnath, 'But he was fine in the morning.' Somnath shrugged, not knowing how to respond. Raju looked up to the second floor, trying to block the sun with a thin, inadequate forearm and asked Ma, 'Can we come upstairs to cheer him?' Ma lied through her teeth, 'He's sleeping.' I crept up carefully to my bedroom window. Although it did not provide the best view of the street, I could tell the disappointment on their puzzled faces even from the distance. How could the hale and hearty cricketer who scored a valuable twenty-five runs to vanquish Dover Road a few hours ago suddenly fall so sick? More bewildered than dismayed, Somnath and Raju walked away, turning once to glance upstairs with the hope that their friend would rise out of his unceremonious slumber and wave to them.

My friends were considerate. They did not disturb me the rest of the day. But they were back on Sunday. This time Anand, Sanjoy and Manas joined them. 'Chinmoy, Chinmoy,' they yelled from downstairs. Ma had appointed Mukul to shoo away the lot. 'Chinmoy is still sick. But he will be fine by tomorrow,' volunteered Mukul without any sign of regret.

'Does he still have fever?' asked Anand in his shrill voice.

'Yes.'

'How much?' It was Sanjoy's turn.

'102 degrees.'

'That's quite high,' Manas looked concerned.

'Don't worry. He will be on his feet by tomorrow.'

Somnath was suspicious now, 'If he has such high fever today, how can he be on his feet tomorrow?'

'Because the doctor said so.'

The boys murmured something undecipherable from the street below. 'Can we see him once?' requested Raju.

'No. It could be contagious.'

Something was definitely wrong. Somnath frowned, 'If the fever is so contagious, how can he play tomorrow?'

'Because the doctor said so,' Mukul's bag of responses was turning empty. He was almost losing patience with the interrogation from the ground level. But the boys had no choice. Mukul's defense was strong. They walked away dejected. I felt bad for them but what could I do? I told myself to hold on for I would be out of hiding in less than a day.

I was restless to be with my friends and my hands were itching to swing a cricket bat. Time stood still and every hour seemed like a month. How far could Monday be? I assured myself of being there soon. Mukul and I shared a room and the double bed. We could hear Baba and Ma whispering throughout the night. Perhaps they were planning what to buy when they got their hands on the vast sum of money. Mukul and I spoke very little right from the beginning of our time together. As always, we kept our thoughts to ourselves. I think he stayed up all night like my parents. But I fell asleep counting the seconds and the minutes and the hours leading up to a new dawn.

Monday arrived with hope. With the ticket placed in the gap between their pillows, Baba and Ma had barely slept the night before. They must have laid down on their sides and stared at it all night long. The winter sun was late to rise. But along with it, the day brought trepidation the Bose family had never known before. Baba was up by 5 a.m. He paced restlessly in small circles in our living room. After nearly three hours of aimless circling, when the tottering hands of the black grandfather clock struck eight, Baba stepped out. By then, he had already downed several cups of tea along with a generous volume of thin arrowroot biscuits.

He briskly walked up to the nearby Southern Avenue to see an old colleague. Sudhir was just back from the fish market and settling down to browse the newspaper when Baba surprised him by a sudden appearance at the unexpected hour. Before he could utter a single word, Baba informed him that he had to take me to the dentist for I had suddenly been struck with a bout of unbearable toothache. Sudhir suggested a home remedy, 'Why don't you ask him to put a clove in his mouth?' But Baba was ready for him. 'I did. But I think the tooth will require extraction. He's been eating too many sweets off late. You know how incorrigible children are these days.' Sudhir nodded in agreement of this terrible crime that children habitually commit. Baba assured him that he would come to work after lunch. Sudhir agreed to convey the message to their superior and said that he would see him later in the day. Baba thanked him for the favour and returned home. As soon as he came back he took a quick bath, finished his morning prayer and put on a new white bush shirt and grey trousers. Ma also dressed for the occasion. After taking a bath and joining him in prayer she wore a neat beige and maroon cotton sari. It must have been new for when she opened the creased folds of the versatile six-yard garment, I could hear it squeak and creak in excitement.

It was a twenty-minute walk to the lottery agent, Munshi & Sons at the corner of Lake Market. Tanmoy and Chitrani Bose reached the kiosk at 9:30 a.m and anxiously waited for Munshi to open the shop. The nearby flower stall had already opened for business. The flower vendor tried to coax Ma into buying some fresh jasmine to adorn the thick bun at the back of her perfectly shaped head. Ma was candid. She told him that she was expecting some good news very soon and promised that she would buy a lot of flowers if expectations were met. Baba kept glancing at his golden brown watch, a wedding gift from his in-laws that he wore only on special occasions. He was struggling not to advance the hands of the watch manually to 10 a.m., the official time for Munshi to open for the day.

Soon it was 10 a.m but there was no sign of Munshi or any of his sons. Every extra minute of waiting was unbearable. Baba kept pacing in front of the kiosk; the magic ticket tucked away in a secret pocket of his underwear, which resembled prison garb. Ten minutes passed. And then twenty. Munshi, the lottery agent had disappeared. Ma was fidgeting with the border of her sari, adding to Baba's restlessness. Baba suggested a walk to the adjacent tea stall to settle their nerves with a cup of steaming tea. Ma agreed. The hopeful couple had just ordered tea when they saw the wooden door to Munshi's kiosk open slowly. Baba, who never wasted anything, promptly paid for the tea and said that he would come back to drink it later. The tea stall owner thought that paying for tea and returning at another time to drink it was unusual, but he accepted the proposal without contest.

The next few minutes changed our lives. Corpulent Munshi's face was the size of a number six football and it rose directly from his chest. He already knew that his agency had sold the winning ticket. He had checked with the same newspaper and knew that he would see the buyer standing in front of his kiosk first thing on Monday morning. 'Then why were you so late?' Baba demanded to know.

'I was at the temple this morning. Today is especially lucky and I offered special prayers. That caused the delay,' Munshi's smile extended from Canada to Australia. He had brought his own copy of Saturday's *Aajker Khabar* and my parents were satisfied that the winning numbers matched with the ones printed on it. Promptly, Baba walked into the nearby Mahaprabhu Mistanna Bhandar, a renowned sweet shop and brought *rasgullas* for Munshi and us. The flower vendor had not lost track of a potential customer in Ma. He kept looking at her from time to time. Ma satisfied him with a reassuring glance that a purchase would follow. The time had come to keep her promise. When she walked up to the vendor, he congratulated her on winning the lottery. Ma was surprised, 'How could you guess?' He smiled and said that her neat sari and restless manner were clear indicators that she had not come to purchase a ticket but had dressed up to celebrate a victory. Although he could not tell how much she had won, he was confident that it had to be a considerable amount. Just then, Munshi yelled from his kiosk. He forbade the flower vendor to accept money from Ma for he wished to pay. Ma was embarrassed and objected. But Baba convinced her with a whisper in her ear that because he had bought sweets for Munshi's family, Munshi wanted to reciprocate. She understood.

Ma wanted to go home without any delay. But Baba reminded her that he had paid the tea stall owner for two cups that lay unconsumed. It was time to celebrate. The winning couple walked up to the tea stall and asked for the prepaid cups. One hand blocked by a *rasgulla* filled earthen pot, Baba handed over a cup to Ma with the other and then gathered his own. They drank the prepaid tea and looked into each other's eyes for the first time since the advent of their children. Life made it so hard for such simple pleasures to be enjoyed. Winning a lottery helped. Tea had never tasted better. The Boses were on top of the world. Good times had begun.

Mukul and I were at home anxiously awaiting their return. Mukul was obambulating in circles like a caged animal. He desperately wanted to own the entire collection of Tintin and Phantom comics and Mandrake and Kerry Drake comics and Rip Kirby and Flash Gordon comics. He would not miss a single issue. Mukul had openly voiced his ultimate desire many times in the past and took every opportunity to confirm it in the past 44.50 hours. He sensed that he was close to his goal. I was excited too. I wanted a new cricket bat with new gloves and new pads and new football boots.

Winning a large sum of money out of nowhere can give one a

lot of confidence. You can forget every care in the world. Tensed muscles can loosen, broken hearts can mend and lost souls can return to roost. Baba and Ma had turned playful. They decided to act as if our ticket number was a misprint and life was going to remain the same. But they were such terrible actors that we knew the truth the minute they walked in. The large earthen pot of sweets was a big giveaway. 'If the ticket was not any good, why did you bring sweets?' I asked. Baba was impressed. But he tried a little more, 'To make us all feel better. So what if we didn't win this time? There is always a next time.' The statement was so out of character that even an infant would have guessed the truth. Baba's normal reaction ought to have been, 'I know we would never win anything. It's a complete waste of time and money. We will never try again.' Mukul had already begun dancing by the time Baba had completed his sentence. Ma could hold back no longer. She broke into tears of joy as I ran towards her. Baba's eyes were smiling and that was a rare sight. Ma confirmed later that Baba would smile in this manner every single day for months after their wedding. But faced with the daunting task of raising a family on meagre government wages, he had gradually lost the virtue. The smile that I knew was always very basic, a perfunctory gesture of acknowledgement, devoid of any serious joy. The lottery ticket had placed before us a new man with a new smile. So what if it took 200,000 rupees and so many years to resurface? It was worth every rupee and every lost day. We dived into the pot filled with sweets and for the first time in my life Ma did not say, 'That's enough. Keep some away for tomorrow.'

# CHAPTER TWO

## Greener Pastures

Over the next few days we visited all the nearby temples. Thanksgiving was important. After all, such a miracle would not have been possible without divine intervention. We prayed as a family and found ourselves bonding like never before. Money changed hands in what seemed like eternity. But actually it was less than two weeks. We retained most of the sum even after deducting Munshi's commission. Within a fortnight, Mukul's dream had come true. He had diligently done his homework and knew where he could buy all his favourite comics. A quick evening walk to the well-stocked Deb Sahitya Kutir and Epic bookstores near Lake Market took care of his life's ambition.

My wish took slightly longer to be fulfilled. It would entail visiting GK Sports near Chowringhee Road, a street immortalised in books and movies. The sporting equipment store was a distance from where we lived. Baba would have to take a day off from work to take me along with him. His weekends had suddenly turned busy and I insisted on the task being performed before school reopened. It was my turn to show off to my classmates. Baba obliged. He took a day off from work, this time on the pretext of taking Mukul to an ENT specialist to tackle an imaginary throat itch.

Baba and I walked up to the Lake Market to board a tram to reach Gariahat junction and connect with buses that would take us to our final destination. Baba had started to wear his favourite wedding watch everyday at Ma's behest. He glanced at his HMT and was preparing for a long wait at the tram stop when I declared, 'We should take a taxi.' After all, we were the Boses. We had won a top lottery. Waiting at a bus stop with every other Boses and Dattas and Roys did not seem right anymore. Baba hailed a taxi and we hopped in. But he had a worried look on his face. 'What's the matter?' I asked. 'Chinmoy, by the grace of a hundred thousand Gods, we are quite well-to-do now.'

'Two hundred thousand Gods,' I corrected him.

Baba ignored my comment and went on, 'But we must not waste.'

'We are buying time, Baba. Imagine how much more you could do with that extra time in your hands,' I stated what seemed to be obvious.

My father was a lifelong government employee. No one complained when he showed up late for work and there was always someone or the other ready to provide proxy if he took time off without good reason. Tanmoy Bose was a good man. But did time and its significance mean anything to him? I don't think so. He followed the same drab routine of living a mundane existence all his life. The lottery was the biggest event in his otherwise ordinary life and he had yet to absorb the event fully. He did not object to my observation. The lottery had won me freedom of speech. My purchase complete, the first time in my entire school life, I waited anxiously for winter vacation to end.

Three months after the win, when one day Baba announced that we would soon have a new home in a very nice area in South

Kolkata, he expected me to cry out in joy. But my life was good and I could not imagine moving anywhere else. I paid little attention to his claim for I thought that he had just floated an idea upon which he would never act. He was surprised that I had not reacted at all while Mukul was so excited at the thought of moving up the social ladder.

Another month later when he said that it was almost time for us to move, I realised that things were serious. The thought of having to leave my friends instantly demoralised me. Baba used to complain that as a little boy he had to travel all over West Bengal with my grandparents. My grandfather was a travelling salesman, selling hair oil for a big Kolkata based corporation. Every time Baba got ready to settle in a new school, it would be time for my grandfather to be transferred somewhere else. Another town, another set of friends, another house. The incessant moving finally came to a grinding halt when he was posted in Kolkata and decided not to move his family ever again. Immediately I pointed it out to him. We would end up moving from place to place like Baba resented doing as a child. We would be subjected to the same nomadic existence he despised. Before Baba could say anything, Ma took his side, 'But your Baba never travels anywhere for work.'

'Then why do we have to go away from here?' I cried out in anguish.

Ma had expected a negative reaction from me for she knew how much I loved my friends. She grew thoughtful for a minute. Then she quietly said, 'This is our chance to own a home. Something that belongs to us. A place where no landlord will come to collect rent at the end of the month. And when we are gone, something that would belong to your brother and you.'

'Where will you go?'

Ma smiled and ruffled my hair, 'I mean when we die.'

'You are not going to die,' I protested.

'Of course we will. Every parent dies. And then their children become parents. That's how life goes on.'

I tried another approach, 'If you are going to die anyway, then what's the point in having the house?'

'Don't you want me to enjoy the comforts of my own home before I die?' Ma said softly.

If I protested any further I would be labeled selfish. My chief aversion to leaving was the fear of losing my friends. I would never be able to make friends like them ever again at some unknown locality. 'What is so special about this new place?'

Baba slumped on his loyal seat and picked up an old newspaper, 'We will be in a better neighbourhood. You will go to an English medium school and be exposed to the good things in life.'

'I always top my English class. Then why do I have to switch schools?' I argued.

'You are doing well but there is ground for improvement,' he reasoned. Ma joined in, 'We can't let you make the same mistake my parents made. To be successful in this country, you must know excellent English and have the right connections.'

'But why...', I began another round of protest. But Baba had had enough. He raised his arm like a dictator from a rogue state and stopped me right on my track. 'Here, we are nobodys but our new address is likely to open doors for Mukul and you.' What was he talking about? I could not grasp it. But I did not possess the audacity to oppose him. Didn't everyone already know us in this neighbourhood? How could we be nobodys here? We would be nobodys in a new place where no one knew us. Baba had everything going right for him and the family. What more did he want? He was being too greedy. Didn't he keep telling us not to give in to greed and remain happy with what we have? Then why this double standard? And why was Ma supporting him in this gross injustice? Later, I learnt that the move and the new school were her ideas. It took me a long time to realise that my parents had turned ambitious overnight for the future of their children way more than enhancing their own social glory.

My world was horribly upset at the thought of moving. Changing schools was not that bad an idea for I had no real friends there. But my best friends from the neighbourhood would be gone! Actually, I would be gone from their lives. My life would be over. I knew the area Ma and Baba had chosen. It was without a doubt nice and appealing, but only from a distance. Owning our own flat there had never before crossed my simple mind. It could be nice but leaving lifelong friends behind was downright treason. I felt that I was about to abandon my comrades on a bloody battlefield.

The following Saturday when I met my friends for a round of football, I broke the news. Their reaction was astonishing. The group immediately resolved to work together and decided to speak with Ma about this troubling issue. The instant camaraderie seemed to be straight out of a foxhole. They would not let me be taken away just like that. I was their valuable friend and they would do everything in their power to prevent the hijacking of an innocent.

There was no football that day. The boys came home along with me. Surprisingly though, Ma was prepared to receive them. How she pre-empted a protest visit by my friends is still a mystery to me. When the team arrived with shoddy, verbal battle plans laid out in their collective minds, they were intercepted with a huge array of the choicest confectionery from Kathleen's cake shop. In the delicious pastry fare that ensued, the sting of the operation mellowed. I nudged Somnath and Raju, the better speakers in the team to lead the protest. They nodded in agreement but could not say much with their mouths full of delicacies offered by my scheming mother. Ma had trapped their mouths shut and rendered their functional minds useless with massive doses of chocolate pastries and lemon tarts. Before they could recover from the cake and pastry blitzkrieg, she called us all to attention, 'Boys, I am going to break some important news to you.' The captive audience, now reeking of spun sugar, hung on to every word she said. 'We are leaving this home.' A muffled noise of instant murmur attempted to escape from pastry-filled mouths. Ma continued, 'But that does not mean that we are moving out of your lives.' She paused for effect. 'We are all very excited to move into our own flat. And you are all welcome to visit your friend like you do now.' There was another half-hearted garbled attempt to protest. Ma did not allow any interruption. 'Chinmoy is free to come over and play with you whenever he chooses.'

'But it is so far,' a dejected Raju managed to speak.

'It's only a twenty minute tram ride and a short ten minute walk after that. Young men like you can walk the entire distance in less than an hour,' Ma presented her counter argument. 'Yes, but...' Somnath had begun to generate a mild opposition when Ma suddenly yelled, 'Time for some ice cream!'

'Yeah, yeah,' came the united response and Somnath forgot the content of his defense. Ma's timing was perfect. The promise of ice cream melted the desire of my warriors to shield me from my now inevitable fate. Ma's presentation was a huge success. There was not going to be any change in our plans. We were going away from Raja Basanta Roy Road.

After the boys had left, satisfied with the promise that I would visit them whenever I wished to, which meant 'not often', I was depressed. Ma realised my state of mind and stepped in to cheer me up. She pointed out that in Raja Basanta Roy Road, there were two big disadvantages to assembling friends. First, one had to step outside the home and get to the main street to reach a friend's place. Second, since we mainly played on the street and Vivekananda Park, it was not possible to stay outdoors after dark. But in a high-rise that would change dramatically. First, I could move from one flat to another without having to step out on the main street and second, the time to return home could be stretched well after sundown as it would be safe to play inside the periphery of the building. I was surprised with Ma's new pitch and raised a question. 'But if I play or visit people in other flats after dark, when will I study?'

'That's up to you. We are better off now, Chinmoy. That means we have more options. This new home will expose you to opportunities you don't have now.' Ma was dead sure of her theory.

'You may be right. But I don't have any friends there. I will be lonely.'

'Wait till you get there.'

'Are there boys like me in that building?' I was trying to be enthusiastic but it was not working.

'There are one hundred flats in that building. Most people living there will have children. Imagine how many friends you'll have there.'

'What's the guarantee?'

'There are no guarantees in life, Chinmoy. But you have to try your best.'

'My life is meaningless now,' I concluded with a wry smile. But the melodrama had no effect on my heartless mother. 'Someday soon, you will thank me,' she stated with absolute knowledge of the future and left me in the room to mourn in solitude.

An ambitious Mukul was happy to be moving. He understood that this was his chance to meet people from a higher economic strata and get ahead in life. He had already visited this new home twice and raved incessantly about the amenities. To whet my appetite, Ma had asked me to join them in a preview, but I could not be bothered. Mukul was about to complete Grade XII and gearing up to study the sciences. He was a good student and in spite of attending a vernacular medium school all his life, his affinity towards everything English was slowly trickling down to me. He was glad with the knowledge that in the upper middle-class set up of his new locality, he would be surrounded by English speaking upstarts. They would know much more about the real world than folks we mingled with in our current lowly avatars.

The big day arrived. I found it hard to believe that we were indeed leaving. My heart was heavy all day. Professional movers had come. They chattered excitedly to work out a plan of action. I was expected to keep a watch on them so that they did not pocket anything while my parents were busy. The movers kept calling our almirahs, Godrej, a brand synonymous with the everlasting steel storage cabinets. They even corrected me once when I referred to the massive contraptions as almirahs. Wedding gifts from my grandparents, they required several able-bodied men to be lifted off their resting spots. The quaint sofa, partially malfunctioning fridge, made-for-life unstylish beds, oil stained plastic combs, half torn shoes - nothing was left behind. Every little thing we had accumulated over the years came along with us. But I was only taking away memories. That's all I cared for. My friends had gathered on the street. They were sad. But no words of protest were heard. They had come to terms with my loss as I had quietly accepted my fate.

After all our household items were loaded into a large truck, Bipin, our landlord, approached us to bid a final farewell. The emotional man who had accommodated the newlywed Boses some nineteen years ago bowed reverentially to Ma and attempted to touch Baba's feet. Baba never allowed anyone to touch his feet. He was of the opinion that the act, if applied to humans, should only be reserved for exceptional people. All the neighbours had gathered with tears in their eyes. The hugs, greetings and bilateral promises to keep in touch continued for a long time until the truck driver got restless and blew his horn to remind us that this phase of our lives was over.

The street that took my running steps on its bare chest every single day during the game of cricket; the street that embraced me during innumerable falls while playing football; the street that left cut marks on my tender skin, casualties of occasional hockey; the street would not be my own tomorrow. All of us were pleasantly surprised to see the number of people that had stepped out on the street to say goodbye to us. My parents were liked but did not have real friends in the neighbourhood. That is why it was more surprising to see such a heavy turnout. Ma concluded, 'This is because we never gossip and respect the privacy of others.'

'That's a possibility,' Baba agreed.

Mukul, the insensitive moron, commented, 'It's Sunday. Everyone's at home and they're bored. They have nothing else to do.' He may have been right. The lazy neighbourhood had risen from its perpetual slumber and found a new activity. In my fourteen years, I had never known anyone from the area to relocate. Baba came up with another explanation, 'Maybe the idea of having more exciting neighbours than us have brought them out of their homes.'

'They have come to say goodbye to me,' I proclaimed as a matter of fact. Mukul stifled a laugh. It was infuriating. He had no friends and did not seem to want any. 'Why did the rest of the family fail to enjoy the attention?' I was wondering when it occurred to me that they were just as sad to leave. This was their strange way of trying to cheer each other up, by underplaying their own importance in the neighbourhood.

We were going away after all. And it could not have been an event to rejoice.

We hopped into a taxi, ready to follow the luggage-laden truck. My eyes turned glassy with tears when I saw all my dear friends and old neighbours choking up at the sight of our departure. As the taxi driver turned on the ignition and the vehicle began to inch ahead, the finality of it all began to bear down heavily upon me. Memories of the neighbouring homes where I witnessed selfless affection and endless days spent with friends crowded my mind in a quick flashback. All of that was being taken away by cruel fate under the cloak of newfound prosperity. I was losing what I loved most and had nothing in my power to reverse my fortune. The taxi sped away as I stuck my head out of the window trying to catch a glimpse of what was to become my past in a short while. I hoped with all my heart that the driver would slow down and allow me to keep gazing at the familiar sights. My eyes were wide open and I did not blink. I could not afford to miss a wink. A cow stood at the edge of a footpath chomping grass as we sped past. Our eyes met for a brief moment. How different our worlds were. She was in sublime bliss and I was in acute agony. Soon we were on another street and heading towards a new world.

Money had done this to me. It had taken away everything that I held close to my heart. I decided that I shall never love money. I knew that I could never be happy again. I cried and I cried and I cried. Ma wept along with me. I noticed the moisture around Baba's sad and quiet eyes. But Mukul was unperturbed. He was busy browsing through *Tintin and the Picaros* while munching away a five star chocolate bar. How could the boy be so cold? He must have a solid stone in place of his heart. 'These useless sentiments mean nothing,' Mukul pronounced. 'People who cling on to the past never move up in life,' he spoke like he knew what life was all about. He sat with a smirk on his face, ready to move on.

After a few minutes we had settled down. Baba asked me to relax and enjoy the ride. 'We are never moving again,' he yawned, tired from the hard work that went behind the move. He was right. My parents never moved again. Death, wedding, divorce and moving are the biggest stress mongrels. My wedding was a breeze; there have been no deaths yet in the family and a divorce, the mini death is not imminent. But that move from Raja Basanta Roy Road a quarter of a century ago was so stressful that every little detail is still embedded in my soul. Ma agreed, 'Baba is right. We are not moving again.' Then she added, 'This is a new beginning for all of us. We must enter our new home with a smile.'

As the taxi approached the intimidating iron gates of the tall white building, Baba mused, 'The name of the building is strange. Don't you think so, Rani?'

'Vanilla Apartments,' Ma muttered and then disagreed, 'I think it's alright.'

'It's an ice cream flavour, not a home where people live,' I complained. The ten storeyed building was painted milk white and the parapets were the colour of green chillies. Baba observed, 'It's like a giant slab of vanilla ice cream with chopped green chillies in it.'

Ma laughed aloud, 'What an imagination. But I think that it'll be the people living in Vanilla Apartments who will add real spice to our lives.'

'You mean they'll be quarrelsome?' Mukul quizzed Ma.

'Spice does not always turn food hot. It brings out its true flavour.'

Mukul nodded like a wise man who had just stumbled upon the answer to another of life's unknowns.

My sadness was short-lived. As the taxi came to a stop outside Vanilla Apartments, we saw a number of people standing at the entrance. Baba said, 'Someone must be having a private function.' Mukul had to have an opinion, 'They have stepped out for a smoke.' Ma was not to be left out, 'Some of the men are smoking. But what about the women?' We did not have to wait very long to find out. The reception committee was for us. At the time, very few people actually inhabited the brand new building. Twenty families had moved in and fifteen amongst them were waiting for our arrival. 'Welcome, welcome,' the crowd roared in unison. Baba was overwhelmed, 'How did you know we would be coming?' The Administration Officer, Jhola Mallick had put up the information on the building notice board informing everyone about the homecoming of the residents of Flat 3A.

We got to know our neighbours right away. Baba and Ma already knew some of them. When they came to look at the flat and then again to book it, they had met a few of them. The spanking new building still smelt of fresh paint and looked like an expensive hotel, a far cry from our old home which had not seen a fresh coat of exterior paint in many years.

The entry to the premises of Vanilla Apartments was marked by a security booth. All visitors were expected to disclose their details. The guard was required to keep the gate closed, opening it only for residents' cars. Visitors had to park on the street. The first four steps of the building were immediately followed by the administration office on the left and a common room to the right. The passageway, flanked by fifty letter boxes on each side led to the Otis lifts. An operator was yet to be hired. The common room had a green Stiga table tennis board and badminton gear, which could be removed for private functions. The front and rear staircases spiraled up the floors like massive anacondas climbing into the skies. The corridors on each floor had two fire extinguishers pinned to wooden holders hanging from the walls.

Flat 3A was spacious with expensive plastic paint on the walls and I found it hard to keep my hands off them. There were two bathrooms and both had sturdy stainless steel showers. Wallpapers matched the coloured commodes. I flushed the commodes and opened the taps to check the flow of water. The crystal clear water flowed like a stream trickling from a pristine glacier. I was dumbstruck, for in the fleeting moments when I had thought of my new home, I had not expected it to be half as nice as this one. Ma checked if the lights were working. Baba had made sure that electricity and gas facilities were set up before we moved in. A little toil and a handful of small bribes had taken care of the two most important essentials. A telephone connection was also in the works.

The kitchen was spacious and there was a functional exhaust fan along with a large window for ventilation. I was glad that my poor mother who spent her life cooking would not have to work in sweltering heat any more. The living room was bright and airy as were all the three bedrooms.

We looked out of place in our old clothes. Our tumbledown, uninspiring furniture was a greater misfit in the beautiful flat. I ran to the balcony and the sight was exhilarating. We were on an important city artery. Our flat faced the entrance of the building and the main road, and our balcony enabled an unobstructed vista of both. The buses and trams and taxis seemed to be so close to us. But then I remembered my friends and was enveloped by old gloom, 'It's so noisy here. We are right on the main road.'

'Look at our location. We have everything within walking distance,' Ma was enthused.

'Except peace,' I complained. Ma ruffled my hair and said, 'Cheer up now.'

The expert movers had worked diligently. Our life in Vanilla Apartments had begun. Ma arranged the kitchen before turning anywhere else and I gave her a hand. Baba and Mukul formed another team and got to work. By the time we were temporarily set up we were dog-tired. Ma cooked some basic lentil soup to go with rice and added fried potatoes to make the meal more interesting. We were hungry and no one complained. She promised to serve fish and meat by the next couple of days once she got a hang of the nearby Gariahat market. I wanted to fall asleep as soon as I hit the bed. But the helpless faces of Somnath, Raju, Manas and the rest of my football team kept flashing in my mind. Eyes brimming with tears, I did not know when I had fallen asleep.

# CHAPTER THREE

# Home Sweet Home

$T$ he next day was the last in my old school. It already felt quite a distance away from where we lived now. Baba had informed them of the blessed reason for my departure. I had taken a transfer certificate, which confirmed that apart from being a good student, my conduct was impeccable. I bid farewell to my classmates. They were unsure why I was leaving. I told them that the daily commute was a big issue, now that we did not live in the area. After school, I ran to Raja Basanta Roy Road. Life was the same there. Nothing had changed. I played with my best friends until dark and then half-walked, half-ran back home. It was past my 7 p.m deadline to return home but Ma did not scold me. I think she knew that it would be impossible to travel back and forth everyday and I would give up soon. That night, I did not sleep at all. Worry kept me awake. I was a prisoner in this beautiful flat.

Although there were some snobs in Vanilla Appartments, most of the residents were friendly. God knows how they would have reacted if they knew that a lottery had brought us in their midst. 3B, the flat next door, was empty and our noisy move had not bothered anyone. The residents of 3F had moved in but the rest of the floor seemed like a graveyard. There was little sign of life. My God, is this where we had ended up after the bustling life of

Raja Basanta Roy Road? I spent the first few evenings in our balcony watching the tortoise-paced trams, packed with fatigued passengers trudge along. The nights at Vanilla seemed strange in the beginning. We were on one of the busiest roads in South Kolkata and there was traffic until late at night. Few drivers cared to refrain from thumping their horns on empty roads, even if it was way past midnight. No one complained and I thought it would not be right for me to throw a tantrum about it. Baba felt the noise too but spoke on behalf of the insensitive drivers, 'The stress of pollution and traffic is too much. They have to deal with it all day long. It doesn't surprise me that they want an outlet.'

'But blowing horns in the middle of the night doesn't really help,' Ma reasoned. 'Maybe it does,' quipped my smart brother.

'Perhaps they pump their horns to stay awake at the wheel,' I suggested.

Ma was impressed. 'Chinmoy always thinks outside the box,' she beamed. Mukul made a face and got back to browsing Asterix and the Black Gold.

A week after we had moved in, Baba got hold of the building carpenter, Kishore. The sorry excuse that was our furniture was littering the new landscape. A new sofa, dining table and bookcase would have to be constructed and tailored to our lonely, snooty existence. Kishore listened carefully as Ma gave him detailed instructions on design and budget. In a few hours, he got to work.

The next morning we woke up to a horrific sight. Kishore had left some varnish on an earthen pot on the frame of the sofa. Some of it had spilled on to the base and a lizard was stuck to it. Mukul spotted the creature and tried to shoo it away. But it could not budge no matter how hard it tried. It was utterly helpless. I would have nothing to do with a lizard but Mukul was brave. He tried to spoon it out. But each time he made an attempt to assist the terrified lizard out of misery, he ended up peeling off its skin. The hapless reptile was combating the unbearable pain of skin being scraped off its chest and stomach along with the frightening possibility that we would bludgeon it to death the minute it escaped its current ordeal.

I left for my new English medium school where I had adjusted without any problem. Mukul had classes to attend for his upcoming board examinations. Baba had to set out for work and Ma was left alone to deal with the trapped lizard in our living room. Kishore came around noon and was surprised to see the sight. He added oil to the base of the sofa with the hope that the lizard's skin would loosen up and it would slide off the frame. But that didn't help either. When I returned in the afternoon it was still struggling to stay alive. Death had not claimed it yet and it was impossible to watch its misery. Mukul was back too. He suggested that a mercy killing was the only solution. His observation was valid. But the lizard had held on for so long that we thought somehow it would slip away from its predicament. Painfully enduring every effort that we made to free it from its miserable state, the lizard breathed its last, late in the evening. There are some incidents time does not fade. This was one of them. Even today, when I see a lizard, the screech of the helpless soul dying a gruesome death at Flat 3A rings in my ears.

That weekend, I was reading a Hardy Boys novel when Ma stepped out of the kitchen and wiped sweat off her forehead with the folds of her sari, 'We have run out of biscuits. Can you run to the store and get some?'

'Sure,' I said. Although it was annoying to be interrupted in the middle of the engrossing drama, I could not refuse as I was Ma's chief help at the time. I picked up some change from a glass bowl next to our new Televista TV set and left.

I walked down the broad staircase for I was yet to get used to the lifts. 'Three floors high up is safe,' Baba had decided when choosing the flat. 'In times of power cuts we could still walk up with a bucket of drinking water.'

'But it's more fun to see the world from higher up,' suggested Mukul when he accompanied my parents on the day of signing the deed.

'Higher may have a better view and lessen traffic noise, but not being dependant on the lifts will be a life saver for us when we grow old,' Ma pointed out.

Mukul had to revert with something smart, 'By the time you grow old, there'll be no power cuts in Kolkata.' Baba supported Ma, 'Having a lift at home is a privilege but we must not become slaves to it.' The lesson has stayed with me. Even today, I seldom avail the lifts.

I jumped down three stairs at a time to reach the ground floor. I had to get back to my reading. As I was heading out of the main gate of the building I heard someone call out from behind. 'Tiger? Hey, Tiger?' I walked on, without turning back when I heard the voice call out again, 'Hey Tiger, wait.' I realised that I was wearing a T-shirt with a print of the majestic skin of the Royal Bengal Tiger. Was someone calling me? I turned to see a well-built boy around my age waving out to me. In a few seconds, he caught up. He had a smile that could win over anyone. He thrust out his hand towards me. I took it with some uncertainty. 'Kirit Banerjee,' he said. 'Are you in 3A?'

'Yes. I'm in 3A.'

'I knew it. Sorry, Tiger I couldn't receive you when you came in. I was visiting my uncle for a few days.' He did not even ask my name. Instead, he was calling me 'Tiger!'

'I have to go.' I was irritated.

'Where are you going?'

'To the convenience store. To get some biscuits.'

'Oh, do you need any help?'

'It's just a pack of biscuits. That's not too heavy, you know.'

Kirit burst out laughing. 'Funny guy, Tiger. You, my friend, are a funny guy.' I said to myself, 'I'm not your friend and never will be.' The pompous boy did not even want to know my real name. I decided that I would not tell him unless he specifically asked me.

'I have to go now.'

'Okay Tiger. Get going. If you need anything, come straight to 10B.'

I nodded and jogged away to display urgency. As I reached the end of the street, ready to move into the next one, I turned to see if the rude boy was still there. Kirit Banerjee was standing exactly where I had left him. He raised his hand and waved to me. Instinctively, I waved back. I was annoyed with myself for having done so. Hadn't I promised myself not to become his friend? Now I had waved to him.

I reached the nearest convenience store in a few minutes. An incredibly fair man walked around the small store arranging items on their proper counters. His hair was so greasy that even from across the counter I could smell the strong hair oil. An elderly gentleman sat at the counter, a pair of old-fashioned eyeglasses precariously balanced on his Pinocchio-like nose. 'Gobar,' he called out. The fair young man replied, 'Yes Baba?' So the fair man was called Gobar and the old man was his father. Clearly no parent would name their child after an animal's droppings even if it were of the holy cow's. The name 'Gobar' must have had some affectionate connotation for the fair young man had not objected to this vile term of endearment.

'There is a young customer. Can you take care of him for a moment? I need to pass urine,' said the old man. I cringed. He could have said that he needed to use the toilet or better yet, nothing at all. The graphic imagery was totally uncalled for. Gobar walked towards me. He was friendly, 'Do you need some help?'

'Biscuits.'

'Do you know which one you want?'

'But what do you have?'

'Look at this shelf. Here you have all the brands.'

I saw the well-lit and well-stocked store, a far cry from the one serving Raja Basanta Roy Road and its surrounding streets. Gobar continued, 'Are you new in the neighbourhood?'

'Yes, we just came to live at the Vanilla Apartments. If you go across the street and turn left...', I began to explain when Gobar smiled, 'Come on, everyone knows where Vanilla Apartments is.'

'Really?' I had not thought about that.

'It's the newest building in this area. Really posh.'

I felt good after a long time. A complete stranger had called my home posh.

'Welcome to the neighbourhood,' Gobar's smile broadened.

'Thank you, Gobarda,' I said hesitatingly. Who knew how he would react to a stranger calling him 'Brother Cow Dung?'

'You know my name?' he looked surprised.

'Your father called out to you. That's when I heard it.'

'Smart. What's your name? Tiger?' he suggested.

A bomb dropped on me. Was everyone in this neighbourhood insane? It was the stupid T-shirt! An ordinary T-shirt bought from a street hawker in Lake Market was getting way too much attention in this crazy neighbourhood. I was not sure if that was a good thing or a sign of bad times to come. But I was getting late. 'I'll take the small pack of Milk Bikis.' I handed five rupees to Gobar. The change came back. It was lesser than what I would generally get back at Raja Basanta Roy Road. 'Everything costs more in this neighbourhood,' Ma had warned. Gobar continued, 'We are expecting a big boom in business because Vanilla Apartments will get filled up by the end of the year.'

'How do you know all this?' I was surprised.

'The whole world knows about Vanilla Apartments.' It was Gobar's turn to be surprised.

'Was Vanilla Apartments that important?' I thought. It was the second time I felt good in less than five minutes. 'Okay, Gobarda. I'm getting late.'

'Your name?'

'Chinmoy Bose.'

'See you again soon, Chinmoy. Tata, Bye-bye,' he waved to me.

I waved back and turned around. As I jogged back home, I could not help thinking about Kirit Banerjee. Would I see him waiting at the same spot? I thanked God, for he was gone. I ran all the way up to 3A without a single break, four stairs leading to the lifts plus thirty-six stairs of the three floors. Ma opened the door, 'I was getting worried.'

'I met a boy downstairs and also spoke to the guy at the convenience store.'

Ma smiled as she took the pack of Milk Bikis from my hand, 'Making friends already?' 'Hardly,' I slumped on our brand new sofa and picked up the Hardy Boys novel. Then I looked up to Ma, 'The convenience store guy's name is Gobar.'

Ma frowned, 'That's not nice. Is he very fair?'

How could she guess? It would be natural to think that Gobar was dark as turd. Ma pulled surprises like no one. 'Yes. He's very fair. How did you know?'

'A name like that must have been given to him affectionately. Otherwise it would be an insult,' Ma applied some common sense into her thought.

'I know,' I agreed. Ma continued, 'Such names stay on with children when they grow up. Parents must be more careful.'

'Gobar knew about our building.'

'Of course he would. His business will flourish because of Vanilla. One hundred flats mean at least two hundred new customers.' Ma, an ordinary housewife, figured out the obvious. I felt stupid. I decided to get back to my book.

At the Bose residence, evening tea on weekends was at 5 p.m. It was special because I was allowed to drink tea. There were no exceptions on weekdays and I had to drink two glasses of milk every day. Ma was serving tea when the bell rang. Mukul opened the door. He called out to me within a few seconds, 'Chinmoy, your friend is here.' My friend? Who? Somnath? Raju? Manas? It must be one of them. But if it was someone he knew why would he not say his name? I was about to walk up to the door to greet my visitor when a beaming Kirit Banerjee strode past Mukul straight into our living room. 'What's going on Tiger?'

What was Kirit Banerjee doing here? He walked up to Ma and Baba and touched their feet. At once, he won over Ma. Baba was also impressed. 'Hello Chitrani Aunty and Tanmoy Uncle, I am Kirit. I live in 10B.' He had obviously found out my parents' names from the black and gold nameplate on our front door.

'Oh, 10B! The Banerjees?' asked Baba.

'You know us already?' Kirit smiled and sat down before an invitation was extended.

'We met your parents when we came for inspection.' Baba volunteered. Ma broke in, 'And they received us the day we came in.'

'Yes, I know. I was not at home that week or else I would have received you too.'

'How long has it been since you moved?' asked Ma.

'It'll be one month next week.'

'Ask your parents to drop by sometime,' Baba said genuinely.

'Sure. Tiger is my first friend in the building.'

'Tiger?' Ma was surprised.

I was yet to acknowledge him properly, let alone call him my friend and here he was, shamelessly calling me Tiger in front of my parents. Mukul had already lost interest in Kirit and walked into his room.

'Your son. He would not tell me his name so I called him Tiger, after that tiger striped T-shirt he was wearing.'

Ma smiled. I was annoyed that she found this whole episode amusing. Suddenly Kirit's eyes went to a pile of *samosas* that Ma had laid next to the tea. 'Those *samosas* look terrific,' Kirit picked up a large one from the plate. Ma was glad that he dived into her carefully created *samosas*. Kirit took a bite and pushed the plate towards me, 'Tiger, you can have some too. Don't feel shy.' I was astonished at his gall. He was devouring my *samosas*, in my house, without being asked and extending the plate to me as if I was his guest. Infuriating! 'Mmm, this is from the heavens. You must be an angel.' Ma was already on his side and this brazen flattery further solidified his position in my household. Kirit went on, 'I will call you Rani Aunty. Chitrani Aunty is too long.'

Mutilating my name was not enough? Now he was set to rename my mother! Baba called her Rani but no outsider did that. To my surprise, Ma consented, 'Suit yourself.'

Immediately he said, 'Rani Aunty, you should teach my mother how to make these *samosas* or else every time you make them, you'll find me here.'

'In that case, I won't teach her or else you won't come to visit,' Ma was reveling in the praise.

'That's impossible!' He exclaimed and put another warm *samosa* straight into his mouth and shut his eyes. Ma was concerned, 'Don't burn your mouth, Kirit.' But Kirit had been transported to another world where he was immersed in the fusion of potatoes, peas and ground chillies. He did not reply. Ma smiled with the knowledge that Kirit was safe. The young resident from 10B had the key to my mother's heart from the moment he walked into our home some twenty-five years ago.

When Kirit returned to his senses, he was pleased to see that Ma had laid out a few more *samosas* for him. He promptly finished two more, then picked one up in his palm and bit into it. He stood up, 'Tiger, make sure you come home tomorrow evening. It's my birthday. Be there at six. I'm having a party.'

'Happy birthday in advance,' Ma said. By then, Baba was reading stale morning news from his twelve-hour-old newspaper and had stopped paying attention to the conversation. Kirit shook his head, 'Thanks, Rani Aunty. But I will settle for nothing less than rice pudding.'

Ma smiled. 'Let's see what we can do.'

Kirit left, munching his half-eaten *samosa*. 'The boy is so rude,' I complained the minute he stepped out. 'He keeps calling me Tiger and doesn't even ask before eating.'

'Kirit is a very good boy, Chinmoy,' Ma was certain. 'Besides, how many people get called, Tiger? It's such a compliment.'

'Just because he praised your samosas,' I complained.

'That's partly true,' Ma admitted, 'But Kirit is the kind of friend who will stay with you all your life, come what may.' She was right.

I wore freshly ironed clothes the next day and stood in front of 10B exactly at 6 p.m. There was no long line-up of young boys and girls. The door swung open when I rang the bell and Kirit greeted me with his winning smile, 'Tiger! Great to see you man. Come on in.' I stepped in with a carefully wrapped birthday present along with a container of rice pudding. Ma had especially taken the trouble to prepare it for Kirit's special day. He graciously accepted the birthday gift and thanked me. But I could tell that his prime interest lay in the stainless steel container. He knew that the rice pudding had reached him. The flat seemed quiet. Where were the other guests? I looked around. The furniture was artistic, the fridge was state-of-the-art and the sprawling carpet in the living room was Persian. Bright expensive paintings hung on the walls rendering a rich and divine glow to the tastefully done flat. Kirit asked me to step into his bedroom, 'Where are the others?' I asked.

'What others?' he countered.

The bell rang. Kirit pushed a cushioned chair towards me,

'Make yourself comfortable. This is your home now. Let me see who is at the door.' He left the room. That was nice of him to say but this fabulously decorated room with every single item reeking of money and fine taste did not remotely resemble my home. This was the ultimate cool. A fine Cosmic stereo system, heaps of audio cassettes, the latest video recorder from Panasonic, a comfortable spring bed and...' My thoughts were interrupted when a boy our age walked in. 'Good', I thought. The other guests were coming in. The new entrant was taller than both of us, with a pair of spectacles that bottomed out below his nose. His face was unusually smooth and completely hairless. He wore a floral full-sleeved shirt with white shorts, which made him appear taller. The boy had a weird sense of dressing. 'Tiger Bose. He lives in 3A.' Kirit introduced me to the strange boy. 'That's what Kirit calls me. My real name is Chinmoy,' I protested.

'Tiger sounds great. I'll call you Tiger,' the boy decided.

'Tiger, this is Pluto from 4G. He moved in yesterday,' said Kirit.

'Pluto?' I was surprised. What a weird name.

The strangely dressed boy must have guessed what I was thinking. 'Aapluto is my real name but everyone in school calls me Pluto.'

'Cool. Like a bloody planet,' Kirit interjected, 'I would give anything for a name like that.' I was slowly relaxing in Kirit's comfortable settings.

'What does Aapluto mean?' I was curious.

'Immersed. Covered. Engulfed. Along those lines,' he said.

'With what?' I could not guess.

'Knowledge. Or love. Or wealth, I guess,' he shrugged.

The bell rang again. Kirit's mother, Sumita Aunty, was back

from the market. The warm smile was exactly the same as Kirit's and it was impossible not to like her. She gave both visitors a warm hug. Then she turned towards her son, 'Have you told him the truth, Kirit?'

'No,' he replied, 'I was waiting for you to get here.'

'Get on with it. I'm here now,' Sumita Aunty urged him. Kirit braced himself as if he was about to reveal the secret of life after death. He looked directly at me and exclaimed, 'It's not my birthday!'

'What?' I was confused.

Sumita Aunty looked at me, 'Kirit wanted to be your friend and this was the best way he could get you to visit.' I was astonished. She knew about his great lie and played along? My parents would never allow a sham of this nature. Pluto had no such misconception. He gave me a knowing smile and took Kirit's side, 'Only to be friends, Tiger.'

Kirit said, 'But since you brought me a gift, I will keep it.' I was not sure how to respond. 'Sure. It's yours.' Although it was not very easy to get over the deceit, it was not that hard either. Kirit was genuinely nice and had a strange mix of shrewdness and simplicity contained in his strong frame. Pluto seemed goofy, displaying intelligence and silliness simultaneously. He was interesting in his own way. Before I knew it, a couple of hours had passed, and a fare fit for kings was served to us.

The food was gourmet. It did not take me long to realise that this type of a meal was nothing special for the Banerjee household. The Banerjees ate like that every single day of the year. By 9 p.m. Kirit's father, Sudip Uncle, had returned from work. He had a very successful import-export business and hobnobbed with the city's top political and judicial brass. A dynamic man, Sudip Uncle dropped out of college when his father suddenly passed away leaving the family in deep debt. He single-handedly turned around the failing family business into a lucrative enterprise. I remembered Sudip Uncle's face and towering presence from the day we arrived at Vanilla Apartments. He was the man leading everyone else to receive us. In the five minutes that he sat down to chat with Pluto and me before disappearing into his bedroom, we felt that we had known him for many years.

Finally it was time to leave. The three of us had little in common, or so I thought at the time. Kirit Banerjee, a glib liar and rich, pompous kid who was impossible to ignore; Tiger Bose, a young man who loved to live in the past and was recently subjected to a name change without consent; Pluto Sen, a distant planet devoid of vegetation and capable of inadvertently making you laugh until you got cramps, were unlikely to become and remain friends. But we had all enjoyed the evening and looked forward to getting together again.

I came back to 3A with a return gift. Kirit asked me not to open the gift until I reached home. When I did, I was overwhelmed. It was the latest Hardy Boys book that I had been searching for. It was hard to find one because it was already out of print. How did he know that I would want this more than anything else in the world? He had seen me holding a Hardy Boys book in my hand when he walked into my home the day before. He must be a magician to have managed to get a copy at such short notice. Mukul was impressed with Kirit right away and immediately grabbed the book from my hand. He went inside his room and started reading it without any delay. When I told Ma about Kirit's cock and bull story about his birthday she laughed it off completely. Somehow I felt relieved. I had begun to like Kirit Banerjee and although I was irritated by his ways, he was indeed my first friend at Vanilla Apartments. I did not want to lose his friendship. The way Kirit came across, I could tell that he was going to be the heartthrob of Vanilla Apartments. 'How did you manage to get that book?' I asked him when I met him the next day. 'My mom's younger brother is in the police. He can get anything from anywhere,' Kirit boasted as he stretched out on his bed. Pluto was listening with great interest, 'I'll have to meet him someday.'

'My uncle cannot say no to me. If I ask for something, I get it. But most of the time, I get things even before I make a wish,' he smiled in the pure knowledge of possessing an uncle who could clearly perform miracles. He added, 'My uncle's real name is Aditya Roy. But since childhood he has always been so popular that everyone calls him by a nickname, a short form of popular - Pop.'

'So what do you call him? Pop Mama?' I joked.

To my surprise, Kirit grinned, 'Exactly. He is Pop Mama to me. Pop Dada to brothers. Pop Kaka to other nephews. And just Pop to my parents.'

'Pop Mama,' Pluto mouthed. 'Cool,' he decided.

By the end of two weeks, Kirit, Pluto and I were becoming inseparable. We spent a lot of time talking about the neighbourhoods we grew up in. We also visited Pluto at 4G. Pluto's father, Nirmal Sen, was a respectable architect and busy with the construction of a newly developing area around the Salt Lake region in Kolkata. Pluto's mother, Urmi, was a successful engineer, and an exception in those days. Very few women engineers had made their mark in their professional lives in the city at that time. But, she was quite well known and respected by her male colleagues. The Sens were busy with their own lives and did not have much time for Pluto. Their marriage had failed. They had not divorced because neither wanted sole responsibility of their only child. Pluto never lacked pocket money but he was neglected. And he sought solace in his new friends. Nirmal Uncle and Urmi Aunty lived under the same roof but rarely spoke to each other. But they never fought, either. They were always civil and kept to themselves. In all their years at Vanilla Apartments there were very few invitations they attended together as a family. Diligence and greed made the fourteen-year old Pluto a fierce competitor in football, cricket and badminton. He did not care much for table tennis.

Every weekend, residents began pouring in by the dozens. We waited impatiently to see how many of them had children who were around our age. It was not that everyone had boys. Some had girls too. Life was looking up.

Since I did not have to step out on the busy main road to play, there was very little objection to leaving the house at odd hours. I could always say that I was going upstairs to 10B or 4G or downstairs to the common room. I was within the premises, simply changing floors. There was enough space to move around and play. Later in the evenings, we used the building facilities to play badminton and table tennis with other boys and girls. But since none of them were exactly around our age, no great friendships formed. Sometimes young parents also joined in for a game or two. We also spent endless hours chatting in the big common room. The building set-up was a great source of freedom for us. Our parents assumed that we were in some flat or the other, when in fact we would often sneak out for a movie or simply loiter around the neighbourhood. Parental vigilance had loosened up and we began to have the time of our lives.

Vanilla Apartments was an amalgam of personalities. There were islands like Parul and Amiyo Biswas and Binoy and Shobha Lagoo. They stuck to themselves and never mingled with anyone in the entire building. Then there were the archipelagos; Tarak and Keya Dutta and Rashi and Taran Agarwal who always mixed with each other and ran away from anyone else they came across.

Bahar and Pankaj Mishra were misfits who had struck gold with their shrimp export business. With new money pouring in, they invited one family after another for lavish dinners. When they were invited back, they sent the host an unnecessarily huge load of fish the next day with a 'thank you' note. Generally people entertained with fish and the Mishra family made it a point to find the same fish they had been entertained with, the night before. The 'thank you' note was an excuse to display their newfound prosperity and it annoyed most people who extended an invitation. But there were some who deliberately invited them knowing this. They knew that whatever they spent on entertaining would be returned several folds, thanks to the strange ways of the Mishras. The next day the choicest fish from the market was sure to be theirs without any additional expense.

In some ways, we were misfits too. We still calculated before we spent. We did not own a car and took the bus or tram to our destinations. But we had learnt some of the ways of the upper middle class. Mukul and I spoke more English than necessary. His glasses were modern now. Instead of the free public swimming pool where swimmers urinated without concern or remorse, it was now the clear blue waters of the tiled pool at Anderson Club.

Vanilla Apartments housed wannabees like Durdanto and Hansini Hazra and their obnoxious children, Elizabeth and Mark. Durdanto Hazra was a voracious gormandiser. When the Hazras came to our place for a meal, we realised that their table manners were abominable. They belched loudly and spoke with food in their mouths. Masticated food often slipped out of their mouths and dropped on the floor while they ate as if it was their last meal on death row. Instead of picking up the dropped particles, they promptly pushed the crumbs under the table with their feet and laughed aloud so that our attention would be diverted. It only succeeded in drawing our attention to where it ought not to have strayed. Elizabeth was a hyperglast and it was difficult to pay attention to any conversation with her sitting in such close proximity. The Hazra kids were younger to me and continuously spoke incorrect English. Durdanto Hazra kept reminding us that they owned a world famous shipping company called Hazra and Sawns, and it took me a while to realise that Sawns was not their British partner but simply meant, Sons. The couple shamelessly exaggerated the profits of their company. Baba and Ma knew they were lying but they went along with the charade. After all, the Hazras were our guests.

The Hazras were a joke. But they did not care. They had money and they flaunted it. They wanted to make their children 'English' and openly proclaimed it. Durdanto Uncle's own English was an embarrassment. A confirmed analphabet, young was *yong* and love was *lyave* in his dictionary. Once after narrowly escaping a fire at a city hotel, his comment was immortalised by a news channel in the form of a sound bite, 'The *phaayaar* was catching the *byattacks* of the *hawtel bhizitors*.' Twenty-five years later, their one-upmanship has not ended.

Politicasters like Surya and Chandra Mukherjee, and Indranil and Vaishali Tagore had spent a lifetime mastering the art of playing naïve residents against one another while the costive speech of Lalit Rai and Piyush Paine was laced with sweet poison. Then came a unique category - The Violent. Sukumar Chaudhry was the star in this category. Within the very first week of his entry into Vanilla, the football coach had beaten up his wife, Runa, with a hockey stick and she ended up in hospital. When the police intervened, Runa protected her husband by saying that she tripped and fell on the staircase. Sukumar's son, Akaash, was our age but never participated in any games or festivals. We went to the same school and bumped into each other quite often. He invariably had bruises on his face and evaporated before I could stir up a conversation. Since it was obvious that he wanted to avoid me in school and the rest of the boys at Vanilla, we let him at ease.

In the beginning, we did not know that Sukumar Chaudhry was an alcoholic. We thought he was a lunatic prone to violence. But one day when Runa Chaudhry returned from work and no one opened the door, she grew concerned that something bad had happened to Sukumar. They were in 2E, so it was not that hard for our security guard, Bheem Bahadur to climb up to the balcony. Initially he was hesitant for he feared that he would be given the treatment if Sukumar Chaudhury caught him climbing up to violate their privacy. But the sight of a fifty-rupee note eased his hesitation and he consented to risk the loss of his Roman nose.

We were waiting downstairs hoping to witness something dramatic. Bheem Bahadur climbed up to the balcony and went into the bedroom where he found Sukumar Chaudhry fast asleep. Without trying to wake him up he opened the main door to let Runa Chaudhry walk in with other members of the building. After exhausting the initial verbal attempts to wake him up, a major clash of cymbals was perpetrated by the neighbours. When that failed, ice-cold water was poured on him. Sukumar Chaudhry stirred a little but for no good. Finally everyone decided to give up and let him sleep it out. He woke up after two days, utterly dehydrated and habitually grumpy and raised a noisy demand for tea.

Soon the news of his being an alcoholic leaked. He would fight taxi drivers on a regular basis. He punched Akaash's class teacher when the boy failed his maths exam. The police intervened again and warned him of dire consequences if any more complaints reached them. He mellowed down for a year or so before he brought down a bagful of groceries on the head of a fishmonger who tried to cheat him. These days, Sukumar Chaudhry is a far cry from his turbulent old self. Cancer has rendered him a recluse and he only steps out in the balcony for a smoke he is not meant to draw into his failing lungs.

'The Strong' must also be a category at Vanilla Apartments only due to the presence of Girin Ghosh. He was as wide as he was tall and being overly hairy he landed with the nickname, Gorilla. When a small fire scared residents out of their flats, the occupant of 9E, Tapan Das refused to come out. Gorilla Ghosh walked up the nine flights, barged into the man's home, physically lifted him like a six-month-old infant, and ran down, never for once stopping along the way. Tapan Das yelled and struggled with all his might to escape from his iron grip but Gorilla Ghosh lived up to his nickname. He created his own legend. Gariahat Market was a good twenty-minute walk from Vanilla Apartments and Gorilla Ghosh often walked back with two dozen green coconuts in his large hands. He was the strongest man in the building and perhaps in all of Kolkata.

Paromita Chatterjee and Aniket Seal were the Vanilla limpets who were incredibly hard to shake off. Paromita was a terror for her raging pyorrhea, a condition that could shoo away wild beasts deep into the farthest corner of their cages at the Kolkata zoo. Aniket was a lecher, using every tactic to say something suggestive to the women in the building. Neither did he have any charm nor did he know anything about the effective use of subtlety in successful seduction, so he ended up with nothing but disdain from the members of the opposite sex. Although Aniket's attempts were indiscriminate and relentless, his hands did not stray. That saved him from being beaten black and blue, an obvious outcome of such advances.

The quidnuncs of Vanilla were many but the queen of nosiness was Rukma Chakravorty, termed BSF by us, an abbreviation for the ever-vigilant and efficient Border Security Force of India. She stood on her balcony at 1A and kept track of who came inside Vanilla and who walked out. She was an insomniac and few nocturnal activities in the building could go unobserved by her watchful eyes. Everyone disliked her habit but also admitted that Rukma was an indispensable security tool of the building.

Then came the whores. Vanilla had a few. But the top contenders for gold were Jonaki Basu and Maakhan Mallik. Jonaki literally meant glow-worm. She had a number of simultaneous affairs in the building. Maakhan, meant butter. It was a name coined by us because of her perfect complexion.

The namesakes were Rajesh Khanna and Sourav Ganguly. The Rajesh Khanna every Indian knew was an immensely popular movie star. Vanilla's Rajesh Khanna only enjoyed the name and copied some of the actor's mannerisms with moderate success. But our Sourav Ganguly had remained anonymous until the nineties when the rising Indian cricket star became a source of great annoyance for him. As the cricketer's stars soared, our Sourav Ganguly was constantly compared with his namesake. When he could take it no more, he changed his name to Gourav. It sounded almost the same, and Gourav meant glory. He thought that he would be finally exempt from the repeated comparisons by making a clever alphabet change. But he was wrong. Earlier it used to be, 'Do you play cricket?' 'Are you a successful businessman?' But after the name change affidavit, it became, 'Are you related to the cricketer?' 'Your name could have been Sourav, you know.' 'You missed being Sourav Ganguly by a single alphabet.' The unfortunate man was now stuck with another malfunctioning name. He could not get back his old name and found no glory in his new avatar. Seeing his misery, his wife Soma asked him to change his name again. But he had had enough. It had taken him a year to get settled into his new name formally and he had paid a heavy price. For us, he had turned into Gourav Uncle from Sourav Uncle and remains so until this day.

# CHAPTER FOUR

# *Fantastic Five*

The next couple of months were the busiest for Vanilla Apartments. Twenty-two families moved in. The moves were invariably scheduled on weekends and Kirit, Pluto and I went downstairs to welcome the new families. Some residents still received the new entrants but the enthusiasm was gradually waning. Established residents had already made friends and efforts to add to their cliques were diminishing with the passage of time. It was astonishing that among the new twenty-two families, there was not a single boy who was either in Grade IX or Grade X. A great couple, Dr. Ranjan Kundu and his wife, Usha had moved next door into 3B. Their son, Vikash was in Grade XI and their daughter, Vani was in the fourth grade. Vikash was a nice guy with a cool nickname, Vick. He was worth including in our small group. Unfortunately for us, Vick wanted to be friends with older boys. We tried to initiate him but a deal could not be struck.

Some girls had also moved in. Sonali, Madhuri, Rituparna were all in Grade X. They were good kids but we were not really going to make them a part of our privileged team. I was giving up hope, 'Doesn't seem like we'll find anyone else to add to our group.' Kirit, the eternal optimist, completely dismissed my negative reverberation, 'More than half the building is yet to be filled.' Pluto rolled his new thorn-encrusted metal bracelet on his wrist, 'It's a serious issue.'

'I guess we just have to accept our fate,' was my best response under such circumstances. Kirit smacked the back of my head with a painless slap, 'Positive. Think only positive.' I nodded in semi agreement. We said a silent prayer for the cause.

The next weekend, we were ritually waiting at the entrance to receive Prasoon and Neelima Raha. They were moving into 5D. A large truck laden with furniture had arrived. A distinguished looking man peeped from an Ambassador car that had followed the truck. Next to him was a pretty lady who was certainly his wife. A little boy, at the most ten years of age, sat next to her. He parked and saw us at once. Ignoring the handful of adults all set to receive them, he waved to us. We were glad to get noticed first in spite of the presence of the adults. He walked up to us and addressed us with a smile, 'Do you live in this building?'

'Yes,' all three of us said at once. Sudip Uncle stepped forward closely followed by Baba, 'Mr. Raha, I am Sudip Banerjee of 10B.' The friendly man folded his hand in acknowledgment, 'Prasoon Raha along with my best half, Neelima and second son, Aurobindo.'

Sudip Uncle smiled, 'I know. We're all here to receive you. And look at our young soldiers,' he pointed towards us, 'They're here too.'

'That is so kind of you,' Prasoon Raha was overwhelmed. Neelima Raha could not believe a reception like this. Although many residents had stopped receiving newcomers by then, it was still a decent turnout.

'I told my older son that he would be making new friends in his new home but he has been quite depressed since last week,' said Neelima Raha.

'Where is he?' Kirit demanded to know.

'We had to leave him at my sister's place for a few days as he did not want to shift here.'

'Which grade is he in?' Pluto got down to business.

'Grade X,' said Prasoon Raha. We looked at each other. The new boy had met the most important qualification.

It was my turn, 'Which school is he in?'

'Don Bosco.'

The boy had scored again. He went to a great school and should easily blend in with us.

'What's his name?' Pluto inquired from behind a pair of ridiculous white plastic sunglasses.

'Rabindranath.'

'No, I meant your son's name,' the inattentive Pluto asked again.

'Rabindranath. Rabindranath Raha,' said Prasoon Raha.

Not many people of my generation were conferred the revered poet's name. Living up to Nobel Laureate Rabindranath Tagore's achievements would be virtually impossible.

Prasoon Raha continued, 'Everyone asks me why we named our sons Rabindranath and Aurobindo.'

Pluto quipped, 'Yeah I was wondering too.' Kirit nudged him to be quiet.

'We thought it would inspire them to write poetry. To create fine music. To be spiritual. They're such inspirations after all.' Pluto was not satisfied, 'But it must create a lot of pressure on them.' Prasoon Raha looked sad, 'You're right. By the time we realised our mistake it was too late. They were stuck with the great names.'

'I'm sorry to hear that,' said Baba who was listening to the entire conversation.

The truck driver had been waiting patiently for Prasoon Raha to get over with the introductions. Prasoon Raha continued, 'Aurobindo is less affected perhaps because he is still too young, although his friends have shortened his name to Auro. But can you guess what Rabindranath is called in school?'

'Robin,' I blurted out.

'How did you know?' Neelima Raha was surprised.

Kirit joined in, 'That's the most obvious option.' Prasoon Raha was impressed, 'These boys are sharp.' Sudip Uncle and Baba beamed in satisfaction with the smart responses of their progeny. I got down to business. 'So when can we meet Robin? You don't mind if we call him Robin, do you?'

'We used to in the beginning but now we've accepted it.' Neelima Raha complained, 'We've had a hard time trying to convince him to come with us today. Can you help us bring him home?'

'Certainly,' said Kirit. Our uncontested spokesman turned towards us, 'We will bring Robin home, right?'

'Right,' Pluto and I joined hands with Kirit.

'That's great to hear,' said a visibly relieved Prasoon Raha. Sudip Uncle granted permission right away. Baba agreed because he had no choice. Pluto's parents were never around and he did not need to seek special permission for such a simple venture. We had already won over Prasoon and Neelima Raha with our gesture. 'How about Wednesday evening, around 7 p.m.?' inquired Neelima Raha. 'We don't want to upset your studies though,' added Prasoon Raha. Pluto let out a mini grunt, 'My maths tutor will leave at seven. Can we go at 7:05 p.m.?' The Rahas found his sincerity amusing 'We will not leave without you,' Neelima Raha promised.

'Thanks,' Pluto nodded and let out a grunt of satisfaction.

On Wednesday, we were ready before our stipulated time of departure. Ma was concerned that I would miss my evening study but since Baba had already granted me the travel permit she could not oppose. 'Try to wind up soon,' she suggested.

'I'm going with others. How can I wind up before everyone else?' I reasoned. Ma realised there was no point in pursuing her attempt any further. I was glad that I would not have to study that evening. Very soon, Prasoon Uncle and Neelima Aunty came to pick me up and introduced themselves to my mother.

Robin knew we were coming and received us graciously. We had expected a grumpy, disgruntled young fellow who would require some coaxing and cajoling to enter his own home. On the contrary, he was really friendly, like his parents. Clearly the Rahas had spoken highly about us for which he was favourably predisposed. Robin had shampoo commercial hair, so perfectly parted in the middle that the partition resembled a road in the middle of dense beefwood forests. He wore fashionable dark blue jeans from FU's and an equally in vogue black Avis denim shirt. Soon, we found out that he was extremely finicky about his clothes. Robin wore Windsor glasses and they gave him a serious appearance. He played the guitar well and loved Elvis Presley. Robin's spoken English was excellent. He had a mild British accent, which sounded like a dream next to my vernacular style delivery. I had an instant complex and promised myself that someday I would speak like him, effortlessly and with panache.

In India, you need heaven to be on your side to succeed if you don't speak English. If you make mistakes while speaking the language, great ridicule is likely to follow. Prasoon Uncle asked

Robin to show us around his aunt's house in Rainee Park and we began the tour from the terrace.

At first sight, Robin was cool. But what he asked us before anything else, threw us off-balance and brought him closer to us right away, 'What's the chick scene like at Vanilla?'

'What?' I tried to recover from his straightforward approach.

Kirit was amused, 'You too, Brutus?' Kirit was studying Julius Caesar in school and every now and then he would mouth lines from the masterpiece. Pluto shook his shoulders ..vigourously, a sign that he was laughing from the inside without letting his exterior reveal it. He contributed, 'We have Loreto, La Martiniere and Modern High School. What more do you want?'

'Great,' Robin looked relieved.

'That's not all,' I chipped in with some icing. 'We have Loreto Convent Darjeeling and Dowhill Girls.'

'They're no good,' Robin shook his head.

'What're you saying man, those chicks set fire to the bloody benches they sit on,' Kirit tried to convince him.

'I know, I know,' he agreed. 'But they don't live in the city. They live in the hills.'

I took Kirit's side, 'They come home on vacations.'

Robin shook his head again, 'Not enough time.'

Kirit nodded. Robin may have a valid point. I had to say something smart now, 'I'd say go for the others and settle for some challenge during the vacations.'

'Tiger, you pull some unexpected ones,' Pluto complimented me and let out a grunt.

'How did you get that name, Tiger?' Robin inquired. Kirit burst out laughing.

'It's because of this ass,' I pointed towards Kirit.

'You like that name. It's far better than Chinmoy,' Kirit protested.

Pluto spoke, 'He used to have a tiger skin T-shirt. That's how he got it.'

'Awesome,' Robin joined in the banter. I was trying to make up my mind about Robin when Neelima Aunty's voice was heard. We were so engaged in our chat that we had not taken the intended tour of Robin's aunt's beautiful home. When we left the terrace together, it seemed that we had known each other all our lives.

First it was 'Lonely Chinmoy,' then it was the 'Tumultuous Two,' followed by a 'Thrilling Three.' Now a 'Fabulous Four' was in the making. All of us had one thing in common. We were desperate to strike friendships at Vanilla. And when you wish for something sincerely, heaven's gate has to open up.

The next day we were restless to get back home quickly after school. We had to nurture our new friendship a little more. We did not go downstairs to play and were at the Rahas by 5 p.m. But whose place would Robin visit first? We flipped a coin. Kirit won. Then came Pluto and I finished last. I reasoned that if Robin visited me last, he would be able to stay the most. 'Tiger always beats us in the end, doesn't he?' Kirit said to make me feel better.

A dozen more families had arrived bringing a handful of additional teenagers. But either because they were already in college, or shied away from us, or were simply too young, they were not fit to be part of our group.

Then one day, with fifteen homes yet to be filled and our hopes of finding more friends lessening, Pluto announced, 'I have a big surprise for all of you.'

'What?' 'What's going on, man?' 'What is it?' The three of us were curious to know. 'Tomorrow, I'm bringing in a present for all of you.'

'What present?' 'Come out with it.' 'Don't behave like a kid. Speak up.' We egged him on.

'Waiting makes it more fun,' said Pluto and before we could catch him and force the secret out of him, he ran away. Pluto had been clever. He mentioned it when we headed home after a round of badminton. Had he spoken about it earlier, we would certainly have dropped divers into his stomach to get the story out. Besides, homework had piled up and we had already switched to study mode.

By the next evening, both Robin and I had completely forgotten about Pluto's promised surprise. But Kirit remembered. When Pluto walked into the common room to join us, Kirit stampeded him, 'Where's the surprise?'

Pluto smiled, 'Three guesses.' Kirit would take none of it any more, 'Do you want a kick in your scrawny ass?'

'You have to work for it,' Pluto was adamant.

Kirit playfully nudged at Pluto's privates with the tip of his new sneakers. 'What's wrong with you man?' Pluto tried to protect his manhood with his left hand. Robin took the cue and tried out the same stunt. With both palms covering the zone rendered vulnerable by the Vanilla hoodlums, Pluto tried me, 'Tiger, you guess.'

'Either you are taking us out for dinner or gifting us all a new pair of sneakers,' I tried. 'Rubbish,' Pluto was disappointed. 'Think beyond mundane material things. Think emotion. Think people,' he continued.

Robin guessed, 'You brought a chick with you whose oranges we can squeeze?'

'Nope,' Pluto enjoyed Robin's participation.

'That's enough, what's the big secret?' Kirit was growing impatient.

'I won't tell you until you guess.'

Kirit had had enough of this game. He looked towards Pluto's nether regions and joined his hands together to mock dive towards his groin. But this time, Pluto was careful enough to have his base covered. 'Not fair, Kirit. Why do you have to act special? Why can't you participate like the others?'

'Oh drama queen, you have my heart crying,' Kirit mocked Pluto. Then he changed his tone, 'Okay, let me guess.' Pluto felt relaxed and satisfied as Kirit had agreed to participate in the silly guessing game. With Pluto's guard down, Kirit dived on him and grabbed the front portion of his jeans, 'I got his duck,' Kirit yelled. Completely taken by surprise, Pluto nearly lost his balance. I caught his chair and saved his crown. Kirit's boorish behaviour made us laugh so hard that Robin nearly toppled out of his chair. While this ridiculous melee was going on, a boy our age walked in from the concealed section of the L-shaped common room. 'Who are you?' Kirit released Pluto and straightened up.

'Looking for somebody?' Robin asked him.

'He is the surprise, you idiots,' laughed Pluto. He was the only one laughing in the room now.

'Hang on, I don't get it,' I was confused.

The stranger solved the mystery. 'My name is Sanket Sanyal and I will be moving in this building on Sunday.'

'What?' we said in unison.

'Yeah,' Sanket confirmed.

'That is a good surprise,' I smiled.

'You won this one Pluto,' Kirit acknowledged.

'Which school are you in?' Robin broke the ice.

'I'm in Pluto's school. Same grade but not in the same section.'

Robin pushed a spare chair towards Sanket, 'Sit down and tell us what's going on.'

Pluto wiped his face with the back of his shirt-sleeve and said, 'Section B and Section D had a joint chemistry lab class yesterday because an expert chemist came to show us an experiment. Sanket and I were paired in that class.'

Sanket joined in, 'I asked him where he lived.'

'And he said that he'd be moving into Vanilla Apartments on Sunday.' Pluto completed Sanket's sentence.

'Unbelievable!' I exclaimed.

'What a coincidence,' Robin admitted as Pluto chuckled in pure pleasure.

Kirit was equally surprised, 'Which flat are you in?'

'2J,' said Sanket, bracing for more questions.

'You have to pass an intelligence test for an entry into our group,' Kirit tested the buoyant youth's temperament.

'That may be a problem,' Sanket looked concerned.

'Why?' demanded Robin.

'Because I'm not intelligent,' Sanket confessed.

I liked his response, 'This qualifies him. I pass him.'

Robin countered me, 'But a test is a test. We all sat for one.'

Pluto laughed, 'Bullshit. You would've failed first thing.'

Sanket solved the debate, 'I'll sit for a test.'

'Excellent,' Kirit said as he took out a broken piece of chalk from his pocket and flung it towards him. Sanket caught it easily, 'Where's the blackboard?'

'There's no blackboard. You'll have to measure the length of this room with this chalk,' Kirit got to business.

Pluto protested, 'That's no intelligence assessment. That's physical labour. It'll take the whole evening and he still won't be done.'

Sanket smiled, 'Any other test or just this one?'

'First take this one successfully and then you can show off,' I mustered up some courage.

'Don't mess with the Royal Bengal Tiger or else, he will *halum* you,' joked Pluto. *Halum* was a Bengali rendition of a tiger's roar.

Sanket looked around the room and spotted a cricket bat lying in a corner. He walked up to it and picked it up. Robin corrected him, 'Not with the bat, Gavaskar,' referring to the legendary batsman. 'You have to use the chalk.'

'I know,' Sanket replied with supreme confidence.

Kirit was observing him intently. Sanket placed the bat flat on to the floor. Then he began measuring the blade with the broken piece of chalk. The blade was sixteen times the size of the chalk. I guessed what he was trying to do. Kirit was already impressed although he did not interrupt the man at work. Robin was quiet. Sanket picked up the bat and walked to the wall on our side of the common room. He placed it on the floor again and began counting the length of the floor with the blade of the bat.

Pluto was still not sure what was going on, 'Sanket, you will never finish.'

'Shh,' I said, 'Just watch.'

Sanket had reached the other side of the room along with the bat in a few minutes. The length of the room was twenty five times the blade of the cricket bat. He stood up and said, '25 X 16 = 240 times the chalk.'

'You pass with a gold star,' Kirit beamed.

'How did he get the number?' Pluto was still not sure.

'Donkey, the blade of the bat was sixteen times the length of the chalk, and the length of the room was twenty-five times the blade of the bat. He multiplied the two and got the result,' I explained to Pluto.

'Genius,' Pluto was amazed but recovered fast, 'Hundred rupees. Take out hundred rupees, each one of you. I've brought in a genius.' No one paid any attention to Pluto's absurd demand.

Robin acted tough, 'But he hasn't passed my test.'

'Come on, man,' I said.

Sanket was ready, 'I'll do your test too.'

'What is the meaning of the word Sanket?' asked Robin.

'An indicator or perhaps a portent of good news, I would say. But if you go literally, I suppose it would mean, a signal.'

Robin exclaimed, 'We'll call you Signal. Sanket is too Hindi. Signal sounds way more cool.'

'Signal sounds ridiculous,' I said. Kirit kicked me from the side gently so that I did not interrupt the ongoing proceedings. 'Actually Sig sounds cooler,' continued Robin, who loved everything American, 'How're you doin', Sig? You got a chick, Sig? You stick up cars, Sig? Your chick's a dip, Sig? Sig's totally awesome.'

'I'm cool with it,' Sanket surprised us with his consent. He must have been desperate to make friends. I remembered what it was like for me only a few months ago when I was new at Vanilla Apartments.

Sanket extended his hand towards Kirit. But Kirit ignored it and gave him a bear hug, 'Welcome to Vanilla Apartments.' Robin joined in and so did I. Pluto broke into a shimmy and exclaimed, 'I told you Sanket…'

'Sig,' Robin corrected him.

'Okay, Sig. See, I told you, these guys are the best.'

Kirit held out his palm and Robin's noisy slap came down upon it hard. I joined in and Pluto's hand added to the size of the mound. Then we turned to look at Sig. Without a moment's hesitation, we felt his hand slam down on the hill to seal a bond of camaraderie that remains unbroken even today.

## CHAPTER FIVE

# Bhitu Bakshi

$\mathcal{T}$ he five of us made a great team. There was a lot of tomfoolery amongst us. Pluto and I were bearers of most of the capers but Kirit, Robin and Sig were otherwise so gracious that we could never remain angry with them for too long. Kirit was the unmatched prankster but we were all gradually turning a little like him. Pluto's hair growth was abysmal and at a time when we wanted to grow moustaches and dense beards, his face did not display a single sign of maturity. He was funny and cool and silly all rolled into one but there was something cold and distant about him. When I pointed it out to him one day, he had a wry smile on his face, 'I'm cold just like the planet.' Although his parents bought him every physical comfort, Pluto did not have the normalcy of a family life the rest of us took for granted.

Eighty-eight flats had already been occupied in the building. Out of the twelve remaining, ten flats were corporate accommodations. These would never see a permanent resident. Executive tenants who would come and go did not interest us for we believed that lasting friendships could not be formed with transient people. When the job moved, they would follow. That left us with two apartments: 7A and 8C. Both were sold but yet to be inhabited.

I had grown accustomed to my majestic nickname although it was inappropriate for someone with a pudgy build like mine. I used it as a pseudonym to write an essay competition in school and won the second prize. That was when I decided that the name was lucky for me and began using it wholeheartedly. Soon enough, I was rechristened Tiger at school as well. Chinmoy had disappeared and Tiger had emerged.

Kirit had a chiseled body and worked out everyday without fail. He had little patience for anyone with excess fat. 'Shows indiscipline,' he complained, pointing to a mini bulge above my belt. I tried to shake him off, 'What about Sudip Uncle and Sumita Aunty?'

'Absolutely. No one is exempt. I've grown tired of telling them. There will come a day when both the old and the new will run to the gym day and night because nothing will matter more than looking good.'

'But fat is a sign of prosperity.' Now I took the side of Kirit's parents.

'It'll all change. How quickly though, that remains to be seen.'

By then, nearly a dozen teenaged boys from the building played table tennis, badminton, football and cricket. But once the games were over most of them did not stay back to chat with us. The girls formed their own groups and some would occasionally join us for a few rounds of badminton.

It was June, 1983. India had entered the finals of the world cup cricket for the first time in history. We decided to watch the match at Kirit's place because he had the fanciest TV set. Plus, we could savour delicacies from Sumita Aunty's creative kitchen. And if India swung a victory, the feast would perhaps be a first of its kind in the history of the entire city.

When I entered 10B fifteen minutes before the match began, a crowd was already busy discussing the possibilities that lay before Team India. Kirit's maternal uncle, Pop Mama was present and it did not take me long to realise why he had landed the nickname. Pop Mama's six pack abs and sixteen inch biceps were evident under a flimsy Levi's T-shirt imported from America. A large Rolex sat like a mini hillock on his powerful wrist. It was impossible to lie to him for he could cut anyone open with his trained police eyes. But his smile and affable manner made us feel that he was on our side. The handsome, young martial arts expert could pass off as a successful movie star and few men in law enforcement could claim to be half as suave. Of all miscreants, he hated drug peddlers the most and rotten criminals convulsed in sheer terror at the sight of the dynamic police officer. But Pop Mama bent the law to his convenience and prospered immensely from the system. When he disregarded the law to eliminate societal bugs, he was hailed a hero by the people instead of being reprimanded by the authorities. By the end of the day, everyone who had met Pop Mama for the first time had taken an immense liking towards the man.

Sumita Aunty was possibly the only person in the entire nation not interested in the match. 'I want India to win, but I don't understand the game. It's too complicated,' she complained. The days of being eternal underdogs were soon over. India won decisively. The scenes of jubilation must be deeply etched in the minds of every Indian who saw the game that day. The entire city descended on the streets. Strangers had converted to blood brothers. The noise of clarinets, bassoons and shrill whistles was deafening and the night sky lit up with fireworks. We began to believe in the impossible. First, it was a 200,000 rupee lottery win for us and then the world cup for India: nothing was out of reach anymore. Overnight, my chest had expanded a few inches like every other Indian's. We were delirious with joy and every evening for the next few weeks, we sacrificed all other sports for cricket. All conversations were centred on the world cup and how our men had proved to be the best. In the middle of all the excitement, a new family had moved in on the day of the finals and not one resident had marked their arrival. We became aware of their existence only after a few days.

The following Saturday morning, I was heading down to the common room when I noticed a middle-aged gentleman seated with a boy of our age inside the administration office. The boy looked so scared and white that he seemed to have been dug out of a coffin. The gentleman was talking to Baba in a hushed tone. Baba had become an important member of the Vanilla Apartments' board and used his weekends to look after the interests of its members pertaining to the residence. At his day job his status had not changed. But with this voluntary position, Baba discovered the respect that he never found at work. The members knew that he was forthright and thanked him for his time and efforts. That was enough to hook Tanmoy Bose for life.

When I reached the common room I found that Robin and Kirit were playing table tennis. Sig was watching the game with keen interest while Pluto listened to a walkman with his eyes shut. 'Hey, did you notice the boy in the office?' I asked no one in particular.

'Must be a visitor,' said Robin after striking the ball back to Kirit.

'Why bother?' Sig said as Kirit smashed a backhand to Robin.

'He could've come to live at 7A or 8C,' I suggested.

'Good point, Tiger,' Kirit caught the ball mid air.

Robin was irritated, 'Shit! Not now. After the game.'

'He may not be there by the time you finish,' I reasoned.

'You go and talk to him,' Robin was anxious to get on with the game for he was winning.

'It'll only take two minutes,' I did not give up.

'Let's go,' Kirit was eager.

'He's sitting inside the office and we can't just walk in,' Robin made a feeble attempt to continue.

'Of course we can. It's our office too,' Kirit had a valid point.

'We can try,' Sig agreed.

Robin gave up. Pluto had heard nothing of the conversation with the music blaring in his ears. But he followed us blindly as we walked out of the common room and headed towards the administration office.

Baba was talking to the ghostly boy when he saw us and looked up. Kirit smiled, 'Tanmoy Uncle, we just wanted to know if he...,' Kirit pointed towards the subject, '...has moved into 7A or 8C.'

'That's right. They're in 8C. This is the Bakshi family.' Baba nodded. Then he turned towards the boy and said, 'You have a new set of friends.' The boy's father relaxed a little. Kirit waved out to the boy but he did not return the favour. 'Do you want to join us?' asked Robin. The boy shook his head. 'How about cricket?' I asked. The boy shook his head again. 'If you don't feel like playing you could be the umpire.' That was the best Sig could do. The boy was about to shake his head again when Mr. Bakshi gestured us to walk into the office. Baba did not approve of us entering the administration office and cramping it. He took the board job seriously and treated the administration office as his own. Kirit sensed there was a problem, 'Is there a problem, Tanmoy Uncle?'

'Yes. No. Kind of,' Baba stuttered.

'We can help,' Robin suggested.

'I don't think so,' Baba shook his head.

'Can you?' Mr. Bakshi inquired.

'Sure. But we'll need to know what the matter is.' I took the cue. It was evident that Baba did not want Mr. Bakshi to discuss the problem at hand with a bunch of school kids. But Mr. Bakshi had already opened up, 'We moved here on June 25.'

'Wow. Historic day!' I exclaimed. India had won the world cup that day.

'Welcome,' said Pluto after a long silence. He had unplugged his walkman and begun to pay attention to the proceedings.

'Thank you. It has been…', Mr. Bakshi had begun to continue his commentary when the ghostly boy suddenly woke up, 'Yesterday I saw a ghost on the stairs!'

'What?' we were completely taken aback by his unexpected revelation. All eyes were on him now.

'Ghost?' Sig asked. Pluto lowered his glasses and looked at the boy from above them as if he was studying a guinea pig in his personal research laboratory. The boy nodded and said, 'Yes. A ghost.' Kirit pulled up a chair and asked us to join in. Baba did not approve of his precociousness but by then we were totally into the discussion. At the flick of an eyelid we were all seated. Robin urged the boy to continue, 'Go on.' The ghostly boy began talking, 'My name is Bittu Bakshi and I live in…'

'Yeah, we got that part,' Kirit was impatient. 'You're in 8C. What about the ghost?'

'Yesterday morning I was walking down the stairs between the eighth and seventh floors when I saw a man emerge right in front of me, all of a sudden. He smiled at me and asked if I lived in the building.'

'Okay. Then?' I urged him on.

'How did you know that he was a ghost?' asked Sig.

'I had bent down to tie my open shoelace. To come in front of me he would have to walk up a few stairs, right?'

'Go on,' Robin needed more information before he formed an expert opinion.

'If he climbed up the stairs, how come I didn't see him?' questioned Bittu Bakshi.

'You were absent-minded,' I reasoned.

'No, there's more. Hear him out,' Bittu's father responded to my rational explanation.

'I was thinking about how the man appeared from nowhere when he asked me if I had watched the cricket finals,' Bittu continued. 'I told him that I saw the action replay on TV for we were not set with our TV connection on the day of the match.'

'You didn't see the finals?' asked Pluto as if it had just been revealed that Bittu Bakshi had been charged with inciting genocide. Bittu continued apologetically, 'He invited me over for sweets at Flat 7A along with my parents.'

'Seems like a sweet ghost,' commented Pluto sarcastically. Immediately he was kicked under the table by Robin and Kirit. Bittu ignored Pluto and went on, 'I had to catch the school bus and told him that I was getting late for school. Then he vanished into thin air.'

'Like he had appeared out of nowhere?' I was curious again.

'Total vanishment?' wisecracked Pluto. This time Sig and I kicked him harder under the table. He grunted as my enterprise landed on his shin.

'Total,' nodded Bittu.

Kirit thought about Bittu's claim for a moment and asked, 'That's it?'

'No,' Bittu was enthused that he had found a platform to vent. 'I couldn't get the incident out of my mind all day at school. Then when I was coming back home…'

'From school?' I interrupted.

'Yes,' Bittu nodded. 'I thought, let me take the lift to the sixth floor and walk up the remaining two flights.'

'To check if you can see him again?' Kirit tried to gauge Bittu's sanity.

'Right. I walked up the stairs expecting to see him but he wasn't there. 7A was locked. There were two big locks hanging from the door. And then all of a sudden I saw him standing in front of the flat.'

'That's quite a story,' Pluto said disbelievingly.

'If you don't believe me, there's no point in my talking any more,' Bittu was annoyed.

Four pairs of legs came rushing towards Pluto from under the table. But this time he was prepared. He avoided my kick and the tip of my shoe landed hard on Sig's shin. Sig twisted his face like a flipped omelet and suppressed a yelp. I gave him a sheepish grin. Robin and Sig had missed their target completely and Kirit's attempt did not have much effect. But he provided cover for Pluto, 'He only meant that it's an interesting set of events. He didn't suggest that you were lying. So please continue.' Bittu hesitated and glared at Pluto, who had by then started on a chewing gum. We had turned into a raptured audience and hung on to every word uttered by Bittu Bakshi. He decided to continue. 'For a few seconds I didn't know what to say. The ghost told me that the action replay of the final match was being re telecast at 9 p.m.' Even though Bittu was uncomfortable in his presence he had managed to ask the ghost, 'Why are these huge locks hanging from the bolt? Are you going away somewhere?'

'I was not at home. I'd been to the market,' the ghost claimed. There were no shopping bags in his hands.

'Didn't you buy anything from there?' Bittu persisted.

'I don't buy every time I go there. Generally in the evenings, I like to walk around the Gariahat market,' he smiled. Bittu Bakshi thought that it was odd for a man to walk around Gariahat market without any intent of purchase. He decided it was time to place a hold on his inquisitiveness, 'I have to go,' he said and started climbing the stairs towards the eighth floor. When he reached the head of the stairs and looked back, the ghost was gone!

'He may have walked into 7A.' Robin shook his head in disbelief.

'7A is vacant,' Baba interrupted. He revealed to us that the owners of 7A lived in New York and were yet to visit.

Bittu Bakshi's case was stronger now. It was impossible for a regular person to enter 7A for Bittu had not heard the sound of the door opening. Besides, if the man had entered the flat, how could the locks still hang outside?

'Are you sure he didn't walk downstairs again?' I tried to make sense of the absurdity.

'100 percent.'

'The ghost may have decided to go for a walk in the market again,' Pluto quipped.

Bittu did not reply. Kirit tried to make sense of the whole episode. 'So you're saying that this man, who didn't look like a ghost, appeared out of nothing and disappeared twice on the same day?'

'Yes.' Bittu confirmed.

'And it happened yesterday,' I liked playing detective.

'Yes,' Bittu was visibly irritated by the constant interrogation.

'None of us have seen this man, have we?' Kirit threw the question towards us.

All of us shook our heads. My opinion was that perhaps we never saw this ghost because we rarely walked between the floors in question. Among the five of us, only Kirit lived above the sixth floor. Since all of us came up from the flats way below, we always took the lift to reach 10B. Everyone agreed that I may have come up with a valid explanation as to why the ghost had managed to escape our prying eyes. Baba was getting restless. There was work to do and we had taken over his office for a discussion about an imaginary ghost roaming around the building.

Ten minutes after we walked out of the administration office, Bittu Bakshi's fate was sealed. He had acquired a nickname – 'Bhitu', the coward. Until this day, he is Bhitu Bakshi to us.

The incident left me agitated that night. What if the boy was not hallucinating? Was there really a ghost lurking around? How come no other resident had ever complained? Could it be that the ghost was only visible to Bhitu Bakshi and no one else? If so, then why? When we met in the common room next morning, I voiced an idea, 'Why don't we walk up and down the seventh floor a few times? We may also be able to see this invisible man.' Kirit's reply surprised all of us. He had already spoken to the Administrator, Jhola Mallick in private and arranged to get the keys for 7A. Jhola had been reluctant at first but a promise of 200 rupees dissolved his resolve. 'But this is too risky,' I cringed at the thought of taking the bull by the horns, even a friendly one.

'We can step into 7A and see for ourselves,' Kirit patted me on the back.

'Without the owners' permission? That's too risky,' Sig played the logical angle.

'Thieves do it all the time,' Kirit was annoyed by our defensive approach.

'If we are caught we could go to jail,' I assisted Sig.

'For what, stealing air from the flat? It's an empty flat for God's sake,' Pluto spoke up.

'No one lives there, so there's nothing to steal. Pluto's right,' Robin agreed.

'What about trespassing?' Sig tried another approach.

'Who cares?' said Kirit.

'Do you expect to find the ghost sitting on thin air, smoking a pipe and offering us sweets the minute we enter?' I was desperate to prevent the impending madness.

'I hope so,' Kirit laughed. Everyone joined in and I realised that I had unintentionally taken the sting out of my pitch.

At Kirit's behest, we decided to involve the ultimate catholicon for all maladies, Pop Mama. We went to his sprawling, ancestral home on Rashbehari Avenue. I was certain that although he spoilt Kirit with expensive gifts, he would never allow us to trespass. After all, he was a licensed upholder of the law. Pop Mama greeted us as if we were members of the parliament. Once we settled down, giddy from the royal reception, I said, 'If we enter someone's property without their consent, wouldn't we be breaking the law?'

'Legally so,' Pop Mama reclined on the custom designed French sofa, grasping my reluctance to get on with the dangerous task. 'But in this case, you're doing something illegal as a social cause.'

'How so?' Sig was puzzled.

Pop Mama leaned forward, 'If there is indeed a ghost in that flat and you can confirm it then something must be done about it. If it's a false alarm, no problem. You did your part for society.'

Sig believed what Bhitu Bakshi claimed to have witnessed, 'I trust Bhitu Bakshi.'

'Bhitu Bakshi?' Pop Mama expressed surprise at this unusual name.

'We have named the boy Bhitu Bakshi instead of Bittu Bakshi,' Kirit said proudly. Pop Mama burst out laughing, 'That is funny. But think carefully, this Bhitu Bakshi actually got off the lift on the sixth floor to check things out for himself. He may have been scared but he isn't a coward.'

'Pop Mama's right,' agreed Pluto.

'But unless we find out that there's really a ghost in the building, the name stays,' Kirit proclaimed.

'Fair enough. It's catchy alright,' accepted Pop Mama. Just then, Pop Mama's cook, Gaja walked in with a tray filled with delicious homemade chicken patties and vegetable spring rolls. Gaja was a culinary God and over the years, his lateral view of life amused us to no end. Once when Sudip Uncle was watching cricket at the MCG in Australia, Pop Mama asked Gaja if he could spot his brother-in-law in the crowd. Gaja squinted and strained hard for a few minutes before he gave up. Then he said, 'The galleries are so crowded. How can we see him among all those people? It's much easier for him to see us. After all, there are only two of us here in the living room.' On another occasion, when the FIFA World Cup was aired in India and every Kolkattan had come alive, the benevolent Pop Mama described the nuances of the game to Gaja so that he could also soak in the fun. After the long lecture on the rules and regulations when it was time for debriefing, Gaja displayed a serene countenance. He asked Pop Mama a simple question. 'I don't understand the big fuss about football. Instead of twenty-two grown up men running after a single ball, why don't they solve the issue by handing one to each of them?'

Pop Mama was ready to assist us in our quest. He took a bite from a spring roll and addressed Gaja, 'Keep them coming, my nephews mustn't go hungry.' Gaja smiled and left the living room. Pop Mama picked up the phone and dialed a number from memory. After a short wait he spoke into the mouthpiece, 'Danger Baba?' We exchanged glances and listened intently. Who was he talking to? Who was this Danger Baba? Pop Mama went on, 'I had a quick question.' Danger Baba must have given him the go-ahead for he continued, 'My fifteen year old nephew, yes, my sister's son, lives in the new Vanilla Apartments on Gariahat Road.' He coughed and trudged on, 'A boy in the building claims to have seen a ghost. Yes, a man who disappeared after talking to him. Yes, disappeared into thin air.' Pop Mama paused to listen to Danger Baba's comments. Then he continued, 'This happened twice on the same day, when the kid was going to school and later when he was returning from school.' Our attention was diverted towards Gaja for he had entered the room again with prized Coca Cola cans, unavailable in the Indian market at the time. It was too precious to waste a single smuggled drop. We dived on our Cokes and stopped paying heed to Pop Mama's conversation with Danger Baba. In a few minutes Pop Mama disconnected the phone, 'There is a way to test the ghost story.'

'Danger Baba? What a name,' said Kirit.

'Danger Baba is a psychic who helps the police. He owns a motor maintenance garage but is gifted with a special power to feel the supernatural,' Pop Mama stated.

'How does he look?' I was curious.

'Maybe one day you'll meet him.'

'So how do we…', Pluto wanted to find out the contents of Pop Mama's conversation with Danger Baba.

'I was coming to that,' Pop Mama did not allow him to finish. 'Danger Baba will give you something that looks like a stick of dynamite.'

'Dynamite?' Sig was scared.

'It's a bunch of long cinnamon sticks tied together with a psychic goat's hair and immersed in some special syrup that Danger Baba concocts in the backyard of his garage.'

'What do we need it for?' I visualised the lethal explosive.

'To check if there's really a ghost. You can call it a ghostometre,' said Pop Mama.

'Sounds dangerous,' I tried to dissuade him from acquiring a ghostometre for us.

'Danger Baba would prepare it for you. He promised that if you have it with you, you would come to no harm when you go in search of the ghost,' Pop Mama's trust in the weird psychic was evident.

'How will the dynamite, I mean…the ghostometre help us confirm if there is indeed a ghost or not? Sig asked.

'I'll give you all the details after I take all other questions,' Pop Mama was pleased with his pertinent query.

'How much will he charge?' Kirit wanted to make sure that this was not an expensive proposition.

'Excellent question,' Pop Mama patted him on the back. 'Short answer to that is, I'll take care of it.'

'Thanks,' Kirit looked relieved.

'How long will it take for him to deliver?' I chipped in, trying to sound as smart as Kirit. 'Spoken like a Tiger,' Pop Mama patted my shoulder so hard that a few drops of urine slipped out of my control and trickled down my leg. I was glad not to sport a pair of shorts that day and grew careful not to act smart anytime soon.

'It'll take him a couple of days,' Pop Mama continued. 'I'm glad that you boys haven't chickened out of the adventure.'

There had been no confirmed agreement of undertaking this dangerous task. We had only gone to consult Pop Mama. It was such a serious matter and Kirit's irresponsible uncle was pushing us towards a probable crisis instead of discouraging us from doing something that was illegal and unsafe. I was dumbfounded at his recklessness.

Robin spoke, 'Where do we pick it up?'

'I'll have it delivered,' Pop Mama had decided on our behalf. 'Now getting back to Sig's earlier question – What do you do with a ghostometre?' He explained that the sticks must be kept balanced on the seat of a commode. If they began to melt, we would have to push it into the commode and cover it with the lid.

Kirit raised a question, 'What if the sticks fall into the commode before it melts?' Pop Mama shifted in his seat, 'You have to tape the ghostometre to the seat to address the balancing issue. If you see it melting, use a stick or a ruler to push it into the commode. Don't touch it with your hands. When it falls into the water, drop the lid. It's that simple'

'So melting is the indicator that there is a ghost,' said Sig.

'Correct,' Pop Mama was pleased with his bright students. 'The lid may be pushed up a couple of times but the ghost wouldn't be able to escape. Do not remove the lid at all. Just get out of there and call me.'

'If the sticks don't melt, then we'd know that there's nothing supernatural at 7A,' Pluto dampened Pop Mama's excitement.

'Isn't there any risk at all for us?' I tried to enhance the risk factor.

'Not unless you don't follow Danger Baba's instructions. I trust that none of you will try any stunts.'

'You're the best, Pop Mama,' Kirit was excited to take on the ghost.

Suddenly Pop Mama looked serious and alarmed us, 'Whatever you do, make sure that you don't sit on that commode to relieve yourselves after the dynamite is dropped into it,' he paused for maximum effect and continued, 'for then the ghost would have only one escape route.' Everyone laughed at the low-brow humour.

Pop Mama was a lunatic to assist such a crazy adolescent venture or perhaps, he was re-living his youth vicariously through us. Sig was getting into the details of 'Operation Ghost Trap', 'How long should we to keep vigil on the dynamite sticks?' Pop Mama did not know the answer to that one, 'My detectives are way ahead of me. I hadn't thought of that. I'll ask Danger Baba and let you know.' Then he inquired if we had already got the keys to the flat. I tried to abort the mission by building as many obstacles around it as possible, 'Jhola, the office administrator wants a lot of money to hand over the keys to us,' I said hopefully.

'How much?' Pop Mama got down to business.

'Rs 200,' Sig understood my defensive angle. Without batting an eyelid, Pop Mama swooshed out a Mont Blanc leather wallet and brought out Rs 500. He handed it over to Kirit and said, 'Good luck, boys.' Kirit took the money as if it was his birthright, 'Thanks.' Pop Mama stood up, 'I'll have to head out to Bajrang now.' Bajrang was a popular body building gymnasium in Triangular Park, a few minutes drive from his home. Once Pop Mama entered the gym, his driver would drop us home. The meeting was over. We stood up. Pop Mama looked at me directly. 'Tiger, I noticed that you drank only a small can of Coke. Don't forget to carry some cans home.' Then he addressed everyone else. 'And that goes for all of you.' They pounced upon the tray and grabbed as many cans as they could. But I was too shy. Pop Mama saw me hesitating. He grabbed four cans and dumped them on my hands. We left precariously balancing smuggled Coca Cola cans in every uncovered crevasse in our bodies.

The deal was sealed. We would be getting the keys to 7A in the wee hours of the following Saturday. Our entry had to be cautious so that no one could see us. We had toyed with the idea of a late night entry but Jhola warned us that the electricity in the flat was yet to be set up. The mounting stress of encountering a ghost gave me sleepless nights throughout the week. On the other hand, I did not wish to return empty handed and look like a fool. At times, I wanted to confide in Mukul but he would surely blurt out the plan to our parents. There were only four people in the world with whom I could share my fears but now they were all party to this madness.

# CHAPTER SIX

# Catch and Release

*T*he big day arrived. It was Saturday and a holiday for most people in the building. We planned to step out very early in the morning on the pretext of a cricket match at Deshapriya Park. There were no early risers on weekends at the Bose residence. As I unlocked the front door, I resisted a strong urge to back out. I could easily tell the boys later that I overslept. But the sheer embarrassment I would have to face for the rest of my life because of the obvious cowardice would be too much to bear. I tiptoed back into my parents' bedroom and stopped in front of Ma's small temple, closed for the night. 'Even the Gods were sleeping,' I thought. It would be ideal to leave seeking 'Their' blessings but opening the squeaky metal doors of the temple at the odd hour would be too risky. Ma slept light. It would be hard to explain the sudden spirituality. I glanced ruefully at the closed doors of the temple, shut my eyes and folded my hands in silent prayer to the out-of-sight deities. Then reluctantly, I left the room.

Kirit was already waiting for me at the base of the staircase on the fifth floor, our meeting point. He gave me the thumbs up as an assurance that our mission was on. He had a small rucksack on his back and nodded to me indicating that the ghostometre was safe and ready to be activated. Robin joined us within a few minutes.

He let out a yawn so big that I almost fell into it. Kirit whispered to him, 'Stay alert.' Robin assembled himself. Sig arrived. His exit from home had not been as smooth as the others. Alok Uncle was awake when Sig tried to put on his sneakers. He told his son to work on his geography, a subject Sig had not fared too well in the last exam. Sig lied to Alok Uncle that he had reserved the entire day for geography, after the cricket match. Although Alok Uncle wondered which of his son's lunatic friends would join him for a game that early in the morning, he did not wish to begin the day arguing with his son.

But there was still no sign of the ever punctual Pluto. Nirmal Uncle was in London for a conference and Urmi Aunty was a late riser. Pluto must have been asleep. 'Should we wake him up?' I asked Kirit, hoping to wage war with a larger army. Kirit, leading our ridiculous mission was thoughtful for a moment. Then he shook his head, 'We want to be inside 7A before the neighbours wake up. The more delay, the more chances of people seeing us. Let's go without him.' I made one last attempt to sabotage the livewire operation, 'It would be a bad omen to go without a soldier.' Kirit spoke like a veteran who had undertaken many similar assignments, 'There's no reason for us to feel weak. We'll do what we have to do. Right?'

'Right,' Robin and Sig agreed. 'Let's go,' Kirit urged. 'Operation Ghost Trap' was underway. Our vertiginous climb began from the rear staircase. Very soon, we reached the seventh floor. It was 4:45 a.m and there was no sign of life in the neighbouring flats. Robin took position on the main staircase between the seventh and eighth floors to alert us of anyone walking down. I stood at the head of the rear staircase on the seventh floor, a less traversed route but one that also needed to be watched. Sig covered the stairs between the sixth and seventh floors to report activity from below. Kirit ran towards 7A like a cheetah after an unsuspecting fawn. Before I knew it, he had opened both the locks and removed the door latch. I saw the door of the flat swing open and my blood curdled. Kirit turned and waved towards me. Abandoning my position, I ran towards 7A and nearly bumped into Sig who was also running in from below. In the next couple of seconds, Robin joined us from above. The door clicked shut. We were inside 7A.

The flat looked really spacious for it was completely vacant. We tried to turn on the lights but as expected, there was no electric connection. The first streaks of dawn helped us before Kirit whisked out two flashlights from his rucksack. We had expected to see a dusty flat but 7A was spotlessly clean. The master bedroom had a great view of the city from both sets of windows. It was open in the north and east. The relatively smaller second room was open in the east and south. The living room and balcony were separated by a decorative glass door like ours.

Our second surprise was waiting. All the windows in the flat were open. We braced ourselves to meet the ghost and tiptoed across the empty space. My heart was beating so hard that I was sure if the ghost had been asleep somewhere in the flat, he would have considered them to be knocks on the door. When we walked into the large bathroom attached to the master bedroom, our reflection in the mirror above the washbasin scared us enough to forget our names for a moment. The bathtub was ornate, although its colour was hard to decipher without direct light. A shower with a fancy hand grip and a commode was all that the rest of the space could handle. The second bathroom was similar but without a tub. The bigger bathroom was the preferred choice for our crazy experiment.

We noticed a familiar smell all around us. 'Do you smell something?' whispered Kirit. 'Chicken curry.' I whispered back. Everyone nodded an affirmative. Suddenly there was a rap on the main door! A few drops of urine escaped my bladder at once and made a small but ugly patch in my shorts. I was glad that it was dark. No one had noticed. All of us jumped out of our skins. Sig stood right next to me and I could see his face clearly. He looked as if his heart had been pushed out of its circuit and ready to pop out of his mouth. 'Who's that?' wondered a wide eyed Robin.

'The ghost,' I announced the obvious.

'It's trying to scare us,' Sig croaked.

It was impossible to meeken Kirit, 'Shh, don't make a sound.' But as soon as he finished, another urgent rap on the door was heard again. My blood had begun to freeze fast and for the first time in my life I knew how it felt to be exposed in sub zero temperature without warm clothing. The ghost was playing games with us before it took us away with it. Should I shout for help? I contemplated. But what if it was a false alarm? I would look stupid. Kirit looked through the eyehole as the rest of us huddled together in terror. He paused for a moment. Then he swung open the door and whisked in a black hooded figure. It was Pluto! The relief was unbelievable. But we had good reason to eat him alive. Kirit held Pluto's neck and mock strangled him as Pluto tried to conceal peals of laughter by covering his mouth with both his hands. The mood lightened. We hurled the choicest of Bengali and Hindi abuses at him. Only Robin used the best expletives conjured by the English language and immortalised by Hollywood. The abuse went on for a few minutes but it was all in whisper mode. Finally, Pluto apologised. He had woken up well before time and thought that he could sleep for a few extra minutes before stepping out. Confidently he had switched off the alarm clock. He woke up late but jumped out of bed, brushed quickly and tucked away some biscuits and a small bottle of water for us in the pockets of a hooded sweatshirt. His thoughtfulness granted him a quick pardon. The excitement had made us hungry and within minutes the biscuits were devoured. We drank some water and got back to our mission. Pluto gave a quick run of the house and smelt the chicken curry. 'Who has been cooking chicken curry here?' he asked.

'What do you think?' I pointed out the obvious. We had assembled in the bathroom, ready to carry out the most frightening experiment of our lives.

Kirit took out the ghostometre from his rucksack. The sturdy and bound cinnamon sticks did give it the appearance of dynamite. Pluto exclaimed, 'Dynamite!' Kirit and Robin taped it to the toilet seat and we gathered around it. I had a foot long wooden ruler in my hand and was ready to push the ghostometre into the water if it began to melt.

The first few minutes were nerve racking. Our heavy breathing could be heard inside the bathroom. The daredevil Kirit was also sweating along with the rest of us. The pressure was on. We were in the middle of a voodoo experiment. If we died here, our parents would never find us. Maybe months later when the owners of the flat came from America to take possession, they would see five skeletons lying in their empty bathroom. By then we would have turned into ghosts ourselves and be roaming around the building scaring the likes of Bhitu Bakshi. My thoughts were interrupted by a muffled sneeze by Sig. Our nerves were edgy and although everyone jumped up in fright, we appreciated that he had at least attempted to reduce the noise. But in a starkly vacant flat even a mosquito belch would sound like a police motorcycle. We had seen each other react to the sneeze and burst out laughing. Trying to laugh noiselessly, we produced a new set of strange musical composition. Kirit and Pluto walked into the master bedroom to control themselves. Robin's eyes were streaming. I was nearly choking in mirth and Sig sat on the bathroom floor holding his mouth. That was when I noticed something that shall accompany me to the crematorium. The taped cinnamon stick dynamite had begun to melt! Since Sig was seated on the floor and closer to the spot where the spectacle unfolded, he was the first to notice the incredible sight. He lost his laugh completely but his hands still covered his mouth. Robin's eyes turned so wide that his eyeballs could have dropped out of their sockets. Kirit and Pluto were back and staring at the phenomenon. None of us had ever known such awe in our entire lives. I had completely forgotten to push the cinnamon sticks into the commode. Kirit was the first to recover. He whispered, 'Push it in.' But I had frozen. Sensing further immobility from my end, Kirit snatched the ruler from my hand and nudged the ghostometre with it. The cello tapes holding it grew loose. 'Be careful, it must not fall on the floor,' Robin warned as the sticks hung from the toilet seat. In the meantime, it continued to melt but mysteriously, there was no smoke. The ghostometre landed into the water with a splash. Kirit lunged forward and dropped the lid of the commode. We were sweating profusely and it took us a couple of seconds to absorb that we had done the impossible. We had trapped the ghost in a commode!

Within seconds we saw the lid of the commode taking a few

knocks from below. The ghost was struggling to come out. We ran. Kirit threw away the ruler and we stormed out of the flat. We had thrown caution to the wind while exiting 7A. Anyone on the floor could have seen us coming out of the empty flat we had no right to be in. But at that point, it was safety beyond anything else. Kirit's hands were shaking too but he was brave enough to lock up. We did not abandon him and stood next to him as he pressed the locks shut. Then we took the rear staircase and ran again. We ran down all the seven floors and reached the ground floor. We did not stop there. We went outside the building premises and headed south towards Golpark. No one said a word. We jogged past the four-street Gariahat Road intersection. Taxis slowed down to see if we needed a ride and sped up in disappointment when they realised that we were not potential passengers. We kept running until we reached the serene white building of Ramakrishna Mission Institute of Culture in Golpark. By then we were all out of breath. Pluto had fallen back. He caught up after several minutes. A tea stall owner had opened up but regretted that we were too early for his *samosas* and *jalebis*. Five panting customers agreed to settle for tea and dog biscuits. The tea helped us settle down. Kirit was the first one to break the silence, 'Did you guys notice something?'

'What?' I asked.

'I pushed the ghostometre into the commode but some of the melted portions were still stuck to the seat,' he said.

'What does that mean?' asked Pluto.

'We may not have trapped the entire ghost,' observed Robin.

'He pushed the lid from below. Remember?' Sig eased our stress. 'Even if he is not entirely trapped, the melted portion is now covered by the lid, isn't it?' We agreed and finished our tea.

Then we started walking back towards Vanilla Apartments. We left the keys in a sealed envelope inside the letter box of Flat 7A. Jhola would come to the office at 1p.m. for a late weekend start and retrieve them.

When we reached Pop Mama's house early that afternoon, we found him talking to another visitor. He guided us to his bedroom and we saw a pile of video games lying around. 'Entertain yourselves. I'll join you shortly. Gaja?' he called out. Gaja appeared from thin air like Aladdin's genie. He enticed us by presenting the lunch menu. It was fried jasmine rice laced with saffron, giant lobsters with a spicy coconut gravy and tender goat meat with spinach and herbs. 'What's for dessert?' Kirit's mouth had begun to water. Gaja was prepared, '*Misti doi* and *kamala bhogs*.' We had already exhausted ourselves by continuously talking about our eventful morning. At the thought of the incredible fare that awaited us, the trapped ghost left our minds for the next few minutes.

Pop Mama joined us in ten minutes. We nearly stampeded him. He raised his arms like a preacher addressing salvation hopefuls, 'Easy, easy. One at a time.' Then he thrust an index finger towards me. 'Tiger?'

'We trapped the ghost,' I said excitedly.

Pop Mama smiled with the knowledge of the obvious, 'Tell me what happened.' I told him everything, not missing a single moment. No one interrupted me for I had covered our venture to the minutest detail. Pop Mama was ready to hear other observations. 'Time to pass the baton. Tiger needs a break.'

'The smell of freshly cooked chicken curry and the super clean flat must mean something,' said Sig.

'Unless the neighbours had cooked chicken curry the night

before,' suggested Pop Mama. Kirit had been quiet for too long. He spoke, 'The smell was really strong. As if someone had just cooked there.'

'Hmm, I can't imagine anyone cooking at that hour,' Pop Mama frowned.

'It was the ghost,' I made a sweeping statement.

'Did anyone see you go in or come out?' Pop Mama asked like a policeman.

'No,' Kirit, Sig, Robin and Pluto confirmed together.

But I thought that I was more observant than the others, 'When we ran out of the building, our watchman Bheem Bahadur saw us. And when we returned, he asked us how far we had jogged.' Pop Mama did not pay much attention to the useless information. He contemplated something and said, 'I'll talk to Danger Baba in a couple of hours or so because he is in Alipore jail now.'

'What? He's in jail?' we were surprised.

'He's talking to a convict on behalf of the police,' Pop Mama glanced at the black and silver Patek Philippe on his left wrist. It was noon. He continued, 'He's extracting some information from him.'

'Beating him up?' Kirit inquired.

'Hypnotising him,' Pop Mama stood up. 'Let's eat now. Then, while you boys catch a movie, I can do some work. After that, we'll talk to Danger Baba. How does that sound?'

'Great!' everyone agreed. With Pop Mama around, it did not seem like we were being supervised by an adult. He allowed us liberties without any fuss.

We had heard much about the bar in the living room with coloured lights and crystal clear mirrors. It housed a galaxy of French wines and I could not pronounce most of their names. Black Dog and Vat 69 along with other whiskies that successfully inebriated Bollywood villains before they deflowered the innocent or murdered the hero's family, were lined up in alphabetical order. However, it would be three more years before Pop Mama served us alcohol from his legendary bar.

The mahogany dining table was covered by a single piece of fabulous Belgian glass. Eight ostentatious throne-like chairs with soft padding complemented the antique table. The food was divine. We ate until we could barely move and after the meal, Kirit administered a bear hug on Gaja. We settled with imported Arabic coffee to watch a pirated video of *The 36th Chamber of Shaolin*. Pop Mama slipped away to work in his study. The movie was engrossing and when it ended, Kirit called out from his seat, still unable to move from the heavy lunch, 'Pop Mama?'

'Is it over?' Pop Mama inquired from the adjoining study.

'Yes,' Kirit yelled back.

'One moment,' came the quick response. Pop Mama was back with us.

'Are you going to call Danger Baba now?' I asked. Accumulated courage from watching a kung fu movie had begun to dissipate and fear crept into my being all over again.

'I already spoke with him,' Pop Mama said calmly.

'What? When?' We were surprised.

'I didn't want to disturb you while you were watching the film.'

'My parents should learn something from Pop Mama,' I thought. They were always asking me to get back to my studies when I was either reading a story book or watching TV. I snapped back at the urgency in Pop Mama's voice, 'The issue needs to be addressed without delay.'

'Do we have to tell anyone that we had entered 7A without the permission of the owners?' I wondered aloud.

'That would tarnish your reputations,' Pop Mama said nonchalantly.

'Looks like we are in trouble,' said a disheartened Sig.

'Tiger, isn't your father the most active member of the building's board?' Pop Mama looked directly at me.

'Yes, but he won't listen to me,' I had to admit.

'Are you absolutely sure?' Pop Mama wanted to be certain that the option of befriending my father was overruled before he proceeded any further.

'100 percent.' I felt bad that I had no clout over my father. But nothing deterred Pop Mama, 'Then I suppose you will have to post a notice on the board.'

'About what?' Pluto looked bewildered.

'The notice should urge the residents to come forward with any information they may have on the matter.'

'You mean, if they've seen a stranger like the one Bhitu Bakshi mentioned?' Sig added. 'Or, if they've seen any unusual activity around 7A?' Kirit tried to ascertain the rationale behind the move.

'Right. I'm quite sure that there are others who've seen the ghost but haven't come forward because people would consider them to be crazy,' reasoned Pop Mama.

'But how will their coming forward help?' I did not get it.

'Even if two adults come forward with something, it would open up an investigation. That's what we want,' Pop Mama was always patient with us.

'Once the investigation begins, many things can be done,' Robin completed his thought. Pop Mama smiled and aimed a false gun towards Robin with his fingers, 'Ditto. I can draft the letter for you.'

'Nothing can get on the notice board without approval from Tiger's dad. Jhola will not give us access to it,' Pluto said in despair. Pop Mama was annoyed with the trivial. He growled, 'Just remove the glass cover of the notice board and paste the damn notice. There's no need to ask anyone.'

'We'll do it this evening,' Kirit was charged.

'Make sure that you don't get caught while doing it,' Pop Mama laughed. Pluto was still pessimistic, 'But what if no one else in the building has seen the ghost?' 'You cannot nab a murderer if you begin on a negative note,' Pop Mama edified us. 'Try this idea. If no one comes forward in five days, we'll think of another approach.' There was a big difference between catching a murderer and playing games with a real ghost. But I chose not to share my thought. Instead, I asked, 'Do you think we could be in any danger?'

'Danger Baba believes that this ghost is totally harmless and likes children. Or else I wouldn't have asked you to get on the task,' Pop Mama said. 'Yeah, right,' I thought. Pop Mama was fearless and hell bent on turning us into mercenaries.

'We're not children, we're fifteen,' Kirit took offense.

'I know that,' Pop Mama corrected himself. 'But if the ghost is your father's age, as that boy claimed, then you're like children to him.' Pop Mama made a valid point.

'Should we pay Jhola to put up the notice?' I hoped that Pop Mama would agree. It would be downright embarrassing to be caught while putting up an unsanctioned notice for public consumption on the building notice board.

'He won't agree to that because he might lose his job. It's

Saturday, so plant it by tonight so that more people can see it when they step out tomorrow,' Pop Mama always knew the answers. A sudden thump landed on my back, 'Tiger, why don't you draft a letter right now?' It was Robin.

Gaja was summoned and he appeared in a flash. A sparkling new Remington typewriter and an unopened ream of bond papers were placed in front of us within a few minutes. I hurried a draft and Pop Mama glanced through it. He was pleased with what he saw, 'You boys are way ahead of your years. I'm proud of you.' Another negative question had popped up in my mind and I thought that this would be the best time to ask, 'What if someone sees us pinning the letter to the notice board?' Pop Mama knew I was scared, 'Smile. Then act natural. Say that you're just helping the administration office because Jhola is not around.' Trespassing and now lying, our list of misdemeanors was getting longer rapidly under Pop Mama's tutelage.

In the evening, while a doubles game was in progress on the badminton court behind the building, Kirit, Sig and I put up the notice. Pluto and Robin kept a watch for anyone coming near the area of the notice board.

The next morning we found out that not only had the word got around, but no less than eight residents had come forward with some information about a strange man. Unanimously, they claimed to have seen him on the seventh floor. Bhitu Bakshi's description was a perfect match. Baba called and chaired an emergency meeting of the board members. It was concluded that something spooky was going on at Vanilla Apartments. But who had put up the notice? No one knew. Since no one saw us, we feigned ignorance. Baba suspected that our group had a hand in this mischief and asked me directly. But I denied the allegation displaying complete ignorance.

By Tuesday evening, two more residents came forward. Another serious meeting was called. It was decided that 7A must be opened to check if everything was in order. In the meantime, Pop Mama played a smart card and visited Vanilla Apartments. He knew that Sudip Uncle would surely bring up this unusual set of events. When he did, Pop Mama volunteered to investigate unofficially. If there were any criminal elements messing with the residents, he would crack down upon them. Sudip Uncle fed this idea to other board members. Pop Mama had already been introduced to many residents in the previous months. Those who had not met him yet knew that Sumita Banerjee's brother was a respected officer with the Kolkata police. They were more than happy to enlist his support and gave him a free hand to do what he thought was best under such strange circumstances.

Pop Mama's interest in the matter was a great booster for everyone at Vanilla. A police officer tagging along with them would not only help in case there was any trouble from the ghost but also assist in legitimising trespass. No one paid any attention to the fact that the Police Academy did not train their officers on how to tackle ghosts.

Led by Pop Mama, Sudip Uncle and Baba went inside 7A. The minute they entered they smelt fresh chicken curry. Baba saw the wooden ruler in the bathroom and pointed towards it, 'How did this ruler get here?' He bent forward to pick it up but Pop Mama grabbed his wrist. 'Don't touch anything,' he warned. Pop Mama had already noticed miniscule movement of the commode lid and quickly guided his aides away from the bathroom on a false pretext. The ghost was still trapped. His attempt to escape was so feeble that if Pop Mama had not known of what had transpired in that flat a few days before, he may have missed the movement altogether. After they exited 7A, Pop Mama knocked on the door of Flat 7B to see if they were cooking chicken curry. Manik and Juhi Datta of 7B were vegetarians.

Pop Mama got the opportunity he was looking for. He declared that he had a gut feeling about the presence of something supernatural at 7A. He suggested bringing in a sorcerer for the future safety of everyone in the building. No one in the building needed to know. If Sudip Uncle and Baba buried the secret deep inside their chests, there would be no negative publicity or opposition. Sudip Uncle placed implicit faith upon Pop Mama but Baba was not in favour of clandestine operations. He insisted that at least the board members of Vanilla Apartments ought to be taken into confidence.

He requested Pop Mama to speak to them. Pop Mama could convince anyone of anything. Who would want to go against this magnanimous servant of the law? The terrified board members joined hands with Pop Mama and promised to keep the sorcerer's visit a secret. Pop Mama brought great relief to the eight assembled directors when he agreed to be personally present at 7A along with the sorcerer. By risking his own life for the welfare of the residents of Vanilla Apartments, Pop Mama became their lifelong friend and hero. Everyone stood up and thanked him. Some hugged him too. Baba was still skeptical about the presence of the ghost and summoning of a sorcerer but decided to accept the wishes of the other board members.

Sanction granted, Pop Mama got to work. While Sudip Uncle stayed back at the administration office with the other members for a chat, Pop Mama went up to 10B. Sumita Aunty was curious to know the outcome of the meeting and he confirmed that a sorcerer would be called. Then he walked up to the phone hanging on the wall and placed a quick call to Danger Baba. But what the ace psychic suggested put him in jeopardy. Although Danger Baba happily agreed to take care of the problem personally, he added that all those who trapped the ghost must be present at the time of his release. 'Why?' inquired a confused Pop Mama. 'As a safety measure,' said Danger Baba, 'Or else their lives could be in jeopardy once the ghost is released.' The presence of all those who trapped the ghost would indicate to him that they were the ones freeing him too. He would forgive them and move on.

When Pop Mama was through with the phone call, Sumita Aunty was ready to interrogate him further. But he said that he could kill for a cup of tea. Curiosity was overpowering Sumita Aunty but when her brother asked for something, he got it without delay. She disappeared into the kitchen. Kirit was using peripheral vision to watch the exchange in the living room, all the while pretending to work on Algebra. He knew Pop Mama had come upstairs only to brief him. The minute Sumita Aunty was out of sight, Pop Mama mouthed to his nephew, 'You guys are coming too.' By the time Sumita Aunty was back with steaming, aromatic Darjeeling tea, Kirit was delirious with joy and resembled a swirling dervish in a magical trance. Sumita Aunty slapped her forehead, 'First I had a crazy brother and now I'm stuck with a loony bin son.' Kirit called us one by one and we assembled at 10B. The job would be done the next day at 5 p.m when most Vanilla residents would be at work. We would be back from school and stepping out to play as we did every day of the week. After a quick sneak in and a quicker sneak out of 7A, along with Pop Mama and Danger Baba, we would be eternally free. Sig and I were reluctant to return to 7A for we were afraid of the ghost's wrath. But when we realised that it was only to ensure our future security, we were left with no choice. What a horrible mess Pop Mama had got us into. First, he handed us the ridiculous mission of 'Operation Ghost Trap' and even before a week had passed, we had to undertake 'Operation Ghost Release?' We were more trapped than the ghost. That didn't seem right.

Next evening we met at Pluto's home for Urmi Aunty and Nirmal Uncle were out of town. There was some solace that we would have to do nothing but watch the legendary Danger Baba at work. Pop Mama was an icon of punctuality and exactly at 5 p.m the bell rang at 4G. Kishlu, the trustworthy servant of the Sens opened the door and Pop Mama walked in along with Danger Baba. Kishlu had seen Pop Mama before but shrieked in abject fright when he saw Danger Baba. He ran into the bedroom where we were seated. 'A ghost has come,' he croaked. We were surprised at his over-reaction. 'From where? 7A?' smirked Pluto. Kishlu did not get the joke.

'It must be Pop Mama and Danger Baba,' Kirit jumped out of the bed. We stepped out of the bedroom and stood rock-still at the sight in front of us. Everyone's face had changed. Along with Pop Mama stood a monster. Danger Baba was no more than six feet tall but his build was like a water buffalo. His skin was so dark it seemed as if someone had rubbed charcoal on it. His eyes were bloodshot from habitual indulgence in *cholai*, the libation of his choice. The eyeballs glowed like coals in a fire and his face was entirely covered with a beard. But what was most frightening about him was the tattoo on his forehead. It was a salamander belching fire. Danger Baba wore a dark green robe and carried a large sack on his back. On his neck he wore a long garland made of beads constructed of cranial bones. When Pop Mama had told us that Danger Baba wore wooden underwear screwed tight with specially designed bronze nails, we had laughed it off. But looking at him for the first time that evening, all of us recalled that little-known fact and stared at him in sheer disbelief.

We trembled from within but put up a brave front. Danger Baba smiled. The gentle smile on his vicious face quelled our fear. 'You boys are very brave,' he complimented us in his soft voice. We acknowledged his smile and waited for instructions. Kirit could not keep quiet any longer. He tried to be funny, 'What's that sack for? To carry the ghost away with you?'

'You're right. If he decides not to leave by the door or the window, I'll have to take him away in the sack.' Danger Baba was a professional. I almost smiled when I saw the baffled look on Kirit's face.

'Are we going to be safe?' I got to the point.

'Of course. I would never allow you to enter the flat if I didn't think so,' assured Danger Baba and continued, 'This ghost is not dangerous. I knew that from his interaction with your friend. The fact that he has allowed you to trap him proves that he is harmless. But still, he's a ghost and should not be taken lightly.'

We nodded as if we understood what he was talking about. Danger Baba went on, 'He hasn't been able to go where he is supposed to be. Traffic congestion perhaps or maybe he didn't have the proper guide map. Whatever it is, we shall soon find out.' Ghost traffic? Guide map for phantoms? I would have thought all of this was absurd until a few days ago. But after what we had done, I was ready to believe anything.

'Ready?' Danger Baba broke my drift.

'Ready!' we said bravely. Pluto was already sweating. He called out to Kishlu but the petrified house help was nowhere to be seen. Pluto walked into the bedroom and found him hiding under the bed. 'Lock the door after we leave.' He walked out and suppressed a laugh, 'You should have seen his face.'

'Operation Ghost Release' had begun. There was no sloppiness of Saturday morning's 'Operation Ghost Trap'. We entered 7A like trained warriors on a rescue mission. Although the sun was setting, it was far from total darkness at that hour. I stuck to Sig who was fast becoming my closest friend among the rest of the group. Pluto was hanging around Kirit. Robin placed his hand on my shoulder. I thought he was offering me support but when I saw his face, I realised that I was the service provider. We smelt the chicken curry at once. Danger Baba drew in a lungful of the aroma and smiled in satisfaction. He nodded to us, indicating that he felt the presence of the ghost. One half of his face was dark and he looked menacing in the diffused light inside the flat. 'How long will it take?' whispered Pluto. Danger Baba placed the index finger of his right hand to his lips. It resembled a thick banana. 'Shhh,' he said.

'Okay, okay, shhhh,' Pluto repeated after him. Pop Mama showed no signs of fear and appeared to be leading an illicit drug heist. He was ready to spring at the ghost the minute he appeared.

Danger Baba walked into the large bathroom and gestured us to follow. Although the bathroom was spacious, it was not meant to accommodate two large adults and five adolescents. Danger Baba asked Pop Mama to stand outside to make more room for the rest of us. Kirit and Robin stepped into the bath and Sig, Pluto and I were closer to the commode. Huddled together with little scope of escaping a ghost attack suddenly made me nauseous and my knees began shaking. Pluto struggled to keep his eyes open. Danger Baba asked us not to worry. He clearly knew what he was doing.

Danger Baba whisked out a butterfly net from his unimpressive sack along with a transparent plastic pouch of liquid and opened it. It smelt of carbolic acid.

'Is he going to wash the toilet?' Sig whispered in my ear.

'Shhhhhhhh,' Danger Baba forbade us again. Sig shut up at once. Everyone tried to facilitate more silence and said, 'Shhhhhhhh' thus emitting more noise than necessary. Danger Baba went on his knees and placed a large sponge on the floor. He poured the phenol-like-liquid slowly into it. Then he placed the butterfly net on top of it and at once the sponge jumped up and stuck to it. He lifted the net, closed his eyes and mumbled something unfathomable.

There was no movement under the commode. The ghost seemed to have been washed away. Or was it ready to spring upon us? We were bracing ourselves when without any warning Danger Baba lifted the lid of the commode. He blocked the passage with a sudden swat of the solution-soaked sponge sticking to the butterfly net. Instantly, we saw the wet ghostometre sticking to the sponge inside the net. How did it climb up from the water below? Mysteriously it did not fall off the sponge even though it weighed much more than its trap. It looked as if someone had pasted it on to the sponge just as the sponge had been pasted to the butterfly net. 'Got you!' exclaimed Danger Baba. Pop Mama pushed his neck into the bathroom and swung it around like a jimmy jib trying to catch a glimpse of the action. Instinctively, we backed away but ended up bumping into each other. Sig stepped on my foot and I barely blocked a scream. All eyes were on the butterfly net when all of a sudden, Pluto spoke, 'Thank you.'

Pluto had spoken. But it was someone else's voice! 'Who are you?' Danger Baba asked him. Pluto had been possessed by the ghost! We stood paralysed with fear as Pluto replied calmly, 'Sushil Sarkar.' There was no change in his facial features but his voice and mannerisms had transformed.

'How long have you been here?' asked Danger Baba.

'Three months,' replied Pluto.

'How did you get here?' Danger Baba spoke with the ghost as if he was getting acquainted with a new neighbour.

'Manik Datta and Juhi Datta called me.'

'Who are they?' asked Danger Baba. I half-lifted my arm to indicate that I knew them. 'You may speak. Sushil Sarkar has no problem with that. Correct?' Danger Baba urged me to participate. 'Sure,' Pluto smiled at me. It was bizarre.

'They live next door. In 7B.'

'Where were you before you came here?' asked Danger Baba gently. Pluto continued with a slight sense of urgency, 'I was going home.'

'And you got dragged in without warning,' Danger Baba assisted him. Pluto nodded sadly and made a glum face quite unlike what we had ever seen.

'Did you answer their questions?' Danger Baba asked.

'I did. They wanted to call some American film actor called James Dean. But got me by mistake.'

'I'm sorry to hear that. But what happened to you?' sympathised Danger Baba.

'I died,' Pluto stated as a matter of fact. We were chilled to the bone.

'I know that. But how?' Danger Baba was patient.

'I was eating when I had a heart attack,' Pluto complained.

'Chicken curry?' Danger Baba said as if he knew the menu at Sushil Sarkar's residence on the day of his death. Pluto nodded, 'Yes.'

'You weren't able to finish the meal,' Danger Baba knew.

'No,' Pluto confirmed.

'Where did you live?' Danger Baba inquired.

'1450 CIT Road. Block B, Flat No 290,' Pluto said without a moment's hesitation.

'I got that,' Pop Mama's voice startled us.

'If I set you free will you promise never to come back?' Danger Baba asked earnestly.

'Absolutely,' Pluto nodded like a much older person.

'Can I trust you to keep your word?' Danger Baba was planning something and we braced ourselves again. Fear gripped me for a moment. What if Pluto dies? Or worse, what if he disappears forever? Pluto spoke, 'I was waiting for someone to free me.'

'It's time to go now, Sushil Sarkar. How will we know that you've left us?' Danger Baba asked.

'The glass from a bedroom window?' Pluto asked.

'Flying shreds may hurt someone on the street below,' Danger Baba said as he pondered an alternative. Pluto looked like a thoughtful and contemplating adult in a teenager's body. 'How about the flush in the other bathroom?' he suggested.

'Sure,' Danger Baba agreed at once. Immediately, Pluto broke the wind. It was an unusually loud and long report and the bathroom was instantly filled with the smell of chicken curry. At the same time, the flush was pulled in the second bathroom on its own. We stood transfixed, finding it hard to believe what we had just witnessed. Pop Mama was also mesmerised with the proceedings.

Pluto looked as if he had just woken up from deep sleep. He was surprised to find everyone staring at him. At the sight of Danger Baba wrapping up his paraphernalia, Pluto remembered our mission and looked towards the commode.

'Pluto?' Kirit asked tentatively.

'Shh,' Pluto pointed towards Danger Baba.

Danger Baba laughed, 'Game over. You can all go home now.' We felt a tremendous sense of relief. I spoke first, 'Is Pluto alright?'

'He is fine,' Danger Baba smiled. Kirit jumped out of the tub and administered his trademark bear hug on Pluto. Danger Baba told us that Pluto would have no memory of the time when he was possessed by Sushil Sarkar's ghost.

Pluto did not believe the events of the previous ten minutes, 'You're all playing the fool with me.' But when Pop Mama and Danger Baba took our side, Pluto said solemnly, 'How long did it last?'

'Only a few minutes,' Pop Mama patted his shoulder. 'That's so cool,' Pluto said finally. We were surprised by his response but were very happy that our wifty, ditzy friend was back among us. 'But why did the ghost choose Pluto?' I asked Danger Baba.

'To escape from our world which was not his anymore, Sushil Sarkar needed someone's help from the team that had trapped him. He chose Pluto because Pluto must have deeply wanted to free him from his misery,' Danger Baba explained.

'But it's not just him. All of us wanted that,' Robin was puzzled.

'That could be true. But as a ghost he knew who wanted his

freedom the most among the five of you. That's why he chose Pluto and spoke to us through him.'

'Wow!' Pluto mouthed.

'You liberated a soul, Poltu,' Danger Baba was proud of Pluto.

'It's Pluto, not Poltu,' Sig corrected him.

'Shit, I missed the whole thing. That's not fair,' lamented Pluto. Everyone laughed. 'How did I look then? Did my face change?' Pluto was curious. Sig spoke up, 'You looked the same. Pretty stupid.' Everyone laughed again. Robin added, 'You were 'you' but your voice was different and you had acquired Sushil Sarkar's mannerisms.' Pluto was intrigued, 'Was it scary?'

'The first few seconds. But after that it was fine,' I assured him.

'You shat in your pants,' Kirit slapped my back. Everyone laughed again.

'So none of you saw him?' Pluto shot his final question.

'He looked like you,' Kirit concluded. Everyone burst out laughing.

Danger Baba was calm, 'He was inside you for which he didn't have a different face. But if you boys wish to see what he looked like, you can come with me to his house.'

'1450 CIT Road. Block B, Flat No 290,' I said.

'That's where he lived. Before he died?' was the next typical Pluto question. Kirit gave him a knock on his head and said, 'Yes donkey, before he died.'

'It's almost six. Let's get out of here,' Pop Mama urged us to move, 'Who wants to join us for a trip to Sushil Sarkar's place?'

As soon as you thought the adventure for the day was over, with Pop Mama around, a new one stared straight at you in the eye. Where there was Pop Mama, there was always hope. Whoever came in contact with him drew positive energy from his perennial enthusiasm and unbound spirit. All our hands went up in excitement.

We packed into Pop Mama's police jeep and he set the vehicle in motion. He turned on the flashing red light on the roof and the jeep embraced the uneven street like a missile that had tracked its target. 'Isn't the light only for emergencies?' I asked.

'This is an emergency,' Pop Mama smiled.

We reached Sushil Sarkar's housing complex on CIT Road. The address was written bold and clear and it was easy to locate the flat. Danger Baba knew the effect he had on people. As he stepped out of the jeep, we had great fun observing heads turn followed by a scurrying of feet. He was like a rock star. People stared at him. But instead of running towards him they ran away from him. In all the amusement though, I could not help wondering how he must feel to be shunned for his unconventional appearance. However, it did not bother him for he was used to it.

We stood in front of Sushil Sarkar's flat and knocked on the pale green door. A fading nameplate read: Sushi Sarkar, Parul Sark r and Samir S rk r. The door opened. A man in his early twenties stood staring at us, 'Who are you looking for?'

'Is this Sushil Sarkar's home?' Pop Mama asked. The young man had not yet seen Danger Baba for he stood concealed at the side of the entrance. 'Yes, but…'

Pop Mama did not waste time, 'Are you his son, Samir?'

'Yes. What is this about?' Samir was clueless about our sudden intrusion.

'My name is Aditya Roy and I am a police officer,' Pop Mama declared, his chest inflated.

'POLICE?' Samir looked as if he might faint.

'Can we come in?' Pop Mama waited for Samir to register his presence.

'I haven't done anything wrong, Sir,' he said sincerely. Pop Mama almost bumped into Samir as the young man made way for the police officer. We followed Pop Mama into Sushil Sarkar's flat and started taking off our shoes one by one. A large picture of a man in his late fifties was centred on the wall. A dry, emaciated remnant of a flower garland hung from its frame. Was that Sushil Sarkar?

'Are these your children?' asked Samir, not knowing how to continue the awkward conversation.

'Do I look that old?' Pop Mama laughed.

'No Sir. Sorry Sir,' Samir was sweating with the apprehension of what was to follow.

After all of us were in, when Samir was ready to shut the door, Danger Baba emerged from the side. Samir's face lost colour and he took a step back, 'What are you?'

'You mean "who" are you?' Pop Mama corrected him, enjoying his predicament. We struggled hard not to burst out laughing.

'He is with us,' said Kirit.

'Who else lives here?' asked Pop Mama as he claimed the most comfortable seat in the room.

'My mother. But now she's gone to the market. I skipped work today because of an upset stomach.' Samir kept glancing at Danger Baba while he answered Pop Mama's questions diligently.

'Over to you Danger Baba,' Pop Mama passed the charge.

Samir was spooked out even more at the mention of the strange mendicant's name. Danger Baba found a seat. Kirit was quick to grab the last chair in the room and there were no more seats left for us. We did not mind standing and watched Samir steadying himself to field more queries. Danger Baba was quick, 'When did your father pass away?'

'Three months ago. But how do you know that he has passed away?' Samir looked puzzled. Danger Baba pointed towards the picture on the wall. My guess had been correct. Everyone stared at the picture. Sushil Sarkar had a pleasant, smiling face and did not scare us. Danger Baba continued, 'What happened?'

'He was eating when he had a massive heart attack,' Samir looked sad.

'Chicken curry, his favourite dish.'

Samir was astonished, 'How do you know this? Who are you?'

Pop Mama intervened. He told Samir. When he was done, Samir was speechless, 'That's incredible,' he mumbled.

'We are here to confirm his story,' Kirit had to have the last word. Emotion ran high and Samir tried to hold back his tears. He stared at Pluto for a long moment making him quite uncomfortable. As Pluto was about to look away, Samir fell at his feet and grabbed his shins with both hands. 'Baba, Baba,' Samir broke into pitiful tears.

'Shit! Fuck. Shit!' Pluto pleaded rather unconventionally to Samir to release him. 'Hey, let go of my feet. Fuck. Shit!'

Pop Mama suppressed a grin. He helped Samir up to his feet. Samir wept like a child for a few minutes. He thanked Danger Baba for undertaking the noble task of liberating his father from earthly bondage. When he recovered, he ran into the room and was back with a handful of currency notes. It was not much but he had grabbed whatever he could lay his hands on. 'This is all I have at home, Danger Baba,' he sobbed. Danger Baba smiled. 'Sit down.' Samir sat at his feet like a cocker spaniel waiting to be patted by his master. Danger Baba placed his humungous palm on Samir's head and it seemed that he was about to spin it like an apple. He was not interested in Samir's money. 'Lead a good life son. Be a good man,' Danger Baba proclaimed and stood up. Samir bowed to him reverentially. Then he realised that nothing had been offered to his guests. 'Please be seated for a while. I shall get some sweets for you and my young friends.' We declined at once and said that we were in a hurry to get back. 'How can I reach you, Danger Baba, if I ever need your help for anything?' Samir asked the large psychic.

'Go to Bagdi Para Road in Metiabruz and ask anyone where I live. They'll guide you.' We were ready to head out when Parul Sarkar, Samir's mother, walked in with a bagful of groceries. She was wiping her face with the folds of her pale blue and white cotton printed sari when she noticed the pile of shoes on the doorway. She looked up and saw us. But when her eyes panned to Danger Baba, she screamed. Samir took a couple of long strides to reach her and helped her to sit down. Pop Mama said, 'Samir, you can explain our visit to her. But we really need to go now.' Danger Baba smiled gently at Parul Sarkar but she was already unfavourably predisposed towards the giant intruder. She screamed again. We barely managed to get out without bursting into a laugh. Pluto started first. And then it grew infectious. Everyone joined in. It was impossible to stop. Even Danger Baba laughed his heart out.

It was getting late and I was headed for a verbal hiding at home. Baba and Ma were not punitive in nature. But they nagged like ninety year olds. Pop Mama drove fast. As we reached the Park Circus *maidan* and the jeep conquered the roundabout that would lead us south towards home, Danger Baba turned serious, 'Manik and Juhi Datta. They have a bad habit.'

'Planchette?' Pop Mama asked.

'Yes,' Danger Baba frowned, 'They summon the dead to answer their questions and don't release them properly. They are not good for Vanilla Apartments. I don't know how you will do it. But they need to go.'

'What did they do, Danger Baba?' I wanted clarity.

'They wanted to call the spirit of an American actor but intercepted Sushil Sarkar instead. The couple endangered the safety of everyone in the building. The dead should be left in peace wherever they are,' Danger Baba intoned.

'But Sushil Sarkar was a good man, er, I mean ghost,' Robin commented.

'You were lucky. What if there is an evil spirit next time?' Danger Baba looked concerned.

Pop Mama was charged, 'I'll get that family out of Vanilla,' he promised as the police walkie-talkie crackled and startled us. 'One moment,' Pop Mama took the call. 'Oh great. Excellent. That's wonderful. Perfect. I'll be there,' he barked into the speaker and hung up. Then he looked at us through the rear view mirror, 'There has been a double murder in the Lake Market area and I'll have to spend the rest of my evening at the site.'

The reality of Pop Mama being a feared police officer slipped us sometimes. His friendly disposition and boyish ways often led us to believe that he was just another important member of our group. He received the call of the horrible double murders as if he had just accepted a dinner invitation. My mind wandered briefly to Raja Basanta Roy Road, a short walk from Lake Market, and the smiling faces of my old friends, Somnath, Raju, Anand, Manas and Sanjoy. To my shock, I was not sad. I had moved on. How fickle our minds were. We forgot old friends when we made new ones. We set aside old loyalties and formed new bonds. The police jeep halted with a jerk and brought me back to Vanilla Apartments before I could turn sentimental.

A week later, a special prayer for Sushil Sarkar was performed at 7A. A priest recommended by Danger Baba handled the proceedings. Pop Mama and Sudip Uncle were present. Kirit wanted to join in but Sumita Aunty would not allow it. If only she knew the whole story! The rituals were dutifully conducted and the priest assured them that the building was safe.

Manik and Juhi Datta were called by the administration. Had they accepted their mistake and apologised, things might have worked out for them. But they made the fatal blunder of not only denying the allegations but also yelled that the board members were aspersing malicious charges against them. The residents' representative committee turned against them and immediately voted for their departure from the building. The Dattas could have gone into a long litigious road but they did not want to have anything to do with neighbours who did not trust them.

When the quarrels began to turn ugly, Pop Mama, who was present during the meeting, stood up and took charge of the proceedings. He warned the Dattas that they could land in jail for disrupting public peace by summoning the supernatural. If convicted, they could go away for several years. Manik and Juhi Datta could not muster the courage to point out that Pop Mama did not live in the building and had no business poking his nose into the issues of Vanilla Apartments. No one messed with the police. They moved to a rental flat within a week and soon, they found a buyer for 7B. We never saw Manik and Juhi Datta or heard of them ever again.

Pop Mama was hailed as a hero. But we learnt a wrong lesson from his example: to take the law into our hands. We were brave in his eyes and began to believe that we had performed a great social service. We basked in the unsung glory for a long time to come. Trapping a ghost inside a commode rendered us a sense of invincibility. It empowered us to take unnecessary risks, which would soon lurch us into more trouble than we could handle.

# CHAPTER SEVEN

# Bad Friends

$\mathcal{T}$he scorching summer heat of 1985 was the beginning of a prolonged nightmare for our next door neighbours in 3B, Dr. Ranjan Kundu and his wife, Usha. Dr. and Mrs. Kundu were a busy couple juggling successful careers in homeopathy and divorce law. Dr. Kundu was experiencing an unprecedented rush in his practice. People were leaning towards homeopathy after allopathic treatment failed to bring them the desired relief from their ailments. The 'divorce business', as Usha Aunty labeled her profession, was booming. She predicted that domestic tolerance would go into a great southern spiral and her business would prosper beyond description. With their professional graphs climbing high, the two established experts found themselves spending more and more time with strangers stuck in miserable conditions rather than enjoying quality time with their children. The money was pouring in like never before and the couple was gripped in its frenzy.

When it came to furthering their own careers, Dr. Kundu and Usha Aunty were fiercely ambitious, but their children Vick and Vani were appreciated for whatever they could accomplish. They were encouraged to do their best but never pressurised to over achieve, unlike most of their counterparts. Vick, a year junior to Mukul, was a better-than-average student and took up Commerce at St. Xavier's college. While we still languished in our staid school uniforms, Vick flaunted his impressive wardrobe. His dream parents rewarded him with the latest gadgets and fashionable clothing. It was their way of apologising for their long hours at work.

Vani was the most adorable kid we had ever known. When she came to Vanilla as a cute nine year old, she boasted that she was ready to waft into double figures. At eleven, she was a darling of almost everyone in the building. Vick maintained a casual acquaintance with our group and occasionally joined us for a game of cricket or table tennis. But he never let us forget that we were younger and kept us at a distance. However, every boy and girl in the entire building, irrespective of age, along with their parents and grandparents, were Vani's friends. She was vivacious and utterly delightful with a winning smile. Every time we needed to raise money for musical functions and sports activities, Vani approached donors as our representative. Not for once would she return empty handed. Such was little Vani Kundu's charm.

Vick had a unique talent. He played badminton really well and won numerous school and college tournaments. Although the Kundus did not oppose his spending a fair amount of time at the courts, practicing a game where there was very little money did not make sense. On one occasion at our place, Dr. Kundu, now a close family friend rather than mere next door neighbour, voiced his concern about encouraging Vick too much. He feared that Vick may take up the game at the cost of neglecting his studies.

Vick represented his college in badminton and was sponsored to attend a coaching camp in Darjeeling, a beautiful hill station near Kolkata. At the camp, Vick shared his room with another ace player, Madan Ruia. Madan was a star player from a lesser-known college of the city. Without any doubt, Madan's talent far exceeded anyone else's in the camp. There was a buzz that Madan could represent India. On one hand, Madan had received quite a mention in the local newspapers but was also dismissed as a potential due to his mercurial temper. He was a loose cannon on the courts and branded by the press as 'Mad' Ruia. Repeated eruptions and constant refute of the umpires' decisions crowned him with a record number of expulsions. This was his last chance at national level badminton.

Mad Ruia came from a poor family and was a known juvenile delinquent. His school records had never been satisfactory and his behavioural anomalies were overlooked by the school authorities only due to his badminton skills. Mad's luck changed when a well-known English medium school in south Koltata asked him to join without bothering about tuition fees. Mad Ruia's poor parents were overjoyed that God had created an opportunity unheard of earlier for their below-average son.

Mad joined the elite school that wanted to espalier him into a refined human being. But in less than a hundred days, Mad received three behavioural infraction warnings. All the charges were serious. When he was not allowed to walk out of History period to use the toilet, something he did repeatedly to disturb the class, Mad defiantly walked to the rear end of the classroom and urinated on the wall. He was let off with a severe warning. The next infraction almost got him thrown out of school. Mad was discovered flaunting his penis to a female classmate during Biology period. Again, badminton saved his skin. But the last infraction proved him to be a serious threat to the safety of other students. Following an argument with a classmate during tiffin break, Mad slid an open stainless steel compass on his seat from the rear. As the boy sat down after a standing acknowledgement of the teacher's entry into the class, a common custom of respect, the window panes nearly smashed with his piercing cry. He blacked out in pain. As the bleeding boy was carried out for numerous stitches, Mad stood up and confessed his crime so that no other classmate could be falsely accused for the shenanigan. He displayed no remorse for the dastardly act. The school had tolerated enough of Madan Ruia's nonsense. He was handed a Transfer Certificate. An involuntary TC was the worst thing a student could receive. No school wanted a student who had been handed a TC elsewhere. His attempt at civil existence would either be completely over or have to be resuscitated somewhat in another city altogether.

Mad Ruia was back in his earlier school with his old set of hooligan friends. But things had changed there. After all, he had abandoned them to attend a snobbish school. Mad Ruia could not settle down comfortably in his old domain. His parents were heartbroken. Never in their grandiose dreams had they imagined their unfortunate child studying alongside the privileged children of the city's bon ton. This was Mad Ruia's golden chance to alleviate the family from their condition and he had ruined it for them. An incredible opportunity had been squandered. Utterly humiliated by their son's behaviour, they came down hard on him.

Mad's disdain for his parents began to grow and he became aloof. The rumour was that he had failed his final exam but the school decided to let him attempt the Grade XII board exam. They feared that if he was kept back and made to repeat the year, the already tarnished image of the school would take a further beating. The teachers got together, falsified his marks and passed him. They told his parents that the school did not want to keep him anymore.

In return for the favour, Mad would have to ensure that he passed the board exam, or else the school would be forced to take him back.

After the meeting with the school authorities, Mad experienced a tremendous sense of rejection. Wasn't this the same school that took him back when the snooty institution showed him the door? Now even they did not want him anymore? He was angry. No favour was being done to him. This was good riddance. The school had rejected him. Now it was his turn to reject the school. He stopped playing badminton and applied himself to a sole cause: to pass his board exam. Mad Ruia passed with reasonable scores, although he did not do well enough to attend the better known colleges in the city.

In the badminton camp, Mad Ruia and Vick Kundu struck friendship gold. Mad introduced Vick to dope and Vick treated him like an equal. When the camp ended, they were back in Kolkata and Vick invited Mad to his home.

Mad stayed at Linton Street, a distance away from Vanilla Apartments. He had to either take the 45A or the No. 10 double decker to reach Vick's home. When he entered his new friend's flat for the first time, he was dumbstruck. Mad Ruia had never seen a more beautiful and elegant home. The comfortable setting was very appealing to him and he made no attempts to hide his indigent existence. Vick's kitchen had stocks of imported cookies and chocolates. The abundance was nothing unusual for Vick but for someone who survived on lentils and rice and a small piece of fish only once a month, this was an unimagined world.

Dr. Kundu left early for work and returned late at night. Usha Aunty was equally busy and when she returned, half-asleep and stifling queen sized yawns, a quick browse of Vani's homework was all she could manage. A languid inquiry about Vick's day would follow and she would be off to bed. On the fast track of life, the successful Kundus failed to read their son's dispirited eyes.

Vick started his classes at 6 a.m and would be free by noon. Although his attendance did not suffer, Vick began to waste precious time. Mad Ruia was enrolled in a college far away from south Kolkata but most of the time he was seen at Vanilla Apartments. He seldom bothered to attend any classes. Vick was getting more and more involved with Mad's friends who were from a different world. Vick had not started on drugs, but reefers filled his smoky existence now. He knew that his parents had a solid social standing and was careful not to be seen buying dope. Mad knew where to acquire the stuff and unhesitatingly went to pick it up for both of them. He got the stuff at ease and proved to be the front man for the task. For safety reasons, Vick would not even be in the area. He would wait at home for Mad to arrive with the pot. In return for the favour, Mad never had to pay a dime for his stimulant.

Before long, Mad was noticeable in branded clothes and accessories, all belonging to Vick. Gone were the days when he would alight from the crowded bus crushed like a plastered sardine in a rust laden tin can. A flashy BSA bicycle was his new vehicle and it did not take a nuclear physicist to figure out the source of his new wealth. Mad had begun to enjoy the comforts of Vick's home, and Vick took full advantage of his friend's daring in acquisition of pot under difficult circumstances. There were long hours to kill and Mad often stayed over. There was enough space in Vick's room and no one considered it to be a problem.

What ought to have struck the family odd was that Mad never needed to call his parents for permission for sleepovers. The hyperopia on the part of Dr. Kundu and Usha Aunty caused serious damage. After a few months had elapsed, they began to notice that Mad Ruia was virtually living with them. In the beginning Mad would go away on the weekends, showing up at Vick's door only on weekdays. But when he started staying over almost every weekend as well, Dr. Kundu and Usha Aunty were resentful. In a four bedroomed flat, however large it was, missing this obvious fact earlier was unpardonable, particularly when they never liked Mad Ruia. Their callousness was about to give rise to an unsolvable problem.

Mad's interest in badminton had waned and doping became his sole activity. When he was sober, he used his connections to get more dope. He had dropped out of college and started dealing to other restless souls without any compunction. Mad was not big but had an uncanny confidence in himself, an aplomb most teenagers lacked. The equanimity worked well on street deals, but the same virtue cost him his place at the Kundu household.

On a particularly gloomy and humid Kolkata morning, when Mad Ruia munched toast laden with copious helpings of butter and orange marmalade at the breakfast table of the Kundus, for the first time, Usha Aunty asked him what his parents did for a living. Startled by the nature of the inquiry, Mad stiffened. But he recovered and said softly that his father was a motor mechanic and his mother was a housewife. He was their only son. Vick was equally surprised as he knew nothing about his friend's family. Badminton had bonded them in the beginning. But later it was dope. Nothing else had mattered.

Usha Aunty's motive was to make the unwelcome visitor uncomfortable. She hoped that Mad Ruia would be embarrassed and cut down his visits. Mad rarely acknowledged the presence of Vick's parents and the initial display of courtesy had evaporated long before. Something about his quiet demeanor made the senior Kundus uncomfortable.

There was a new arrogant air about Mad Ruia. For some time Dr. Kundu and Usha Aunty chose to ignore him for they had other pressing matters on their minds. The Kundus were large-hearted and Mad Ruia hailing from a working class background had not been a deterrent to his forming a friendship with their son. But, like in most badminton tournaments, Mad had lost the favourable position with which he had begun.

For the first time in his entire student life, Vick fared poorly in his college exam. The Kundus were taken aback. Sensing the reason for his deteriorating performance, they asked Vick to associate with boys and girls from similar backgrounds. Vick flared up. He accused his parents of picking on an unfortunate kid who lacked opportunities. What had Madan Ruia done wrong? He was born in a poor household. That was his crime. Wasn't Madan Ruia an ace badminton player? How could they be so insensitive?

Usha Aunty was firm, 'That's not true. First of all, you don't practice badminton together. Secondly, he had a great opportunity at a good school but you told us that he got himself expelled.' Dr. Kundu agreed, 'That boy's contribution in your life is a big zero. But being in your environment, he benefits immensely.' Vick was not prepared to give up without a fight, 'So what? Doesn't he deserve to pick up a few good things from us?'

'Most certainly. But not twenty-four hours and seven days a week and at our expense,' replied Usha Aunty.

'What do you mean by that?' Vick took an angry stance.

'Don't act stupid, Vikash. A blind person can tell that he wears your clothes.'

Vick stormed into his room, out of the sight of his concerned parents.

Mad was almost the same size as Vick. Although Vick's clothes were not tailored for Mad, they fit him quite well. But his shoe size was exactly the same. In our group too, we exchanged clothes and shoes regularly, but this was extortion! Whatever new came to Vick, Mad was seen wearing the very next day. Vick received a hefty pocket money but off-late seemed to need more and more. The Kundus complied for they believed that their son deserved to enjoy the fruits of their labour. But they had unwittingly created a crater that would soon grab their son into its entrails.

Initially Vick would participate in some games, but gradually he found some excuse or the other to avoid us when we invited him for a match or two. Irritated by what we read as growing conceit, we avoided him. We knew that he had started on dope. It was obvious to us that Mad had a hand in the supply. But we had not realised that things had gone so out of hand.

Matters came to a head one Sunday evening. Vick and Mad walked in, their entire being doused in dope. As they mumbled their way into the living room, they saw Dr. Kundu and Usha Aunty intently following a news-based program on TV. Instead of disappearing into Vick's room, they decided to join his parents.

Without warning, Mad leaned towards the glass bottomed centre table, picked up the remote control and switched over to a popular sports channel. Dr. Kundu was more surprised than angry. But Usha Aunty stared directly at Mad and asked angrily, 'Don't you think it's necessary to ask?' Mad should have taken the hint, apologised and departed quietly. Instead, he glared back at Usha Aunty and said, 'You have a TV in your bedroom.'

There was a stunned silence in the living room. Usha Aunty, unable to withstand the presence of Mad Ruia in her home any longer, rose from her seat, snatched away the remote from his hands and asked him to leave.

'Leave my house, right now!'

'Why?' came the defiant response.

Another awkward silence followed this unconventional reply.

'Because it's my house and I don't want to entertain you.'

'Why?'

Dr. Kundu looked at the impertinent guest in wonder and suspected that he was intoxicated.

'Because of your manners,' screamed Usha Aunty.

'You're the one yelling at me,' Mad stated as a matter of fact.

Another quiet second of stupefied silence followed. Vick supported his friend's lunacy, 'He just suggested an option. That's all he did.'

Dr. Kundu realised that it was time for him to take over before things turned uglier, 'Vikash, why don't you visit his house and behave like this with his family? See what they will have to say to you.'

'But we don't have TV at home,' Mad replied in his usual calm manner.

Dr. Kundu could not believe his ears. As it is, the situation was bad. But the boy seemed to be pushing the limits. Suddenly, he noticed that the top three buttons of Mad's shirt were open and his chest displayed a fairly large tattoo. Dr. Kundu could not tell what it was, but it gave the impudent visitor a menacing look. How could he have missed that strange tattoo all this while? Or was it very recent? Was this tattoo related to a gang? Dr. Kundu bounced out of his thoughts and tried a different approach. He stood up and walked up to Mad. Then he put his arm gently on his shoulder and tried to reason with him, 'Look, Madan....', but before he could finish, Mad pushed away Dr. Kundu's arm from his shoulder and shoved him away. It was not a violent shove but enough to affright. Dr. Kundu slightly lost his balance but broke his fall by slumping back into the fawn coloured leather sofa. Speechless and now scared, Dr. Kundu and Usha Aunty thought of what to do next.

Mad said calmly, 'I didn't mean to push you.' Vick repeated, 'He didn't mean it.' Mad turned away from Dr. Kundu and stared at the TV screen. A football match was on and he began to take keen interest in the game, completely ignoring the presence of Vick's parents. Dr. Kundu realised that he was dealing with an unusual phenomenon. He was shaken but tried to act normal, 'Madan, I think it's time you started for home. It's a long distance back.'

'He's staying over,' Vick interrupted.

'No, he's not,' Usha Aunty was furious, 'and if you wish to go with him, you can leave too.'

'You want me to leave my own house?' Vick's pride was hurt. 'Fine. I'm leaving. And I promise you that you will never see me again.' He leaned towards Mad and pulled at his sleeve, 'Not another minute where my friends are not welcome. Come on, Madan.'

'I'm too tired to go anywhere,' Mad stifled a yawn. It was time for Vick to be jolted. He was at a complete loss for words.

Usha Aunty came up with an ultimatum, 'I'm warning you, Madan. If you don't leave in the next two minutes, I'll be forced to call the watchman.'

'Bheem Bahadur knows me. He won't do anything,' Mad yawned with his mouth wide open.

'What do you want?' asked Dr. Kundu, feeling helpless.

'Nothing,' Mad shrugged.

Dr. Kundu began to lose his cool, 'That watch you're wearing. Doesn't it belong to Vikash?'

'I'm just wearing it.'

'We've been noticing things, Madan. Every time Vikash buys a new shoe or gets a new watch, you seem to start wearing them right away and he keeps going back to his old stuff. What's going on?'

'Vick owes me money.'

'What for?' Usha Aunty asked disbelievingly.

'You ask him.'

'I'm asking you and if you're in my house, you have to answer me.'

'I don't have to answer to you or anyone else. If he pays back the money he owes me, I won't take his things.'

'This is extortion!' Usha Aunty screamed in anguish.

Dr. Kundu cut in, 'How much does he owe you?'

'Why do you want to know?'

Vick restlessly fidgeted with his shirt collar. The gesture would go against him later when the time came to present his defense.

Dr. Kundu continued, 'I can give you the money right now.'

'50,000,' Mad said coolly.

'What?' Usha Aunty fumed so hard that you could boil an egg on her head.

'50,000? What did you buy with that kind of money, Vikash?' asked Dr. Kundu.

'Er, well, nothing...well, generally...well, stuff..,' Vick mumbled, finding himself in a sticky situation.

'Stuff? What kind of stuff?' asked Usha Aunty.

'Not stuff, general expenses.' Vick gulped.

'We need to know the truth,' said Dr. Kundu.

At that point, the bell rang. Usha Aunty walked up to the door and opened it. Vani stepped in. She had gone to play with Dolly, Kirit's new Labrador. Vani's beaming face revealed that her past hour had been well spent. She immediately sensed that something was wrong in their peaceful household.

'What happened?' she asked innocently.

'You should get to your homework,' Usha Aunty tried to dismiss her from the living room.

'I finished my homework before I went to play with Dolly. Remember?' she reminded her mother.

Before Usha Aunty could come up with another plausible excuse to extract her daughter from the ugliness of the scenario they were confronting, Vani ran to the sofa. She sat with a thump and cuddled up to her father. Dr. Kundu put his arms around her and indicated to his wife to let her stay on. Then he took a deep breath and tried to appear sincere, 'Madan, if you can produce a receipt, or an agreement, or in some other way prove to me that Vikash indeed owes you that absurd sum of money, I will clear his debt.'

'Receipt?' Mad gave a cackling laugh that sent a shiver up Dr. Kundu's spine, 'I don't need your money. I have lots of money.'

'And can I ask how did you get a whole lot of money?'

'You can. But you may not. It's none of your business.'

'Fair enough. But it's my business to make sure I don't entertain anyone I don't like. And I don't like you. So you should leave. Or else I will have to call the police.' Vani's large eyes had widened more in fear. She moved closer to her father.

At the mention of police intervention, Mad decided that he had had enough. He addressed Vick in a loud voice, 'You owe me money and now your father insults me. You will pay for this buddy. You will.'

Vick was terrified, 'Please Madan. Don't mind him. He doesn't know what he is saying.'

'Oh, he knows what he's saying. I can hear him. He's not even five feet away from me. If you don't pay up soon you're in trouble,' Mad stood up, ready to depart from the scene.

Usha Aunty was firm, 'Could you please leave Vick's watch on the table?'

Mad ignored her completely and kicked the elegant turquoise blue ceramic flower vase on the centre table. It went down with a crash on the carpet, making a mess of the orchids, but did not break. Vani cried out, terrified. Mad stomped out leaving behind a room filled with gloom and dread of the possibility of more encounters to follow. Usha Aunty was shaking with rage. New worry lines had developed on Dr. Kundu's forehead in the previous half hour. Vani snapped out of her stupor, 'Why was he behaving like that?'

'I wish I knew,' was Dr. Kundu's unsatisfactory response.

Vick had already walked into his room and shut the door behind him. Usha Aunty started towards Vick's room when Dr. Kundu stopped her. He asked her to allow Vick to recover from what had just transpired. 'Let him be on his own for a while.'

'He must be drunk,' said Usha Aunty.

'I don't think so.'

'How can you be so sure?'

'He wasn't smelling of alcohol.'

'Oh my God. Drugs then?'

'I don't know, Usha. I hope not.'

'What are we going to do now, Ranjan?'

'It could be marijuana or something like that. Let's pray it's nothing worse.'

'Oh my God, oh my God,' Usha Aunty slumped on the sofa in despair.

Vani interrupted, 'Can anyone please tell me what is going on?'

'Nothing that will stop me from taking you out for some ice cream,' Dr. Kundu smiled. Vani knew it was a bribe but she was prepared to take it.

'Two scoops?'

'Two scoops it'll be.'

'Dada must have done something really bad,' Vani smiled. Dr. Kundu forced a smile in an attempt to revert to normalcy.

The night was long. Vick did not come to the dining table. He slept throughout the evening and the entire night. Dr. Kundu and Usha Aunty talked their hearts out through a sleepless night. But they let Vick be.

The next morning, Dr. Kundu called his office first thing to announce that he would come in after lunch. All appointments for the early hours were postponed. He had begun to understand that his long hours at work had drifted his son away from the family. Although Monday was meant to be a murderously busy start to an up-to-the-neck work week, Usha Aunty called her juniors and asked them to hold fort until she came in later in the day.

The perturbed couple tried to act as if everything was normal in the household. Vani was overjoyed at being dropped off to school by both parents instead of her regular school bus. The Kundus figured that if they did not reduce their hours of work, they would ultimately be left with only money, for their children would be long gone on their own paths, distinctly different from what any parent would prefer.

It was 9:30 in the morning. The sound of running water in Vick's bath indicated that he was finally up. Dr. Kundu and Usha Aunty patiently waited for him to emerge. They had a long day ahead of them. Clients would demand attention, patients would require treatment. In a bid to save time, they were already dressed to leave for work. Just before the clock struck ten, Vick appeared out of his room, looking miserable. He came to the dining table like a zombie and sat down. He looked so drowsy that Ranjan and Usha Kundu thought that their son had not noticed them. Dreamily, Vick ignored the platter of neatly cut and salted fruit placed there by the part-time cook and decided to go for an uncut apple from the bowl.

'Talk to us, Vikash,' attempted Dr. Kundu.

Vick bit into the apple, lifted his eyebrows, assimilated the statement and ignored the suggestion.

'If you don't talk to us, we won't be able to help in any way,' continued Usha Aunty.

'I don't need your help,' Vick said calmly.

'Your parents were insulted by a low life and it doesn't matter to you?' fumed Usha Aunty.

'You insulted him too, remember?' Now it was Vick's turn to be adamant.

'Oh, so now you're calling your mother a low life?' Usha Aunty said sarcastically.

'I didn't say that. You did,' wiping off some apple juice trickling down his chin.

'What do you owe him money for?' Dr. Kundu inquired.

'I don't owe him any money.'

'Then why was he saying so?'

'I don't know.'

'If you don't cooperate, we can't help you.'

'Cooperate? What are you? Police interrogators?'

'Calm down, son. This is making matters worse.'

Vick paused to take another bite from his already finished apple. When he could see no flesh left in it to bite off, he tossed it back on to his plate.

Usha Aunty took a deep breath, 'So you don't owe him any money?'

'Didn't I just say so?'

'I noticed your reaction when Madan brought it up. He seemed to be telling the truth. You didn't protest.'

'I told you. I don't owe him any money!' Vick was losing his temper.

Dr. Kundu spoke softly, 'That's a relief to know. But then why didn't you object to his claim?'

'I didn't care.'

'Do you have anything to tell us?' tried Dr. Kundu.

'Nope.'

'Then don't expect any help from us,' Usha Aunty stated clearly.

'Okay.'

Usha Aunty was tired of her son's non-cooperation. She stood up. 'I need to go now. I'm already very late.'

There had been no disclosure, let alone a resolution. Dr. Kundu made a final attempt, 'You still have a few minutes to decide if you wish to talk to us.'

'There's nothing to talk about,' Vick was relieved that the family meeting was nearing an end. He walked back to his room and slammed the door. Dr. Kundu and Usha Aunty left for work feeling miserable. They addressed the woes of the entire world but when it came to their own child, they failed to assist him.

The day passed quickly and when the troubled couple returned home, they found that Vani had done well in her exam. After the nightmare of the previous day, Vani's report card made them forget their grief, if temporarily. Everything seemed to be settling down. Vani was chattering away excitedly. She was recounting the praises showered upon her by her teachers and describing her fruitful day when matters took a serious turn. In the course of the conversation, Vani mentioned that Madan Ruia had visited the flat in the evening along with two of his friends. Usha Aunty was enraged, 'What kind of person would come back after what happened yesterday?' Dr. Kundu began to fear that they were dealing with an issue way more complicated than visible to the regular eye.

Vani added that the boys accompanying Mad Ruia looked scary. They wore chains on their necks, their shirt buttons were open and they had tattoos on their chests and wrists. Dr. Kundu feared that Mad Ruia might be a part of a gang. He had read in the papers that some gangs had special tattoos to distinguish them from rookie troublemakers.

Vick was not at home. When he returned a couple of hours later, the house exploded. Dr. Kundu could not bear this nuisance any longer. Vick was given an ultimatum that the police would be called on Madan Ruia if he did not stop visiting their home.

At this point, Vick confessed that he was not strong enough to ask Mad and his friends to stay away. Although he had never taken any money from Mad, like he claimed, Mad assisted him in buying weed. He did not know if Mad belonged to any gang or what the tattoos symbolised.

Vick's confession immediately drew sympathy from his parents. They viewed their son as a victim. When Dr. Kundu asked Vick if he was willing to take a drug test, he was ready. Usha Aunty came to his rescue. She said that it must be embarrassing for him and they were prepared to take his word for it. The hallmark of good parenting lies in understanding and encouragement. Vick found himself blessed with both. The family bonded instantly as pent up words of confession began to flow out of Vick like a tributary heading swiftly towards its source.

Dr. Kundu was confident that half the battle of wiping out the affliction in question was won because the patient wanted nothing to do with it anymore. A master of mind games and the victor of many court battles, Usha Aunty was also convinced that now the truth was out and overcoming any obstacle would be easy.

But their relief was short-lived. They realised how helpless their son felt in the company of this anti social element. Vick was concerned that he may get into trouble with Mad Ruia and his friends if they were not allowed into his home. But he was unsure of what kind of threat he would have to face. Vick Kundu had become a puppet in the hands of Mad Ruia and his thug friends. He constantly parted with his trendy clothes, shoes, watches and a steady supply of pocket money not only with Mad but also with his friends. He further confessed that his precious BSA racing cycle had also changed ownership.

'Some household items have gone missing too,' complained Usha Aunty. 'That's when I first began to suspect the crook.'

'I don't think he's a thief. At least he didn't take anything in my presence,' Vick's protest did not appear very sincere. He wanted out, but was scared to disclose more information that might get him into trouble.

Dr. Kundu and Usha Aunty knew that there were more skeletons in the closet but agreed not to probe their son. They chose to support him. 'Vikash, you have a good future ready to embrace you.' 'You have always been a good student and that's what you truly are.' 'You must get back on track.' 'He is a college drop out. You have nothing in common with him.' 'You have shown great generosity in accommodating him for so long. But he took advantage of it.' 'You have nothing to worry. We are with you.' 'You chose us over him. We are proud of you.' The injections went on.

Vani had been quiet for too long. She had to contribute, 'They were scary. But they could not scare you. You are too brave for them.'

The next day, Dr. Kundu came to our place after work. He would drop in from time to time for a cup of tea, so I did not suspect anything unusual. He had taken Baba into confidence and discussed their crisis with him. When Baba recounted the Kundus' predicament at dinner, we were all shocked at Mad Ruia's audacity. 'There's something creepy about him,' Ma said. In the afternoons she would see Mad Ruia walk in and out of 3B all the time. Baba remembered him from an old newspaper item which had first coined his ominous name. He took his friend's side, 'This is unacceptable. The boy is so rude.' Mukul was indifferent, 'I didn't know Vick would have friends like that. I thought he was smarter.' I made a wish, 'I hope Mad Ruia never comes back.'

Our watchman, Bheem Bahadur was summoned. When Dr. Kundu asked him if he knew Mad Ruia, he claimed to be able to identify the boy at midnight with a scarf tied around his eyes. Dr. Kundu and Baba instructed him to stop Mad Ruia from entering the building again.

Baba also accompanied Dr. Kundu to the nearby police station and spoke to the Officer-in-Charge, Tej Thakur. Thakur's aged parents were long time patients of Dr. Kundu and he bestowed extra attention on the case. He brushed off the issue by saying that these problems were not uncommon and generally fizzled out with the passage of time. If the delinquent had half a brain, he could guess that the watchman would stop him from entering the property next time. But he promised to assist if the boy troubled the Kundus again.

The following week passed without incident. Vick had no idea that his father had spoken to the police. He was too scared to ask Mad Ruia to stay out of his life. Instead, he met Mad near a marijuana den close to his college and requested him to space out his visits. That way, things would even out and change the scenario in his favour. To his relief, Mad complied.

Two weeks later, as Vick sat preparing for a class test, the doorbell rang. He opened the door and found Mad Ruia along with a man he had never seen before. Mad's new friend had long locks of unkempt hair and reeked of *ogoru* perfume, usually applied to corpses on their way to the crematorium.

'What're you doing here?'

'What a strange question.'

'I mean, how did you get in? Bheem Bahadur…'

'Oh, I took care of him.'

'How?'

'I gave him 300 rupees.'

'I'm surprised that he took money from you. He's very loyal.'

'Everyone is loyal to money.'

'I have an exam next week.'

'Are you asking us to leave?'

'Don't be ridiculous. Come on in.'

Mad introduced the new person as Jata as they walked into his room. Anyone could tell that Jata got his funky name because of his ringlet curls. Bheem Bahadur had been bribed. Mad Ruia and Jata scared him but he decided that it was best to inform Dr. Kundu and called him at his office. He admitted coyly that he had allowed Mad Ruia to come in along with a friend with strange hair because he was scared to handle them on his own. Dr. Kundu called the police station and spoke to Thakur right away. Then he dashed out of his office leaving his patients waiting and wondering.

As he drove past Vanilla Apartments to reach the police station he had an urge to get home. But the prospect of tackling the ruffians on his own unnerved him. Thakur was ready for him. In less than twenty minutes, Dr. Kundu was driving back to the building closely followed by a police car. Thakur smoked a cheap scented cigar while a massively built uniformed constable drove the vehicle.

The trio met an anxious Bheem Bahadur at the entrance. He promptly handed over the three hundred rupees he had collected from the boys to grant them entry into the forbidden zone. Thakur congratulated him for his honesty and quickly pocketed the sum. He casually reminded Dr. Kundu that the police dealt with real criminals every single day of the year. In comparison, these thugs were only rambunctious children. Dr. Kundu requested Thakur not to raise his hand on the boys. He reluctantly agreed.

Soon the trio stood in front of 3B. Dr. Kundu found his hand shaking as he pressed the doorbell. There was no answer. Sweat broke out on his forehead. He rang the bell again and waited impatiently. No response. The constable took over. He leaned forward and pressed the bell with all his accumulated might. He did not release his finger for what seemed like an eternity. When there was no response, he began to play it like a piano key, unsuccessfully attempting to create music from the button with a single note.

The madness worked. Vick swung open the door, irritated at having his marijuana induced paradise violated by a vile musician in khaki. He was well within his senses to realise that he was staring at his father and two policemen. Loud music could be heard from his bedroom. Sheepishly he made way for the trio. No one said a word. The trio walked towards Vick's room and Thakur gently pushed open the door.

Mad Ruia lay on the bed, a cigarette dangling from his lips. Jata lay on the floor, his eyes shut. 'Who are you?' Mad demanded to know the moment he saw Thakur and the constable.

'Turn off the music,' bellowed Thakur.

Jata opened his eyes, disturbed by the sudden loud voice.

The room reeked of pot. Vick had consumed a generous amount and it had started kicking in. He had a smile on his face and looked at his dad as if a long lost friend had just returned after a long sojourn. Jata switched off the music.

Thakur addressed Mad Ruia, 'Were you asked not to come to this house?'

'Which police station are you from?' Mad countered him.

The constable slapped Mad's face so hard that the room shook with the noise.

'Answer my question.'

Vick trembled in fear. Dr. Kundu held his son and tried to ease the tension in the room, 'Officer Thakur, you had promised…'

Thakur lifted his arm and stopped him from interrupting the proceedings.

'Answer my question.'

'What are you charging me with?' Mad Ruia asked again.

Another slap resounded across the room. This one was harder than the last one. Dr. Kundu had never advocated corporal punishment as a solution to problems but he realised that these were extenuating circumstances.

Vick made a feeble attempt to protest, 'Hey, who do you think you are?'

Dr. Kundu addressed his son, 'The police are here, Vikash. Do you want them to take you away?'

'Model father,' mumbled Vick.

Thakur leaned menacingly towards Mad Ruia. 'For the last time, were you asked not come here? If you fail to answer, you will be taken to the lock up.' Mad stood calmly, without any trace of fear.

'Yes,' he replied, looking directly into Officer Tej Thakur's eyes.

'Yes, what?'

'Yes, I was asked not to come here.'

'Then why are you here?'

'I came to meet my friend.'

'When your friend has a house of his own, you can go meet him there. I don't want to see you, or hear of anyone else seeing you in this flat, or anywhere in this building, or even this neighbourhood. If I do, you'll be in jail. Is that clear?'

'Yes.'

'Now, where did you buy the marijuana?'

'There's no marijuana. Only cigarettes.'

Another slap landed on his cheek. This one was so hard it must have rattled his teeth. Mad Ruia's mouth began to bleed. 'You can search all of us. You can also search the room if you wish.'

'Hmm, that means everything is inside you. Well, get up and get out.'

Thakur moved up to Jata. He held him by the dirty, ebony tresses and forced him on to his knees. 'I remember you, you swine. But I don't remember your name.'

'Jata.'

'Jata. Yes. Now I remember.'

'I had been in your lock up.'

'Thank you for reminding me. What were you in for?'

'Theft.'

'What did you steal?'

'Chicken. But it was a false charge, Sir. That's why you had released me.'

'Is that the only time we've met?'

'No Sir.'

'I'm listening.'

'I was in your lock up on another occasion.'

'For?'

'Selling bottles of blood.'

'Spurious blood.'

'I didn't know that the blood was spurious.'

Dr. Kundu felt nauseated at the knowledge of the company his son kept. Just then, Mad Ruia tried to sneak past the constable towards the door. Thakur caught hold of his shirt collar. 'Where do you think you're going?'

'You asked me to get out. I'm leaving.'

The constable stepped up towards him, ready to strike. 'You aren't going anywhere until Sir has finished talking.'

'I didn't know because he didn't say that,' Mad Ruia replied cheekily.

The constable would not let any opportunity slip past. The room resonated with another thunderous slap. The knock was so hard that Mad's head almost snapped from the impact. Mad Ruia's eyes burned with hate but he did not utter a word of complaint. He stood his ground. Thakur dragged Jata on to his feet by his complicated hairdo and warned him. 'Jata, you got lucky both times. But don't push your luck. I don't want you to meet this boy here or come into this building. Ever!'

'Sure Sir. As you say,' Jata played along.

'Now out of here before I put a larceny charge on you. Out!'

Thakur and the constable kicked the boys' keisters with considerable force and they hurtled towards the door. But in spite of the deliberate humiliation inflicted upon them, they took their time, assembled themselves, tied their shoelaces and calmly walked out without looking back.

Vick, suitably high by then, sat on the bed mouthing flummadiddles. Dr. Kundu looked at him with disgust. The constable walked across to the balcony to make sure that the boys left the building. He saw that Mad Ruia and Jata were strolling out as if nothing had happened. The boys were gone but Thakur had a worried look on his face.

'Will everything be alright, Officer Thakur?' inquired Dr. Kundu.

'You know, the other boy, Jata, worries me. I'm sure that he'll head some criminal gang in a few years. We nabbed him twice on small charges but he got away.'

'How?'

'He's backed by a political leader.'

'Do tattoos mean anything?'

'Yes, tattoos can denote which gang they belong to.'

'So I had guessed right.'

'I've spent half of my life in the company of criminals and I know that this boy, Jata is a criminal of the big league - in the making.'

'What about Madan Ruia?'

'If he stays close to Jata, he will get sucked in. At the outset he displayed all the necessary qualities.'

'And they are?'

'Very similar to the skills of a doctor.'

'What?' Dr. Kundu was astonished by the unbecoming comparison.

'For one, remaining calm under pressure.'

'Oh, I see what you mean.'

'The boy was fuming inside but was quite calm outside.'

'What else?'

'He was fearless. That is a crucial key for surviving in the crime world.'

'What will we do then?'

'I hope the threat works and they never come back.'

'Do you have doubts?'

'I'll be honest with you. Yes, I have my doubts.'

'Please suggest a solution to this mess,' Dr. Kundu pleaded.

Thakur thought for a moment. 'Can you send your son out of the city for a few days?'

'Where?'

'To visit a relative or a family friend. That'll help.'

'That's not a problem. But for how long?'

'In such situations, physical distance diminishes love. These boys are likely to drift towards a new victim.'

'I could pack him off by the middle of next week after his exam.'

'Is a college break coming up?'

'He has three weeks off after the exam.'

'Count your blessings that the timing is right. Had it been in the middle of the term, he would not be able to get away for that long.'

'I hope he wants to go on vacation.'

'What're you talking about, Dr. Kundu? Your son, what's his name again?'

'Vikash.'

'Vikash must not be given a choice. He will have to take a vacation whether he wants one or not.'

'I understand. Let me work on that as soon as Mrs. Kundu returns home.'

'Pick him up yourself after the exam next week to make sure he doesn't disappear with these scums. Then at the first opportunity, put him on a train.'

'I don't know how to thank you.'

'Keep me posted.'

'Thank you Officer Thakur.'

All of a sudden, Vick spoke, taking everyone by surprise, 'Thank you, Officer.'

Thakur shook his head in disappointment at the wasted youth. But he acknowledged with a slight nod. Then he walked out with the constable.

Vick seemed to have returned to his senses, 'What was all the police fuss about?'

'You're going to Delhi to be with Shinjon Uncle for a few days.'

'But he was here last month.'

'I know that. This is to get these sociopaths to stay away from you.'

'I'll be alright. I don't need to go anywhere.'

'Wash your face and eat something if you haven't eaten since morning. It makes me cringe in shame to see my son drifting into nothingness after dissolving in pot at two in the afternoon.'

'Have you never tried marijuana when you were my age?'

'I hate to disappoint you. But I haven't. Look at me. Become even half of me and then talk.'

'You're twice my age. How do you expect me to achieve the same things?'

'Going by that principle, show me that you're half of what I am.'

'Yeah, whatever.'

Dr. Kundu glanced at his watch. His patients were waiting. He walked out in a hurry.

That night, Ranjan Kundu spoke with his brother, Shinjon Kundu, a successful businessman in New Delhi. He explained the situation in great detail. Shinjon had no inkling that such a horrible brew was in the making during his short visit to Kolkata the month before. Vikash appeared to be normal and an ideal son. Brotherly love ran high and Shinjon was more than willing to assist. He asked

Dr. Kundu to put Vick on the first available Rajdhani Express from Howrah station to the capital city. Vick's protest went unheeded and he reluctantly acquiesced.

A day after Vick left for New Delhi, Dr. Kundu visited our home again to share his woes with Baba. He bravely admitted that he was partially responsible for the calamity, for he had neglected family duties in the pursuit of money. Baba encouraged Dr. Kundu by saying that he worked that hard only to solidify his children's financial future and must not nurse any guilt because of it. Ma joined in and made him feel better by mentioning that she was certain of a tremendous comeback by Vikash. Dr. Kundu confessed that he feared the boys might show up again after his son's return. Baba disagreed, 'They'll forget all about it by then. I'm sure they won't take a chance after the warning from the police. Everything will be fine.'

The boys had not made another attempt to come back to Vanilla. Life was slowly returning to normal for the Kundu family. At the end of the third week, when Vick was due to return from his forced vacation, the latent tension began to resurface. When he arrived at the Howrah station the entire Kundu family was present to receive him. They acted normally without bringing up the topic looming large on all their psyches, but the subtext of the conversation was thick in the air.

Vick resumed college. The first week was peaceful. Then one day, as Vick parked his new shiny blue Yamaha RX 100 motorcycle to buy a pack of cigarettes, Jata appeared with two boys and blocked his way. They asked him if he wanted some marijuana. Alarm bells started clanging in Vick's mind. Politely, he declined. His young accosters cribbed that old customers needed to remain faithful so that honest tradesmen did not go hungry. The cigarette vendor sensed trouble for he had overheard the conversation. Since Vick was a regular at his kiosk, he tried to facilitate a speedy escape for him. Ignoring other customers he handed over a pack of twenty Gold Flake King cigarettes to Vick, his preferred brand. 'Vikash babu, I don't have change today. Pay me tomorrow.' Vick picked up the hidden message, agreed at once and removed the motorcycle from the stand without any delay. Just as he put the key into the ignition he felt a sharp object pressed against his stomach. 'Turn the key and I'll push the blade inside you.' Jata held a knife to his stomach. The knife scared Vick but he acted brave, 'I'll buy some stuff from you.'

'You said you didn't want any,' the second interceptor smirked.

'If it helps your business, why not?'

'So you are doing us a favour? We're charity seekers, are we?' asked Jata

'I didn't mean that.'

The third interceptor, who was yet to utter a word, yanked Vick off the motorcycle. It was back on its stand and Vick found the young man's arms around his shoulder.

'Take my wallet if you want.' Vick tried not to panic.

'Why did you disappear without saying a word?' Jata asked.

'I just went on a vacation.' Vick felt a sharp pain on his left kidney. He realised that he had been punched from the back by one of the two unknown faces.

'Where did you go?' Jata asked.

'To see my uncle in Delhi. It was winter break.'

'You know me,' said Jata. 'You could have informed me.'

'I don't know you that well.'

'What about Madan? Isn't he a good friend of yours?' Jata probed.

'Yes, he is.'

'Then?'

Vick realised that no matter what he said in defense, the group would pick a fight anyway. He tried to proceed sensibly.

'I've been forbidden by the police to associate with him,' he hoped that the mention of the magic word, 'police' would shoo away the nuisance.

'Forbidden? Are you a slave of the police?'

'I live in my father's house. He said he would throw me out.'

'So get out. Or do you prefer to choose your father over your loyal friends?'

Vick noticed that he had been guided into a narrow lane and tried another approach, 'Look guys, I'm sorry I didn't tell Madan that I was going out of town. I will call him and sort it out with him.'

'You will call him? How? Does Madan Ruia have a phone?'

'No.'

'Then? Will you visit him?'

Vick tried to think of a way to escape.

'Go on. How?' Jata urged.

'I don't know his place.'

'No phone, no address. How will you reach him then?'

Vick hesitated and looked around. He was plastered to the wall and completely cornered.

'Take his shoes,' said Jata. The second interceptor bent down.

'Wait. I'll give them to you,' Vick protested.

'The watch.'

'Here, take it.'

He slipped out of his sneakers and removed his watch as fast as he could.

'And here's my wallet. There must be 200-300 rupees in it.'

'This guy is in a hurry to go home,' Jata smiled.

The attackers closed in on Vick. Jata's long locks hung like a string of bells close to his face and he could feel the second interceptor's onion breath on his face.

'I gave you what you wanted,' pleaded Vick.

The third interceptor grabbed his throat and squeezed hard. Out of breath, Vick opened his mouth to breathe and Jata stuffed a handkerchief into it. The second interceptor grabbed his hand and began to twist his fingers backwards. Before Vick could put up a serious resistance, three fingers in his left hand were badly broken and twisted backwards. As he slid to the ground and blacked out, he was kicked all over a few times. But he felt no pain for all the pain had now descended on his broken fingers. Jata and his team left Vick unconscious in the lane and jogged away.

Luckily for Vick he did not lie unattended for very long. Within a few minutes, a milkman came into the lane whistling the tune of a popular movie song. He saw Vick lying unconscious on the street with a twisted look of pain on his handsome face. He jumped off his age-old Raleigh cycle, tied his *dhoti* firmly and attempted to shake the young man back into consciousness. He noticed that Vick's arm was limp in an unusual way.

A couple of hours later, Vick's fingers were dressed. Slightly sedated with painkillers containing soporifics, he was driven back to Vanilla Apartments in his father's brand new beige Fiat. The milkman had taken him to a hospital and within a few minutes,

Dr. Kundu had been contacted. When Dr. Kundu wanted to reward the poor milkman for helping his son, he refused the tip and walked away.

Wonder of all wonders, Mad Ruia showed up at Vanilla Apartments the next morning. He told Bheem Bahadur to deliver a chit to Dr. Kundu. He stood patiently outside the gate and made no attempt to enter the building. Bheem Bahadur asked the liftman to take the urgent message to Dr. Kundu. The chit read, 'I heard that Vikash has had an accident. I have come to see my friend. Madan Ruia.' Dr. Kundu gathered courage to step downstairs in his dressing gown. Mad was alone.

'What happened to Vikash?' he feigned ignorance.

'I thought you knew.'

'I heard that some thugs beat him up.'

'Your friends.'

'If that was true why would I be here?'

'He recognised that boy, Jata.'

'I am not friends with Jata since the day we left your home.'

'I'll give you 50,000 to get lost forever.'

'Can I see him?'

'He's asleep.'

'I can come back in the evening.'

'Officer Thakur has strictly warned you against coming here.'

'He won't know unless you tell him.'

'I won't tell him you came in spite of his warning. Please go away.'

'If that's what you want. But remember that Vikash has made some bad enemies and without me you may find it hard to protect your son.'

'He'll be fine.'

'If you change your mind, you won't know where to reach me. That's why I'll wait for a few minutes for you to reconsider your decision.'

'My mind is made up. Save yourself the time.'

'Suit yourself.' Mad shrugged and turned to leave. Then he quickly turned back and flashed a smile that chilled Dr. Kundu.

Dr. Kundu was no match for Mad Ruia. He felt bile rise to his throat from his insides. He was a respected homeopath in a big city, but right now he was a helpless pawn in the hands of a budding hustler.

Again it was a rush to the police station. But this time Dr. Kundu was in for a rude shock. Thakur said that Jata had now become untouchable because of his political affiliation. Due to his close association with Jata, Madan Ruia was also exercising the new muscle at every opportunity.

'Could changing homes be an option?' Dr. Kundu inquired.

'But how many things will you change?' came the most discouraging reply. Thakur was right. An established doctor like Ranjan Kundu had a large and loyal patient following at the very accessible Ballygunge Circular Road. It would be a professional setback for him to leave the area. It would take many years to re-establish a comparable practice somewhere far away. But most importantly, it would not serve the greater purpose - buying peace. A doctor of his stature could be traced easily wherever he went. Plus, all their friends and relatives were in South Kolkata.

The Kundus were going insane with worry for their only son and his future when, of all the experts, my mother came up with an idea, 'Send him overseas for higher studies.' Mukul had already expressed deep interest in going abroad for graduate studies and the topic was regularly discussed at the Bose residence. Ma dispensed her ever-effective common sense solution to our neighbours. It was a worthy proposal but applications and admissions for international students did not happen overnight. The Kundus pondered much and contacted Usha Aunty's cousin, Komal Panja, a dietician who had immigrated to Canada. Komal's husband, Bhaskar was an academic and the couple lived in Vancouver. Komal could assist with information. When she was consulted, the Kundus were pleasantly surprised to see her enthusiasm. Komal was glad that a member of the family might join them soon while the Kundus sulked. The thought of the light of their lives brightening a home in a distant, cold place gnawed at them.

In 1984, the Kundu family had visited Komal and Bhaskar in Vancouver. Vick's previous trip to Canada worked in his favour as the Panjas had liked both the Kundu kids immensely. They worked out a game plan for Vick and relevant papers were readied.

After the attack, Vick realised that he was in grave danger. But he was more scared for his parents and considered it cowardice to leave them at the mercy of the crooks. However, he was short on options.

Dr. Kundu and Usha Aunty were relieved that Vick had acknowledged that the errant boys were criminally oriented, even if they were yet to be convicted for their transgressions.

It was an emotional departure for Vick. He had no real intention of leaving the country. It was a terrible feeling to be hounded out. Reluctantly, Vick bid farewell to his parents. Vani sobbed uncontrollably at the sudden departure of her beloved dada. Usha

Aunty wept at the sight of her son walking into airport customs, away from her sight. Dr. Kundu placed his arm on her shoulder in a desperate attempt to console her. Travelling to the West for higher studies was becoming a major fad at the time. However, tuition costs and living expenses were prohibitive with the weak rupee. Realistically, such luxury was out of reach of most middle-class folks. Mukul's blood raced at the news of Vick's sudden exit. He was also a contender and envious of Vick's good fortune. Uncharitably he remarked, 'I would have gladly let a bunch of hooligans break my fingers to study in Canada.'

Vick's hand was healing. The sympathy and care of his relatives in Vancouver helped him overcome the stress with which he entered Canada. Vick found comfort in the breathtaking beauty of British Columbia and the mild winter was manageable. His assimilation was smooth. His English was superb. Instructors liked him for his impeccable manners. The coursework did not require him to stretch too much as he was used to a far more rigorous academic regimen before Mad Ruia had entered his life. Moreover, being the only Indian student in his class, friendly Canadian classmates took extra interest in him. Vick did very well in his first term exam. Komal and Bhaskar Panja were ecstatic to have assisted Vick in the adjustment to his new life in Canada.

Vick was totally off dope and about to embark upon a great chapter in his life, leaving behind the few haunting dark days, when fate took an ominous turn. Bad luck had followed Vick to Canada. At a college party, cannabis formed part of the menu and Vick indulged all over again. The resilience he had displayed in shunning pot so far turned to dust. The wrong crowd took notice and welcomed Vick with open arms. Vick started on pot again. But he kept improving in every exam throughout the first year, eventually outshining all the local students.

In Kolkata, the menace of Mad Ruia had subsided. Nothing was heard for a year. The Kundus were free. Vick was restless to go home to see his parents. To be in his own room. To hold Vani in his arms. To finally stop living the life of a fugitive. Since Mad Ruia was nowhere to be seen, why not go home for a short break? After much discussion, the family concluded that it might be worth the effort. The day school broke for Christmas holidays, Vick was on a flight to India.

Vick's homecoming was as teary as his departure. But this time it was a gush of joyous tears. He was driven home without incident. In his short time abroad, he had developed a mild accent which amused the Kundus. Vani started pulling his leg about turning Canadian in less than a year. I was leaving for Maths tuition when I saw Vick excitedly jump out of their car. 'Hey, Tig, what's going on?' He extended his right arm. It was strange as we rarely shook hands with people we saw every other day. But then, I realised that I had not seen him for nearly a year. He shook my hand vigourously.

'You look great Vick. Working out?' I asked.

'Off and on,' he flexed his bicep.

Vani gave me a hug in sheer joy, 'Tiger dada, my dada is back.'

'Isn't that cool?' I participated in her excitement and turned to Vick. 'Usha Aunty said that you're doing very well in Canada.'

Vick smiled, 'How's Tanmoy Uncle and Chitrani Aunty?'

'Come over while you are here and see for yourself.' No one ever asked about Mukul.

'They're okay, right?'

'Yes, yes. They talk about you quite often.'

'I'm here for three weeks. Sure I'll come and see them.'

'Bring along some pictures of Vancouver. Mukul would be thrilled. He's also looking to study abroad.'

'Oh, awesome. I'll get the pictures.'

I still regretted that Vick and I were not friends. Since we were next door neighbours and our parents were quite close, we made it a point to be nice to each other. As I walked to my tuition I could not help thinking of Canada. What was it like? Snow all around, McDonald's burgers, fast cars, broad highways, huge shiny buildings, white people in dark suits. I also imagined the comforts of a loving aunt's home in the dream world. A honking car brought me back to the real world. I had stepped off the footpath during my musings and was almost run over.

Vick's arrival was a hot topic of discussion at our dining table that night. Baba and Ma were glad that the trials were over for the amiable Kundus. Mukul had stopped joining us at the dining table and usually watched TV while he ate. Otherwise, I am certain that he would have had something nasty to say about Vick. Two days later, I rushed back from school thinking of my favourite rice pudding Ma had promised to make. When I entered home, the smile on my face evaporated. Ma was sitting quietly in the balcony, colour drained from her face. 'What's the matter?' I asked, gravely concerned.

'There's some very bad news,' she said.

'Where's Baba?'

'No, no. He's fine.'

'Mukul?'

'He's gone out.'

'What is it?'

'Vikash.'

'What about him?'

'He came from Canada on Sunday.'

'I'm the one who saw him first.'

'Oh yes, that's right.'

The suspense was oppressive.

'Ma, what happened to Vick?'

'He was coming out of Gobar's convenience store when some ruffians beat him with bicycle chains.'

'What?' I could not believe what I heard.

'He is in hospital.'

'My God! He has only been here for two days.'

'It's horrible.'

'How did you find out?'

'I saw some people carrying him back.'

'Why did Ranjan Uncle and Usha Aunty let him step out on his own?'

'The driver was with him. He was also hurt.'

'The driver is also in hospital?'

'I don't know exactly.'

'Is it that Mad Ruia and his group?'

'Who knows? They jumped on him when he stepped out of the store. It seemed that they were waiting for him.'

'That's strange. How would they know that he would go to Gobar's store at that time?'

'I don't know.'

'It would be too much of a coincidence that they just saw him by chance. They must have seen him leave the building and followed him.'

'But how could they know that he was back in Kolkata?' Ma raised a valid question.

'You're right. This doesn't make sense. It's hard to believe that they were watching the building for one whole year.'

'Dr Kundu said that only some close relatives knew that Vikash was back in town.'

'And us.'

'I'm sure some other folks in the building must also know.'

'Baba will be shocked to hear this.'

'What if Vikash dies?'

'Ma, please. Think positively.'

'He was unconscious. I read somewhere that if a person stayed unconscious for a long time, he might die.'

'Nothing like that will happen,' I was unhappy to see her unusual negativity.

'How can you be so sure?'

'Ma, I don't know. But I don't want to think like that. And you mustn't think like that either.'

'I hope the police does something about it this time.'

'I thought the Mad Ruia chapter was over for them.'

'I still remember that boy's face so well.'

'Naturally. It hasn't been that long. I didn't like the look of him right from the very first day.'

Vick took two months to recover. The culprits were rounded up by the police. Vick identified them but he had never seen them before the attack. The rowdies claimed that it was a case of mistaken identity. But Dr. Kundu refused to believe them. Mad Ruia was picked up by the police but he had a solid alibi. At the time of the attack, he was in a movie theatre with three vagabond friends who testified. They produced four tickets of the show and answered all questions pertaining to the film without making any mistakes. It did not conclusively prove that Mad Ruia was watching the movie at that particular show but the police could not hold him any longer. As a feeble measure, the police issued a newspaper notice requesting anyone who had been on the adjoining seats to come forward and testify if they had seen the boys in the cinema hall. No one came forward. The public found better things to do than to get unnecessarily involved with the police. Mad Ruia was released. Physically healed but psychologically scarred, Vick went back to Canada. We thought we had seen the last of him, at least for many years to come.

Vick had run away due to the presence of bad friends in his life. And bad friends became his nemesis in a land thousands of miles away. Vick's pot smoking friends in Vancouver were not only weak students, some of them had started dealing too. From East Hastings to West Pender and from Homer Street to Burrard Street, they had a fan following. Vick hung out with the waywards and his grades began to suffer.

Komal and Bhaskar Panja attributed the vicious attack on Vick as the prime cause of his dropping grades. Bad grades over a period of time had serious implications. Vick would not be able to continue studying in Canada. If his student visa was discontinued, he would be forced to return to the nightmare from which he had narrowly escaped. One evening, when the supportive couple was brainstorming solutions for their nephew, they heard a loud knock on the door.

Two RCMP investigators in casual clothing asked for Vick. They showed him a few pictures and asked him if he knew the people in them. They were Vick's dealer friends. Vick agreed that he had seen all of them in college but did not know them personally. The investigators had no solid evidence but they were seasoned experts who could tell that Vick was lying. They warned him of the consequences of associating with the racketeers in the picture. The threat was subtle but as clear as a neon light.

Bad friends are bad news. Vick was drawn towards them like a moth to fire. He needed a joint and these friends were his only source in Vancouver. He exercised caution and lay low for a few days, out of the sight of the RCMP. When he bought from his dealer friends, he was furtive.

Vick had found a weekend job at a café on Robson Street. His grades had begun improving when one day he was apprehended while buying a joint. Guns drawn, RCMP officers enveloped them. In the chaos that ensued Vick was charged with dealing. He had thrown away the purchased stuff and when he was handcuffed nothing was found on him. When the police asked him why he tried to run away from the officers, he protested, 'I didn't run from the police. I thought there was trouble somewhere around and that's why the police were running. I didn't realise they would catch me and pin someone else's crime on me.'

The excuse didn't fly. Vick was deported. The RCMP accompanied him to Komal and Bhaskar Panja's home on Laurel Street and gave him an hour to pack his things. The devastated couple was too aghast to protest. Vick's Canadian dream was evanescing and they were powerless to prevent it. Vick was handcuffed again and put on an Air Canada flight to Switzerland, his long time dream destination. He spent a night swallowing verbal insults from the commanding officers at a detention centre in

Zurich and lost appetite for Swiss chocolates forever.

Twenty-four hours later, he was back in New Delhi boarding a connecting flight home.

Dr. Kundu and Usha Aunty were demolished. The untoward incident created a severe dent in the relationship between the two families. While Komal and Bhaskar Panja accused Vick of taking undue advantage of their hospitality and nearly dragging them into trouble with the police, Dr. Kundu and Usha Aunty felt that the Panjas should have fought the unfair and drastic step taken by the Canadian authorities.

While Vick was being deported from Canada, another strange set of events were unfolding in Kolkata. Mad Ruia had been apprehended for murder. He was all over the local news. Apparently he had expressed a desire to sell his father's puny tenement on Linton Street to start a business. But fed up with the daily nuisance and the accompanying shame resulting from Mad's tumultuous life, his parents made it clear that the family tenement would not be sold, especially for their neurotic son's business needs.

Contempt at both schools, exclusion from Vick's home and parental rejection pushed Mad Ruia over the edge. Soon after his father's declaration, he drugged his unsuspecting parents' dinner. A thin lentil soup, an everyday fixture in their frugal household was laced with opiates. As his parents fell asleep, he tiptoed out of his bed and opened a small rear exit from the tenement. The ill-fated parents of Mad Ruia were in deep sleep when Jata walked in with two accomplices. They gagged the groggy and disoriented couple with handkerchieves and bound them to wooden chairs. In an abhorrent follow up, the group hacked them to death with meat cleavers.

To throw the police off-track and avoid suspicion, Mad's gangster friends also gagged and tied him up like his parents. Then they beat him black and blue. As they walked out the front door, Jata smashed an empty whisky bottle in the corridor to alert the neighbours. He wanted his friend to be discovered soon. The noise woke up the next door neighbour of the Ruias. He heard the sound of scurrying feet closely followed by a loud groan that seemed to originate from the Ruia household. He got out of bed to investigate and saw Mad Ruia tied to a chair croaking for help while his parents were drowned in blood. Mad testified that he was sleeping when the three assailants had entered. 800 rupees was stolen along with a thin gold chain and a set of gold earrings that belonged to his mother.

The news of the gruesome Ruia murders made headlines for weeks. Although Mad Ruia won public sympathy right away, the police knew his shady past. His parents were ordinary folks with no enemies who would inflict such a macabre fate on them. Brutal murders for such a paltry financial gain did not seem right. It could be the handiwork of obdurate criminals who had a grudge with Mad Ruia. But the police reasoned that if it was indeed the truth, why was there such an obvious disparity in their treatment? They would have beaten up his parents and killed him and not the other way. Mad Ruia's story did not fit.

The initial sympathy wave was over. Mad Ruia became the obvious suspect of the heinous crime. He sensed trouble and protested the preposterous insinuation by suggesting that the attack could be the handiwork of some of his creditors. But the Kolkata police was in no mood to buy this balderdash.

Until the incident, Mad Ruia had enjoyed the protection of

the corrupt politician who also sheltered Jata. But when the politician realised that the occurrence was drawing unnecessary attention towards him, he decided to withdraw support. The police got the opportunity they were seeking and swooped in. In a damp and dingy lock up, they extracted the truth from a shieldless Mad Ruia. He received a life sentence for the first degree slayings of his parents. Jata and the two accomplices joined him for the same time.

Ironically, instead of breathing a huge sigh of relief on the day the case was decided in the court of law, Vick Kundu was boarding a flight back home with a deportation order stamped in his passport. After a week or so, Vick visited us and spoke to all four of us. We listened. He spoke of injustice, humiliation and the unfair treatment meted out to him. We did not have words to console him.

Sadly for us and everyone else in the building, Dr. Kundu and Usha Aunty moved from Vanilla Apartments two months after Vick returned from Canada. Word of Vick's deportation had got out and they knew that they had lost the respect they once commanded. It was best for them to depart as gracefully as possible. They went away to the newly developing Golf Green area, a more than half hour drive away from Vanilla Apartments. The Kundus held on to Flat 3B for three more years after their unceremonious departure while we hoped that our best neighbour ever would return to the property one day. 3B was sold to a multinational financial corporation and residents come and go every year.

Gradually we lost touch with the Kundus. Ten years later, Baba was suffering from acute acidity and decided to visit Dr. Kundu's office. Dr. Kundu was very glad to see him after so many years. Baba was deeply saddened to see that he had greyed completely and his skin was wrinkled like a much older man's. What was worse, he had lost his charming smile. Usha Aunty and Vani's pictures were placed on his desk but there was no picture of Vick. Baba was curious to know their whereabouts but being a decent man who disliked probing, he waited until Dr. Kundu opened up to his old friend and neighbour. Vani had moved to California for higher studies and met her husband at the same university. Vick had moved to Bangalore. He was always in and out of jobs. Being in the technology sector, he was seriously limited due to his inability to travel overseas. Promotions were hard to come by. He was forced to turn down lucrative offers regularly in the west due to his travel record, a permanent scar that was slowly sapping the life-blood out of him

We felt bad with the way Vick's perfect life had turned out. But our hearts ached more at the loss of our favourite little Vani, the apple of everyone's eyes at Vanilla Apartments. When will Madan Ruia see the sun again? He won't. Two weeks into his sentence, a prison riot killed him.

# CHAPTER EIGHT

# Bad Debt

Winter was most suitable for cricket. The cool air helped the bowlers while the lack of humidity assisted the batsmen to stay in their creases for a long time. We played on a narrow street across the busy main road in front of Tulip Montessori and had our own set of rules. Three wickets, substituting for real ones, were painted on the long white exterior wall of the school. Our initial attempts to steady the real wickets between large bricks failed and quite often batsmen heard their wickets hitting the ground, even before the bowlers had released their deliveries. The wind was the chief obstructer of the game but we did not take long to find a workable solution to the problem.

No permission was sought from the school for we knew that no sane person in a position of authority would allow us to damage the school wall. Pandey, the school watchman enjoyed our weekend matches, even taking sides to cheer. It never occurred to him that we had drawn ugly lines on the property he was supposed to guard, right under his nose. The lines were perfectly straight. The height was ascertained by using real wickets and the two crowning bails were painted in red. A nearby construction site provided the red and black calligraphy stones that completed the defilement.

The wall bore our torment in silence and the lines were left undisturbed for five years. We touched them up every couple of months so that they remained fresh.

Street cricket had ceased for us by the late 80s. The wall-wickets that bore the marks of many an exciting game lay unattended. Like everything else, they required maintenance. By the time we were in university, the wicket lines had faded away and I missed those days filled with cricket. Even Pandey remembered nail biting finishes as vividly as I did. We had moved on with more pressings things in life and our wickets had been claimed by the most ruthless bowler of all: time.

On a Sunday in the winter of 1987, we played cricket from ten in the morning and finished by noon. The match drawn, we headed back home for a quick shower before catching a popular quiz show on TV. Along with the other players, Robin, Pluto and Kirit had left early. Sig and I followed with the cricketing gear. We dumped the equipment in the common room and headed towards the stairs when we noticed an Afghan man striding into the building. Spotting an Afghan in their traditional loose clothing was not unusual in the area. Our neighbourhood tea stall was their favoured haunt. When we played cricket they took great interest in our matches but did not take sides. They supported every one who played well. In turn, we ended up trying harder when we had an audience. Our Afghan supporters liked hard hitting batsmen. They clapped and cheered when the ball flew into the distance after taking a smack from our bats. Sometimes, after the matches, they offered us delicious raisins, pistachios and cashews from cloth pouches hidden in their large pockets. That would be their treat in return for a great match. Although we hesitated initially, their faces became known to us gradually and we savoured the goodies. I was always curious to know about other nations and inquired about their homes. They spoke no English but managed a conversation in broken Hindi. Nostalgia swept over them as they spoke of their beautiful land with great sentiment and lamented the ravages of war. When they spoke of Kabul, their large hearts seemed to melt and their tough exteriors softened. There was one particularly friendly man in the assembled Afghan group who confessed his obsessive love for biryani from the famous Shiraz restaurant in Park Circus. It was his staple for breakfast, lunch, tea and dinner. When we wondered how he could digest such rich fare every day, he simply laughed and said that digestion was a mind game. It had nothing to do with the capacity of the stomach. If the mind loved the biriyani, the body would follow. He added that he could never leave Kolkata because of his addiction. We did not know his name but he was a source of great entertainment for us. Often we came face to face with him and asked him if he had biryani that day. The man would break into a guffaw of admittance which amused us no end. We did not know any of their names but were familiar with their friendly faces.

But we had never seen the Afghan who walked into Vanilla Apartments that Sunday. Built like a gigantic refrigerator on wheels, he was easily six and a half feet tall. He could devour our very own strongman, Gorilla Ghosh along with dried fruits. Fridge on Wheels wore a headgear so large that a band of musicians could perform a concert upon it. His thick beard resembled the dense forests of the Sunderbans and a Royal Bengal tiger could easily stay hidden in it. He had not bathed in weeks and smelt like rotten tofu. When he spoke with Bheem Bahadur, our head of security, the petrified watchman quickly disintegrated into the position of the 'head of insecurity'. Sig and I were at a distance and could not hear the exchange. But at the outset, we knew that trouble was brewing. Fridge on Wheels was angry. Curiosity got the better of us and we had to find out what was going on. Bheem Bahadur pointed his finger towards a flat on the front side of the building. It was evident that Fridge on Wheels was looking for someone. Bheem Bahadur did not attempt to reason with the goliath and let him in. Fridge on Wheels marched away towards the stairs. Bheem Bahadur ran towards the administration office when we intercepted him, 'Who was that, Bahadur?' I asked. Bheem Bahadur was glad to see us. 'He was looking for Prasoon Sir.'

'Which Prasoon Sir?' Sig was alarmed that the giant may have come in search of Robin's father.

'Robinbabu's father,' he was surprised with Sig's ridiculous question.

'What did he want?' I inquired.

'He said that Prasoon Sir owed his friends money,' Bheem Bahadur said wide eyed.

'He must have made a mistake,' said Sig. But before we could say anything else, Bheem Bahadur walked away from us straight into the office. Jhola Mallick was lazing in the administration office with a cup of tea along with our electrician, Bonka and the building carpenter, Kishore while Baba and Sudip Uncle discussed the building agenda. When Bheem Bahadur explained the situation, we heard Baba reprimanding him, 'You should not have allowed him to walk in without permission.' Jhola was less patient, 'Idiot. Why did you show him Mr. Raha's flat?'

Bahadur croaked a confession that he feared for his life.

'Call Gorilla Ghosh,' Sudip Uncle instructed Bonka. Gorilla

Ghosh was the only person who could stand next to Fridge on Wheels and command respect. But could King Kong take on the The Hindu Kush? Everyone rose from their seats and headed for the lift. In the meantime, Sig and I took the rear staircase to warn Robin of the visitor in transit. As we ran up the third floor, we heard a blood curdling scream. The dense hair on my head rose like a porcupine ready to release its deadly quills. We peeked from the stairs and saw an unbelievable sight. Fridge on Wheels had made an error. Seething in rage, he rang the doorbell of my neighbour in 3D instead of the Raha residence in 5D.

Dev Rakshit, the owner of 3D was a perennial pessimist. He had entered his name into the bad books of all the residents, way back in 1983 when India won the World Cricket Cup. Rakshit commented that only a handful of insignificant nations still played the game and the win meant nothing. Maligning the victorious Indian cricket team was blasphemy and getting away with it, no less than a small miracle. But everyone hated him since then. He made his position worse when he attended Sunit and Milly Roy's infant's rice eating ceremony in the building's common room. When all other guests were going gaga over the baby, he commented that having children was the worst form of selfishness and narcissism. Sumita Aunty was present and asked Dev Rakshit for an explanation of his weird philosophy. Rakshit reasoned that children were non-existent when their parents chose to have them. This meant that parents wanted children for their own entertainment rather than any altruistic intent. My mother took Sumita Aunty's side, 'So children are just for entertainment?' she asked angrily. Realising that he may have treaded on a few corns, Dev Rakshit countered, 'Not always. They are also conceived as an investment.'

'Investment?' Ma was taken aback at this new angle.

'Yes. People have children with the hope that their kids will look after them when they grow old. We educate them so that they get good jobs and make money to feed us when we are incapable of feeding ourselves.'

'What nonsense, I don't care for my children's money,' protested Neelima Aunty.

'You may not care because you have a lot. But many others do,' Dev Rakshit was not to be cowed down.

'That's rubbish,' refuted my mother.

'Why do you think there's this absurd fascination with a male child?' Dev Rakshit continued.

'You are generalising. I adore my daughter,' said Usha Aunty.

'Of course, I am generalising. But what I'm saying is that the motive is always selfish. Be it for entertainment, investment, fear of mortality or just following a tradition – it is always selfish.'

The host, Sunit Roy stepped in finally, 'Fear of mortality?'

Dev Rakshit was not to be cornered, 'We want to keep on living. But there is no such elixir. No matter who you are or how much fame and fortune you acquire during your stay on earth, when the call comes, the curtain falls. But we don't like that, do we? We want to keep on living. And we can only do that through our children.'

'I don't want to be immortal,' said Sudip Uncle.

It took some gumption to continue an argument like this against stiff opposition. Prasoon Uncle entered the debate, 'What is this rubbish about tradition? I did not have children because everyone else was having them. I wanted my children.'

'That could be true in your case. But it has to be for any one of the four reasons. It can't be outside of that.'

'What was your reason for having Mufti?' asked Sudip Uncle.

'Anita and I fell for tradition but when we realised our mistake, we made sure that we didn't have a second one.' As if dismissing India's glorious victory was not enough, calling all parents of the world selfish and all children, bearers of their parents' greed was too much for the guests to digest. Dev Rakshit was blacklisted.

Dev Rakshit's daughter, Mufti was the most uncouth child in the entire building. Unfortunately, they were on our floor. Mufti had the habit of casually tossing food from their balcony. Even when caught red handed, Dev and Anita Rakshit would blatantly deny their daughter's involvement. When Mufti returned from school in the afternoons, feeding her lunch would turn into a World War. Anita would scream instructions and the obstinate Mufti's loud shrieks of resistance kept the neighbours praying for their daily ordeal to end. On weekends, it was Dev Rakshit's duty to feed Mufti. The fight would erupt a little after noon and invariably end up with Mufti vomiting all over the table. In the name of discipline and not wasting food in a nation where many children went hungry, Dev Rakshit would gather the vomit in a spoon and forcibly feed it to his only child. More vomiting and hair-raising screams would rock our floor until the job was done. Neighbours suggested a change in her diet and alternative methods of child rearing but Dev Rakshit refused to pay any heed.

Dev Rakshit was in the middle of this weekend ritual that Sunday, when the doorbell rang. His mind occupied with the task at hand, he opened the door without looking into the eyehole. He was lucky that the collapsible gate outside the door was locked. As soon as he opened the door with a plate filled with vomit in one hand, a massive, hairy arm darted through the gap in the gate and grabbed his shirt collar. The very next moment, he was lifted off his feet. The plate from his hand hit the floor and the vomit splattered around. Aghast at this sudden attack, he yelled for assistance. In broken Hindi, Fridge on Wheels asked him to clear his debt or die. Dev Rakshit was clueless about the matter and begged Fridge on Wheels to put him down. Soon his collar gave way and he fell to the ground. Sig and I watched from a distance and enjoyed every bit of Dev Rakshit's plight with perverse mirth. But we were concerned about Robin's father. What if the Afghan's claims were true? It couldn't be, we told ourselves. There must have been some mistake. Prasoon Uncle's business was doing so well. They had even bought a new car last month. Mufti had heard her father's pitiful cries and reached the door along with her mother. She was ecstatic to see the vomit smeared on the floor and the wall from where it would be impossible to extract. Dev Rakshit looked like a traumatised rabbit facing a hunter with a shotgun. Mufti cheered for Fridge on Wheels as Anita yelled for Bheem Bahadur and the police. Fridge on Wheels was confused at the unexpected support from Mufti when Baba, Sudip Uncle, Jhola, Kishore and Bheem Bahadur stepped out of the lift. Fridge on Wheels was least perturbed to see the group of men heading towards him. Dev Rakshit could not slam the door shut for Fridge on Wheels had positioned his big toe as an effective door stopper. Even from the distance we could tell that his *chappals* were a special 'yeti' size from Jumbo Footwear, a store in North Kolkata.

Sudip Uncle requested Fridge on Wheels to calm down. But the angry Afghan kept repeating one sentence that he had rehearsed well in Hindi, 'I want the money.' Dev Rakshit had derived sudden confidence at the appearance of the men from administration. He had just begun complaining about the inefficiency of the security at Vanilla Apartments, when Fridge on Wheels shook the collapsible gate with both hands. The entire steel structure shook and sounded like the bells of *ghungroo* anklets on a dancer's feet. Dev Rakshit stopped bawling. He looked like a notorious animal trapped in a hunter's net, searching for an escape route without success. The assembled men requested Fridge on Wheels to explain his grievance to them and promised to solve his problem. Fridge on Wheels said that he had come to take Dev Rakshit away. The woeful victim cried out again with the protest that he did not owe money to anyone. Sudip Uncle stepped forward cautiously and began to mediate in a gentler voice. Finally, Fridge on Wheels calmed down and confirmed that his friends, a set of Afghan moneylenders were owed money by a person whose name was written on a chit. He had come to collect the amount or take away the man if he failed to deliver. Merciless beating would follow. We found out for the first time that the friendly Afghans who always cheered our Sunday cricket games and shared their delicious dried fruits with us were a band of moneylenders. Their rates were much higher than the going market rates, often exceeding usury. No papers were signed and no questions were ever asked. Fools who believed that they could disappear without paying, confronted reality the hard way. Few law enforcers wanted anything to do with the Afghans. It was suicidal to borrow from them if one could not pay up. Those who took from them were typically in the last stages of ruin.

When Sudip Uncle saw the handwritten chit with the culprit's name on it, he was shocked. It was Prasoon Raha! Whether Prasoon Raha had anything to do with the problem or not was a matter for future debate. But Dev Rakshit's innocence had to be conveyed. It took a while but the group finally managed to convince Fridge on Wheels that the man he was looking for lived in the flat two floors above. Fridge on Wheels was about to climb upstairs when Sudip Uncle told him that the Rahas were out of town and expected back the next morning. Fridge on Wheels stopped in his tracks, unsure about his next step. We seized the moment and ran upstairs to warn Robin. It was a coincidence that Prasoon and Neelima Raha were visiting their farmhouse in Kakdwip, a couple of hours away, along with Aurobindo.

Robin was settling down to watch the quiz show on TV when he heard a loud knock on the door. At the sight of us he realised something was gravely wrong. We dragged him out before he could say a word. He did not protest and ran along with us towards the rear staircase.

In the meantime, Fridge on Wheels acknowledged his folly and asked Dev Rakshit to step out for a friendly hug. But Dev Rakshit was not ready to take any chances.

We had a great view of the entrance of the building from our balcony. Robin could see the Afghan from there. When we walked in, Ma was about to remind me that my favourite quiz program was on. But she stopped when she saw the urgency with which we ran to the balcony. She followed us. 'What's the matter?' she asked. 'First look at that guy. Then I'll tell you everything,' I said as I pointed towards Fridge on Wheels. He had just exited the building. Like a mountain in motion, he walked up to a parked Royal Enfield Bullet 350 motorcycle. With the drop of an eyelid he released the rusted vehicle from its stand. The large Enfield motorcycle had disappeared!

'Where the hell did it go?' asked Robin.

'He ate it,' replied Sig.

The heavy motorcycle had actually got concealed under the flowing pajamas of Fridge on Wheels. It looked so puny that we barely noticed it. But we heard the growl of the powerful engine. From the third floor balcony, it seemed as if Fridge on Wheels was running away from us with a cloud of smoke emitting from his gigantic rump. Only when he turned into the main street, did we catch a glimpse of the motorcycle's tires. 'What was that all about?' asked Ma, awestruck at the sight of Fridge on Wheels. 'Case of mistaken identity,' I said.

'Must be a money lending issue,' Ma bowled me over. How did she know all these things? She was just an ordinary housewife.

'He thought that Prasoon Uncle had borrowed money from his friends,' Sig informed Ma. She listened to what happened and asked Robin to stay with us until his parents were back in the evening. Although Robin tried to act normal, it was an anxiety ridden afternoon for him. He kept glancing at his watch, hoping his parents would return soon. When the Rahas returned, they heard what had transpired in their absence.

Prasoon Raha was socially adept and everyone believed that the barging in of the incensed Afghan was a grave mistake. But they wondered how he would prove his innocence to Fridge on Wheels when he came back the next morning.

Later in the evening, Sudip Uncle visited us. He told Baba that he was going to speak to Prasoon Uncle in private. Sudip Uncle was solution oriented. He had to know the truth for the safety of the Rahas and other members of the building. Prasoon Uncle would either have to cough up the demanded sum or find a suitable explanation to satisfy the collector. Baba was reluctant to delve into the personal matters of the Rahas but since it entailed security concerns of the entire building, he could not refuse to join Sudip Uncle.

Around 8:30 in the evening, Sudip Uncle and Baba entered 5D. After some small talk about the weather and how India was faring in the current cricket series, Sudip Uncle got to the point. 'Mr. Rakshit was really lucky today. Thank God the collapsible gate was locked,' he paused, expecting Baba to contribute.

'He could have killed Mr. Rakshit had it not been for the collapsible gate,' Baba tried his best. Sudip Uncle realised that he would have to take the conversation further as Prasoon Uncle had not volunteered any information on his own. He decided not to waste any time. 'Mr. Raha, is there any truth to what the Afghan claimed?' Prasoon Uncle's face was expressionless and it was impossible to tell what was going on inside his mind. There was an awkward silence. Sudip Uncle shifted in his seat, 'Look, Mr. Raha, if there is any way we can help, you must tell us. We're your friends, aren't we?' Prasoon Uncle gave him a weak smile, 'Of course.' Baba made another attempt, 'How did the Afghan make such a terrible mistake?' Prasoon Uncle gave in, 'Well, he did not make a mistake.' Sudip Uncle knew that from the start. An Afghan collector would never bother an innocent man. He leaned forward and lowered his voice, 'What happened?'

'I had a small property near Mumbai,' Prasoon Uncle said.

Sudip Uncle and Baba listened intently. Prasoon Uncle reclined on the sofa, 'Last month I sold it.' He paused for reaction and comments. When he received none from the two men seated across him, he continued, 'I took most of the money in cash. You know how unfair the taxing system is. People like us work so hard all year and at the end of it the government takes it away. I was just trying to protect what was legally mine.' A shrewd businessman, Sudip Uncle understood Prasoon Uncle's motivation. At this time Neelima Aunty appeared with tea and imported biscuits. As she poured the piping hot liquid into the fine bone china cups, the aroma of the expensive Darjeeling tea engulfed the tastefully done living room. Sudip Uncle took a sip, 'This tea is divine.' Neelima Aunty smiled and said, 'Fried potato fritters are on their way.' Baba protested, 'It's already late. We won't be able to have a proper dinner if we have the fritters now.' He liked fritters immensely but tried to save her the extra work in the kitchen. Sudip Uncle's rotund face lit up in glee, 'Mr. Bose speaks for himself. I'm ready for fritters,' he raised his arm like a schoolboy who knew the answer to the teacher's question. Neelima Aunty was pleased with his enthusiasm, 'It's always a pleasure to feed you. But Tanmoyda is always on a diet.' The mood had lightened and everyone laughed. Sudip Uncle ran a circle on his belly with his right hand, 'Look where my indiscipline has taken me and see where this slim and trim young man stands.' Baba was not skinny but seated next to Sudip Uncle he could pass off as being lean. Neelima Aunty knew that it was time for her to slip away. As soon as she walked out of the living room, talks resumed. 'You were telling us...', Sudip Uncle prompted Prasoon Uncle to avoid repetition. Prasoon Uncle picked up the hint, 'I converted the cash into gold and took the Kolkata Mail from Mumbai.' He paused for a reaction. Then he continued, 'I thought that no one would be able to guess that I had so much gold with me if I hid it inside a tin of *ghee*.'

'If you don't mind my asking, how much was it?' Sudip Uncle

was direct. Prasoon Uncle hesitated for a moment and continued, 'Well it was worth 600,000 rupees.'

'That's not a small amount,' Sudip Uncle suggested. Baba was about to take a sip from his tea cup when he heard the amount. He turned into a statue. Prasoon Uncle went on, 'I put the gold at the bottom, covered it with *ghee* and sealed the mouth of the can.'

'That's a risky thing to do,' Baba commented. Prasoon Uncle nodded in agreement. 'I had sprained my shoulder on the train and called a porter at Howrah junction.' Baba and Sudip Uncle were listening intently when the fritters arrived. It was a crucial point in the story but Sudip Uncle snapped out of it at the sight of the fritters. He dived straight into the plate exactly in the manner Kirit did the first day he stormed into my home uninvited. But in a quick display of tremendous restraint he requested Neelima Aunty, 'No more. This is a lot.' Baba agreed. Neelima Aunty smiled, 'Are you sure?' Fritters had already filled Sudip Uncle's mouth and he could not speak. Baba acted as his spokesman and joined in for a bite. He had also succumbed in the end. Neelima Aunty left. Prasoon Uncle picked up a fritter with his well manicured fingers, 'I had no choice because of the bad shoulder. He placed two suitcases on his head, balancing them with one arm and picked up the can with the other one.' Baba was stupefied, 'You let the porter hold that can?' Prasoon Uncle shook his head in deep regret. 'My shoulder was killing me. I had thought that the porter would never guess what was in a simple can of *ghee*.'

'He must have realised that it was unusually heavy. Gold weighs far more than *ghee*,' observed Sudip Uncle. Prasoon Uncle recounted the great tragedy, 'You guessed it right. He understood that this was no ordinary can and I was guilty of a false sense of comfort.'

Prasoon Uncle walked out of the train and followed the porter at the worst time of the day. Train after train were coming in and leaving the station. To make matters worse, hundreds of people had gathered to witness the inauguration of a new train by an important minister. To get lost in the vast sea of thronging commoners was the easiest thing.

Prasoon Uncle and the porter walked towards the exit. He kept a close eye on the porter but in a fleeting moment of inattentiveness, the man escaped with the can. As soon as he realised that the porter had vanished, Prasoon Uncle raised an alarm. But to single him out from a multitude of porters in their red uniform and ragged headgears was impossible. The crowd swelled with every advancing step as an overzealous announcer began yelling the arrival of the much awaited minister. Members and volunteers from his political party raised their voices in cheer, downing out Prasoon Uncle's desperate plea of assistance from the assemblage. Notwithstanding the pain in his shoulder he waded through the crowd, his desperate eyes searching for the dishonest porter. After a few minutes of struggle, he discovered one of his suitcases lying on the floor. It had been trampled out of shape by hundreds of callous feet. The second suitcase and the most valuable can of *ghee* were gone.

There was a sad silence when Prasoon Uncle finished his sorry tale of being duped by an illiterate porter at one of India's busiest railway stations. Not knowing what more to add, he finally looked at the fritter he had picked up a while ago but forgot to put in his mouth. He began munching it while Sudip Uncle and Baba waited for him to tell them how this story was connected to the arrival of Fridge on Wheels.

Prasoon Uncle finished the fritter and continued, 'I had

purchased some export quotas on credit from a few local companies. They were waiting for my payment.'

'And the payment would be in gold?' Sudip Uncle guessed.

'Exactly,' Prasoon Uncle looked miserable.

'You borrowed money from the Afghans to pay off the creditors?' Sudip Uncle was irritated at Prasoon Uncle's stupidity. Baba inquired, 'Aren't their interest rates much higher than the market?' Prasoon Uncle nodded, 'I made a mistake. But I needed some money fast and acted in haste.'

'That's all in the past now. But how do you propose to tackle the issue tomorrow when the collector shows up?' Sudip Uncle was frustrated.

'I'm not sure,' Prasoon Uncle had a lost look.

'It's a lot of money,' Baba blurted out.

'I owe the Afghans two hundred thousand,' Prasoon Uncle declared. Sudip Uncle and Baba realised that Prasoon Uncle had somehow managed to cover the rest of his loss.

'I have an idea, Mr. Raha,' Sudip Uncle proposed. Prasoon Uncle leaned forward with the eagerness of a grizzly that had spotted a salmon. Sudip Uncle was a hero in the community and his simple bailout plan saved Prasoon Raha's life.

'Why don't I loan you the money? You can pay off the collector tomorrow.' He suggested. Baba was speechless and Prasoon Uncle could not believe his ears.

He hesitated, 'It's a lot of money, Mr. Banerjee.'

'I know that. But my concern is that you may not be able to raise the money by tomorrow morning.'

'You're right about that.'

'Let's hear your alternate plan for tomorrow?' Sudip Uncle probed.

'I don't have one. Yet.'

'You're fast running out of time.'

'I guess so.'

'Let's take the easy way out of this situation. You can pay me back whenever it is convenient for you. It's safer to be in my debt than the Afghan collector's.'

'It's embarrassing,' Prasoon Raha hesitated.

'It'll be worse if the collector doesn't get paid tomorrow.'

'I don't know how to thank you,' Prasoon Uncle was overwhelmed.

'That means you accept my proposal.'

Prasoon Uncle's hand darted towards Sudip Uncle like a snake reaching for a rodent from a hole in the ground.

'I don't keep that kind of cash at home,' said Sudip Uncle. 'But let me get on to it.'

'Do you think it is safe for me to face the collector tomorrow?' Prasoon Uncle was apprehensive.

'I'll be going to the office slightly later tomorrow. So when he comes in the morning, I'll take care of him.' Sudip Uncle assured him.

'We will ask Bheem Bahadur to send him to the administration office to collect the money. He won't bother to walk up to your flat if he is satisfied,' Baba added. Sudip Uncle stood up. Prasoon Uncle shook his hands again, 'I don't know how to thank you.'

Baba returned home. He was distant during dinner. Ma asked him how the meeting went and he wondered aloud, 'How will Mr. Banerjee manage to get 200,000 rupees by tonight?'

'They have connections,' I butted in. Mukul had to act smarter than me, 'He won't run into debt to help a neighbour. Obviously he has the money.'

'Even a goat knows that,' I countered. Mukul wanted to snub me but could not come up with something more intelligent. He went back to eating and acted as if I was not even worth fighting.

The next morning, Fridge on Wheels was back. As he entered the administration office and pulled up a chair, Sudip Uncle received him with a smile. Jhola wondered if the wobbly chair could hold his weight. The door of the office was closed. Before Fridge on Wheels could even bring up the topic, Sudip Uncle handed him a parcel wrapped with a newspaper. It was full of currency notes. He stated that Prasoon Raha's father had been taken ill outside town for which he could not return to Kolkata. But when the honest Mr. Raha heard that the collector had come, he apologised for the delay and sent the money via a messenger. Fridge on Wheels immediately turned sympathetic towards Prasoon Raha and wished his father a speedy recovery. He assured Sudip Uncle that Prasoon Raha was a free man and suggested that he could also borrow again from his friends, anytime he wished. Bheem Bahadur arrived with tea. Fridge on Wheels looked at the small cup and its content. He picked up the cup and gulped down the boiling liquid even before Sudip Uncle could take a sip. Then he stood up, lifted his massive arm and bid farewell to Sudip Uncle and Jhola.

From his bedroom, Prasoon Raha watched Fridge on Wheels ride away in his Enfield Bullet 350. He shut his eyes in a silent prayer, shuddering at the thought of landing in the Brobdingnagian hands. When Sudip Uncle returned home, Sumita Aunty asked him if he truly believed Prasoon Uncle. Sudip Uncle could not be certain. Some things did not seem to add up. But still, he deserved a chance.

'What do you mean?' she asked. Sudip Uncle walked into the

bathroom and raised his voice to speak as he soaped his hands, 'Raha isn't stupid. Agreeing to pay such a high interest is harakiri. He must owe more to others.'

'What a nasty situation to be in,' Sumita Aunty was sympathetic. Sudip Uncle sat down for an early lunch. Sumita Aunty sat next to him and served him hot basmati rice from a large cooker. Sudip Uncle spread the rice on his plate and waited for it to cool down. 'Another thing was evident,' he said.

'What?' Sumita Aunty was all ears.

'Raha was unusually calm. He should have been terrified.'

'He wasn't scared at all?' Sumita Aunty was surprised with Sudip Uncle's observation. Sudip Uncle shook his head. 'I think it was an act. He's desensitised to it. Raha is way more cunning than he appears.'

'Then why did you lend him such a large amount?' she frowned. Sudip Uncle spoke with food in his mouth, 'I think he will return the money soon. My guess is that he'll borrow from someone else to pay me back.'

'And pay that person back again by borrowing from someone else,' concluded Sumita Aunty. This time Sudip Uncle's mouth was too full. He simply nodded in agreement.

It turned out that he was right. That evening, Kirit came to my place and asked me if I could keep a secret. He knew that I must have known of his father's generosity towards Prasoon Uncle for Baba was also present at the time at Robin's place. But he shared his father's thoughts with me.

'Prasoon Uncle is a hustler then?' I was astonished. Kirit valued his father's judgement and believed in his theory.

'Yes', he said confidently.

'So what can we do about it?' I wondered.

'Nothing. If he is that way, we cannot change him. But do you think Robin knows?' he inquired.

'I don't think so. Or else he would have spoken about it yesterday when he had the opportunity,' I said. Kirit struck my head with an Archie comic, 'Dimwit. Are you crazy?'

'But we're friends, right?' I was surprised.

'You are naïve, Tiger. His confession would mean washing his family's dirty linen in public.'

'You have a point there, but let's wait and see when the money comes back to Sudip Uncle,' I suggested.

'Or not,' sighed Kirit.

Kirit and I agreed that we did not have this conversation. Within a few minutes we stepped down to the common room. Cricket followed. Some of the boys in the building had heard about the collector and thoughtlessly asked Robin about the incident. Kirit and I noticed the ease with which he laughed it off. He also made fun of Dev Rakshit and acted out an imagined impersonation of Rakshit's face when Fridge on Wheels had grabbed him. Everyone was in splits. Kirit and I laughed along with the others. But when our eyes met during the melee, our suspicion that Robin had full knowledge of his father's flagrant ways was confirmed.

One morning, a couple of weeks later, Kirit pushed me awake. I woke up sluggish and sleepy eyed, 'What's the matter?'

'Wake up, idiot. It's 8:00 a.m.' Kirit had already completed a round at the gym. 'Prasoon Uncle returned the money last night,' he said.

'And?' I was alert by now.

'He also offered to pay interest.'

'And?' I asked again.

'And what?' Kirit was irritated by my naïveté. 'Dad took back his own money and refused the interest.'

I thought for a moment and agreed that Sudip Uncle may well have been right. I pointed out that the chapter would be closed, now that the debt had been settled. But Kirit shook his head, 'Far from it. If what dad fears is true, it will only escalate. But since we can do little about it, let's just forget it. But I thought I'd share the news with you first thing in the morning.'

'By waking me up at eight on a Sunday morning,' I grumbled. Kirit lifted my pillow and struck my face with it when Ma walked in. 'Would you like some tea, Kirit?'

'No, Rani Aunty. I've been exercising. No tea or coffee for me. I just came to get this lazy mongoose out of bed.'

'How about some milk shake?' Ma tried. Kirit gave up, 'I can never win with you. I'll go with the milk shake.' Ma walked out with a smile. Since the very first day he intruded upon Flat 3A, Ma enjoyed feeding the rich, overfed kid from 10B.

After the Fridge on Wheels incident, every time we came across Prasoon Uncle, we could not help thinking about it. But time heals everything. Kirit and I had set aside our judgemental attitude within a few weeks. Prasoon Uncle was always so nice that it was impossible to picture him as a foxy deadbeat.

Three months had passed and the incident had become ancient history. One evening, Kirit and I had stepped out for a smoke at the neighbourhood *paan* shop belonging to an eternally spaced out man called Dhumki. Robin was taking guitar lessons, Pluto was assisting his grandfather in his gardening hobby and Sig was sucking up to a family friend visiting from New Jersey. A torpid Dhumki was spreading small pieces of betel nuts on a customer's *paan* when he saw us approaching. He handed over two loose sticks of Peter Stuyvesant. Kirit and I shook our heads as we wanted Marlboro. 'This is also from *Amrika*,' Dhumki claimed. Even he recognised our implacable affiliation to everything American. At his insistence, I reached out for the unfamiliar brand, another budding connection to America. As I lit up, Kirit playfully asked the name of the supplier of this contraband. Dhumki protested vehemently by stating that all his foreign cigarettes were legitimately acquired and legally sold. Kirit liked to fool around with Dhumki and was preparing to tease him some more when I spotted Prasoon Uncle in a blue and white bush shirt on the opposite footpath. He was trying to pacify an irate man. I nudged Kirit and pointed out the scene. Immediately Kirit forgot his agenda and handed out two extra rupees to Dhumki. The unexpected tip was enough for Dhumki to shut up and allow Kirit to concentrate. 'Something's up,' Kirit was certain.

'Money lender?' I guessed.

'Could be.' He said and positioned himself on the side of the shop to be partially out of sight. I stepped behind him. Prasoon Uncle stood in front of 'Akaash Kusum', a high-rise two hundred metres away from Vanilla Apartments. He looked all around and quickly stepped into the building, leaving his agitated companion waiting. We were wondering why he had entered the building, when he did the most unbelievable thing. 'Akaash Kusum' had a side entrance from Garcha Road, an adjoining narrower street. Since we had an angular view from the side of Dhumki's shop, we saw him step out of the building from the side and briskly walk into the street. The unsuspecting man who was waiting for him kept staring at the main entrance while his scheming debtor had slipped away from the side entrance from right under his nose.

We crossed the street and went into Garcha Road. In the distance we could see Prasoon Uncle walking away really fast, almost jogging. He turned to make sure that the creditor had not discovered his guile. Then, he darted into a connecting lane that could eventually bring him back to Vanilla Apartments from another side of the same street. It was a clever move. It would be highly improbable for the waiting man to unravel this deceit, unless he knew about the side entrance and the connecting getaway street. Twenty minutes had passed. We quickly returned to check on the probable creditor and found that he was excitedly talking to a man who had stepped out of 'Akaash Kusum'. We stood in the vicinity and overheard his loud voice. He was complaining to the stranger about a man called Sundar Sinha who had borrowed ten thousand rupees from him and disappeared for three months. He had given up hope of finding him when by sheer chance he came face to face with Sundar Sinha on the street. When he asked for his money, Sundar Sinha said that he lived in 'Akaash Kusum' and asked him to wait while he got the money. He had disappeared into the building some twenty minutes ago and was yet to return. The sympathetic listener shook his head and said, 'I've lived in this building for twenty years. I'm sure there's no one here by the name of Sundar Sinha.' We knew what had happened. The stranger did not know how to console him. To break the awkward silence, he asked, 'What was Sundar Sinha wearing?' The dumbstruck creditor barely mumbled, 'A blue and white bush shirt.'

# CHAPTER NINE

# Gravy Train

*A* few days before the Mad Ruia episode began in the lives of our neighbours, Mukul declared his desire to move to America the way an astronaut addresses a press conference before a mission. He pretended to be passionate about pursuing higher studies there. But like most of his contemporaries, his keen interest lay on landing there somehow. The soil of America called much louder than the draw of great scholarship. Investment in education was common for the middle-class. But a small fortune was necessary to pursue it successfully in America. Families were prepared to toil endlessly for a better future for their offspring, and the definition of a glorious future invariably translated into an American one. Prohibitive tuition, added to housing and travel expenses would cripple them, and their children would not be able to visit them for many years. But they were ready for the selfless sacrifice. Imagine the pride when neighbours, friends and relatives would know how their children were rocking America with their brilliance. Does reflected glory reduce the bask? Not if one doesn't think so.

Mukul was no Einstein but had always been a decent student. More importantly, he was blessed with long-term vision. He foresaw that Health and Wellness studies would grow in popularity as Americans continued to grow in size. We were certain that Mukul would bag some scholarship to attend graduate school in America. It did not matter if it was a very prestigious one. He applied to lesser known, low tuition schools and planned to transfer to a more reputable institution when his situation improved. When Baba praised him for his consideration to curtail expenses, Mukul quickly corrected him by saying that the move was only to facilitate his quick entry into graduate school.

In 1988, Vanilla Apartments witnessed an exodus. Six students left for higher studies to the United States. As expected, Mukul managed a scholarship. But he would be attending a virtually unknown college in Henderson, Nevada. He knew that his better heeled co travelers from Vanilla Apartments looked down upon his choice. After all, they were set to spend the next few years in the manicured quads at the various Ivys or live it up in New York, Los Angeles or Miami.

The possibility of losing a son to America became real now but my parents had absorbed the jolt. It was painful enough for them to let their first born go. But the knowledge that I wanted to follow Mukul in a few years had created an unfathomable emptiness in their lives. The strain showed on their faces but their smiles concealed their grief. They had resigned to embrace their sons' dreams as their very own. In spite of the partial financial aid from the college, Baba and Ma were sad for Mukul. They were about to spend a lot of money to assist their son, but still he could not go to either New York or Los Angeles. They had never heard of any other American city and thought that these were the only two real cities in the nation. Mukul foresaw that his days of struggle would stabilise after graduate studies. 'I'll be riding the gravy train after school is over.'

'Gravy train? Where does that go?' Ma was puzzled.

'It can go as far as you can take it. It doesn't have to stop,' Mukul laughed as his eyes gleamed with the prospect of a golden future.

'But if the train won't stop, how do you get off?' Baba was equally baffled.

Baba, an old-school simpleton from Kolkata could not visualise the compartments of the gravy trains of the American railways. But he did not wish to dampen his son's spirit. Ma was happy that Mukul was so gung-ho. My relationship with Mukul was nippy from the start but off late, we quarreled over the trivial. But I was not indifferent. In fact, I felt great joy that his ambition to study in the United States could well be fulfilled soon.

At Ma's prodding, Baba had purchased a small plot of land in the Baguiati area off the Eastern Metropolitan Bypass, close to the airport. The idea had been floated by Sudip Uncle when he visited with Sumita Aunty, right after we had moved into Vanilla Apartments. When they left, Ma asked Baba to think about it seriously. Sudip Uncle had instilled a sure-fire confidence in the investment. Trusting Ma's instincts completely, Baba took the plunge. He was dead right. By the time Mukul was applying to colleges in America, the price of the small marshland had risen almost eighteen times. That seemed very satisfactory on paper, but it was not enough to fund both our graduate studies in a country where so many of their own failed to afford college. One of us could go through with a little scholarship and a good deal of financial assistance from home. This put Baba and Ma in a spot. They were very supportive of Mukul's dream but were faced with a legitimate concern. Ma knew that I had also set my sight on the same shores. If Mukul used up all the money from the sale, what would Tiger be left with? Baba found a simple solution to this complex issue. He declared that only one of his children could board the famous gravy train in America. The other would be remembered for his sacrifice. But Ma was not ready to give up that easily. She asked Baba to call a family meeting, something we had never experienced before.

It was our first and last family meeting. Ma urged Baba to open the proceedings. However, Baba was unprepared and Ma took over. I tried to make it easy for her. 'Mukul is older and that's why his chance has come before mine. He should go.'

'Exactly,' Mukul agreed.

'But you want to go to America too,' said Baba.

'Graduate school. Three years from now.'

Baba failed to understand why any sane person would study hard to complete their graduation in India and then travel all the way to a distant land to study the same thing all over again.

'But in three years what's going to change so dramatically? Where will the money come from?' Ma asked me.

'You mean, if you spend everything on "my" education?' Mukul was defensive. Ma read the hostile note in his voice. But she remained calm and continued, 'Put yourself in our shoes, Mukul. You are both our children. We love you equally. We don't want anyone to be left out.'

Mukul was restless, 'You mean that you don't want "him" to be left out.'

'That's not what she meant,' I said, as I saw the pained look on the faces of my dilemma-ridden parents. 'Why don't you take what you need now and when my turn comes, help me out?' Mukul had expected some retaliation from my end. My magnanimity caught him off guard.

Ma grabbed the straw, 'I'm sure you will be in a good financial position by then because you will have a head start.' Baba nodded his greying head vigourously in support of the idea. Mukul shrugged, 'Sure, I will. But let me tell you that if you study Humanities you will not get a good scholarship.'

Ma took my side. 'Why?'

Mukul stated a fact, 'You're an average student, Chinmoy. So you will have to choose a subject that will become popular in a few years. Only then will you get a decent scholarship.'

'English is my subject of choice. I will study what I like,' I protested.

'And be what, Shakespeare? And remain unemployed?' Mukul was disgusted with my preference. He had a point but I was not going to be overpowered by him. 'I didn't know that Shakespeare suffered the tragedy of unemployment,' I said and laughed it off. Mukul gave up. Ma butted in, 'Mukul, you have our help and our blessings. But you will have to promise that you will help your brother when his time comes to go to America.' Mukul made a face, 'The way he is going, his time won't come.' Baba was annoyed with his negative energy. 'We need to have your word,' he said.

'When I make money in America, yes. But I can't help if I don't make money,' he tried to slip away from a commitment. My parents had not been able to get a real promise out of their first born. Ma did not give up. 'But you are going with the belief that you will ride the gravy train. You are taking your parents' help, their entire lives' savings to study hard and do well in America. Right?'

'Of course,' Mukul was surprised that Ma was stating the obvious.

'Just as it is our duty to assist you to the best of our ability to realise your dream, you should give back to the family when your time comes. And your nearest family member is your brother.' Mukul was ready to object again but decided to play along. He nodded, 'Sure. I'll help him. Didn't I just promise that?'

'If you had, I missed it,' Ma was vexed at his insincerity. But at least the painful family drama was over for now.

The confidence of youth rode high. I told myself that I would get a good scholarship and work my way to America with or without Mukul's mercy. If he helped, good. If not, I'd take on the challenge on my own. I was naïve. Selling our plot of land was as easy as frying an egg. The area was fast turning residential and promoters lapped up the offer. We made good money. But we were competing against the powerful American dollar far greater in value. I was sad that although we made many times the investment, Baba and Ma would not be able to enjoy any of the kill. Mukul did not require every cent that came from the sale right away, but he would use up a substantial amount in the following two years.

An American visa stamped on the passport was the dream of many a young student. Mukul was ready for the big day. It was gloomy and raining when he appeared for the visa interview. Baba, Ma and I waited outside the American Consulate on Ho Chi Minh Sarani as Mukul stood in the long serpentine queue. Baba considered it to be an unholy omen for the sun to not show its face on this important day. But Ma was of the opposite opinion. She said that it was only a mere drizzle and not a downpour, and that meant the sun would appear soon. It turned out that she was right. The drizzle stopped and our soggy umbrellas slowly dried up as the sun peeped from behind the clouds and smiled at us.

Ma occasionally waved to a tensed Mukul to assure him that all would be well, but he was too pre-occupied to return the gesture. My four best friends wanted to join us to cheer him up, but Mukul had declined their support. They knew that Mukul had no friends of his own and their generous show of camaraderie was for my parents. Soon Mukul walked into the fortress and disappeared from our sight.

In a short while, a girl walked out in an orthodox skirt and blouse. She looked as if her heart had been pierced by an angry soldier's bayonet. We remembered seeing her enter through the intimidating gate of the Consulate. She had a defeated look on her face. Her parents were waiting outside, side by side, along with us. At the sight of her father, her knees buckled but the athletic man hurled himself towards her. She collapsed into his arms in pitiful tears. His pre-emptive move had saved his daughter from certain skull fracture. It was an overwhelming moment. To witness the young lady's dream shatter before our eyes was moving beyond description. We tried to look away and let the family mourn, but it was impossible. A crowd gathered at once. No one asked what had happened. The street housing the American Consulate was no stranger to the sight. Artificial consolations and insensitive comments along with practical advice poured in until the cacophony became unbearable. 'This is not the end of the world.' 'Why do these kids want to go to America when our education system is the best?' 'Time heals bedsores. This is nothing'. 'Get married to a boy settled in America.' 'Serves you right. That's what happens to traitors.' 'They don't know the meaning of patriotism. Look at us. We've never even stepped outside our country.' 'Apply again. You may get a better visa officer.' 'Next time try from Mumbai.' The admonition and exhortations got our heads spinning. The girl was too dazed to register the din all around and continued a low murmured sob. She could barely walk and had to be lifted by her father to reach their car.

I was wondering what fate awaited my brother, when after an unusually short interview, Mukul walked out from behind the gated barrier. Our hearts skipped a beat. He was not smiling. Had he been refused too? Ma stood next to me. Baba's hand turned into a fist and Ma grabbed my arm for moral support. 'What happened?' Baba barely managed to ask him. Mukul shook his head and my heart wasted a beat. I felt Ma's grip tighten. 'They rejected my application,' Mukul said. For a split second, I felt incredible disappointment. Baba froze. But Ma knew that Mukul was lying, 'I don't believe it,' she said confidently. Mukul burst out laughing and lifted both his hands in victory mode. He had been granted a first class ticket to the gravy train! 'What a nuisance,' I thought. Did he even realise how Baba's face fell for that one moment? But I did not turn that wonderful moment into a confrontation. We hugged each other for the next five minutes before any one of us could say a word. The first time ever, someone from our family would be going abroad. And that too, to America! Everyone knew that gold and precious gems lay scattered on the streets of America and green dollar bills grew on trees for anyone to collect at will.

Soon, it was time for him to leave. Baba and Ma were glad that Mukul was on top of the world. Baba had a distant cousin called Barid Baran, aka BB in Sacramento, California. He had written to BB Uncle for advice when Mukul had begun his applications. But BB Uncle was of no help. Unperturbed at not receiving a response to his letter, Baba wrote again seeking important travel tips for

Mukul. This time we heard from him. Granted, Mukul had never traveled by himself, let alone boarded a plane across an ocean, but we were more intelligent than grasshoppers. BB Uncle's long list of instructions was overbearing and condescending.

Hey Mukul,

Below you'll find a list of do's and don'ts. If you memorise the pointers, you'll be fine.

Bon voyage,

BB Uncle.

1) An hour or so before your flight is ready to land, a flight attendant'll give you a Customs form. Fill it up. To fill it up, keep a ballpoint pen. It must be a working ballpoint pen.

2) They'll ask you if you're bringing in any food items, firearms etc. Don't steal airline grub. Firearms don't mean firecrackers in your arms. It means guns! Don't bring any guns with you.

3) If you don't follow anything on the form, ask the flight attendant. If you don't see one around you, check if your fellow passenger speaks English and ask him. I'm guessing YOU speak the language.

4) You'll have to put down the address of your destination on the form. Write it down with the ballpoint pen.

5) If the form requires you to state the sum you're bringing into the country, write down the exact amount truthfully. Don't hide dollar bills either in your underwear or inside your anus.

6) If your ears pop during the flight, there's cotton wool. Use it to plug your ears. Don't plug your co-passengers

ears with it.

7)    Don't drink whisky or beer on the flight, even though it's free. Chances are you'll go overboard and vomit. However, if you are nauseous, use the vomit bag kept inside the flap of the seat in front of you. Don't vomit into the ears of your sleeping co-passenger.

8)    After you get off the plane, follow other passengers. But don't follow them blindly. If someone enters the restroom, don't just walk in behind them. You use the restroom only if you need to.

9)    When an immigration official asks you a question, always reply. How will you know that the person is an immigration official? He will be behind a counter wearing a uniform. Speak loudly and clearly so that he understands your accent.

10)   Once you are through, don't look for porters. Don't ask strangers to help you with your bags. It's your load and you're expected to carry it. This is America. Here, you are on your own.

We were exhausted and insulted by the time we were through with BB Uncle's lofty and patronising letter. It was evident that BB Uncle would not be of any assistance if there was any crisis. In America, Mukul would indeed be on his own.

A food binge began a week before Mukul left. Ma spent most of her time cooking for him. Baba asked him to make the best use of this opportunity for Mukul was heading for starvation in the faraway land. Cooking lessons began. Ma began to teach him how to make rice, dal, chicken stew and fish curry. Mukul was focused and benefitted immensely from the training. He hardly stepped out of the kitchen and took notes in a small diary. Ma asked him to participate in the practical aspect of it more than memorising the theory.

Baba and Ma were concerned that there would be many people waiting to feed beef and pork to their unsuspecting son. 'How will you know if they tell you that it's chicken,' Ma worried. Mukul dismissed her concern, 'I know what chicken tastes like. I've had it all my life.'

'But you don't know what beef or pork tastes like,' Baba sided with Ma.

'How about he doesn't take anything that doesn't taste like chicken?' I suggested.

'But for that, he would have to at least bite it once,' Ma always came up with a surprise every time I thought I had outwitted her.

'That's a risk I'm prepared to take,' smiled Mukul. Lessons complete and with only a few days left for him to leave, Ma asked him to prepare any one dish for the family. The exercise would demonstrate his skill. But Mukul was not interested in cooking for anyone else. Baba and Ma were bouncing between emotions but Mukul had already been transported into a world unknown to us. He was physically in Kolkata but in his mind, he had already left home.

On the day of his departure, Flat 3A was full of chatterbox relatives and neighbours. Mukul was bombarded with an equal measure of advice and blessings, none of which he sought. Sudip Uncle and Sumita Aunty came to wish him good luck and gifted him an expensive camera. Mukul accepted it as his birthright. Relatives had fed him a large fish head for lunch. The general belief was that his intelligence would never desert him in time of need, thanks to the nourishment provided by that specific fish head. By evening, Mukul was exhausted. Ma had packed enough stationery for him to last his entire lifetime. Erasers, pencils, ball point pens, fountain pens, note books, half a suitcase was filled with them. At around 6:30 p.m., five hours before the time of his actual departure, we headed for the airport. It would not take more than an hour to reach the airport from Vanilla, but Baba insisted that this was a cautionary measure to make sure that Mukul did not miss his flight.

No family member had ever flown in an aircraft and Mukul's fantasy trip was a surprise to all our relatives. Loud prayers were uttered and Mukul's forehead was smeared with yogurt before he stepped out of the door of 3A. The yogurt would help him keep his cool under tremendous pressure. Noisy relatives wanted Mukul to write to all of them at least once a month. Mukul readily agreed to avoid negotiations. They all knew that he would not keep his promise. Uncles and aunts asked for his specific date of return. When I pointed out that he had not yet left, they were embarrassed and let it pass as a joke. Two taxis were summoned. Kirit had set aside one of his three family cars for our use. Mukul had not liked Kirit from the very first day he visited in 1983. He maintained his old disapproval and preferred a taxi to Kirit's car. Baba, Ma and two of my four uncles went in the cab with him. I joined Kirit and the rest of the gang in his shiny black Peugeot purchased from a European consulate. The second taxi followed us with two uncles and corresponding aunts. There were thirteen people to see him off.

The Eastern Bypass eased traffic jams to and from the city. But flights and trains could still be missed, if one did not leave well in advance of their scheduled time of departure. Mukul's fleet had left together. But the taxis had sneaked through traffic signals while Kirit's new driver had slowed us down. The result was our delayed arrival at the Dumdum airport by ten minutes. When we reached the airport we saw a strange sight. Mukul was sitting on the cemented floor at the side of the entrance. Both his hands rested on his head. Everyone surrounding him chatted excitedly making it impossible for us to grasp the problem. Soon we found out that Mukul had left all his educational certificates in the taxi. Even the letters from the school were gone. How could that happen? He was clinging on to them when he had hopped in. Mukul howled that he had lost his life.

He was sanguine that the cab driver would notice the papers at some point. But how could the driver gauge their significance? He would certainly dispose them. Kirit differed. He had hailed the taxi while Mukul's departure paraphernalia was on. The amused driver had inquired where his passenger was headed. Kirit had told him that this was a student flying to America for the first time. The driver knew the building and it would be most natural for him to return the documents. Kirit stepped towards Mukul and pulled him up to his feet. Everyone cheered for him. He looked into Mukul's eyes and ordered, 'Get going.'

'But I don't have the admission letter from the college. They'll send me back from the airport,' he cribbed. Robin stepped in and dismissed the idea at once. 'That's impossible. Your passport has a student visa stamped on it. No one can stop you.' Everyone cheered him up. Reluctantly, Mukul left.

It was not Mukul's day. The cheap East European flight had three long stopovers and aircraft changes before it transported him to his final destination. In the second sector the airline forgot to load water on the flight. Vexed passengers had almost torn the seats off their hinges. With no access to water and several hours delay either due to technical snag or bad weather at every juncture, when Mukul finally reached the city, he had no strength left to pick up a telephone receiver. The dehydration exacerbated his jetlag. Three days later he called home to describe the ordeal.

My considerate parents were anxious to hang up before Mukul completed his sordid tale of suffering. They did not want him to waste money on phone calls. Baba asked him to write a detailed letter, 'That way we can exchange more information. Or else, you have to constantly keep your eyes on the metre,' he worried. Ma urged Mukul to share a quick word with me before he hung up. I sprinted to the phone and began to speak excitedly into it. But the dull humming noise of a dial tone greeted me. Mukul had hung up. We assumed that the connection had been severed. But when the act was repeated thrice in the next six months, it became quite evident that I was not welcome in his American world.

We received a letter from Mukul after his first month in America. Ma tore the letter with great care. She did not want to miss a single word destroyed due to careless ripping. Mukul had settled into a shared accommodation with three male students from different parts of the world. It was a two bedroomed apartment on the second floor of a four storeyed building within walking distance of the Department of Nutrition. Two Vietnamese boys from the same school had rented it and illegally sublet to Mukul and a Pakistani student. Mukul's letter cast a shadow of great concern on my parents. 'Of all the people in the world, Mukul's roommate had to be a Pakistani?' Baba's face was glum.

'What if the boy harms him?' Ma had developed worry lines

on her charming face. I laughed at their undue tension, 'You know how shrewd your son is. I'm concerned for the Pakistani.' But no matter how hard they tried to brush the thought aside from their afflicted minds, they spent a few sleepless nights over the non-issue. An elaborate letter expressing their concern was written. They decided to post it to his college address. What if the Pakistani opened the letter at home and unleashed his wrath on their docile son? They could not take a chance with his life.

Mukul laughed hard when he read the letter. Ishaaq, the Pakistani menace was the most wonderful person he had ever known. He was a great friend, helping Mukul in every possible way and never expecting anything in return. With their stereotype dashed, Baba and Ma began to feel better. Then one day when Mukul called, he put his best and only friend in the world on the phone to speak with his parents. It was Ishaaq, the dangerous Pakistani. Baba did not know what to say to him. But Ishaaq's friendly voice and courteous manner bowled him over. When Ishaaq insisted on speaking with Ma as well, she took the phone coyly. She could not match his chaste Urdu but managed with a broken, local version of Hindi. Ishaaq asked Ma if she was truly the fantastic cook that Mukul boasted of. Servile to flattery, Ma quickly warmed up to the former spy. 'You have to come home to find out,' was her smart answer. My simple mother had overcome a lifelong prejudice in minutes. She made me proud. Ishaaq was equally touched by her generosity, 'You are my Indian mother from today,' he said. When the phone call ended, my parents felt guilty of harshly judging Ishaaq simply for his nationality. Ma placed the receiver back on its stand and announced dramatically, 'If I am Ishaaq's Indian mother, then he is my Pakistani son.'

# CHAPTER TEN

# The Caregiver

Travelling by train was unlucky for Prasoon Uncle. Two years after the Fridge on Wheels debacle, he suffered a massive heart attack on another Kolkata bound train from Mumbai. After the train left Nagpur, he experienced acute chest pain and collapsed on his berth. Fortunately for him, his co-passenger in the first class sleeper turned out to be a cardiologist. The doctor read the symptoms correctly, attended to him and administered a few medicines that he was carrying. He saved Prasoon Uncle's life.

Prasoon Uncle was brought to Kolkata and admitted to Bellevue, a private nursing home on Loudon Street. His condition was improving when an iatrogenic problem delayed the recovery. Finally, when he returned home, he required live-in help. Neelima Aunty was an important administrator at a South Kolkata college and could not stay home indefinitely. Robin attended college in the morning and his afternoons were free. But he was not qualified to handle a recovering heart patient. And Aurobindo was too young to be of concrete help. The family decided to hire a trained nurse to watch over Prasoon Uncle during the weekdays when Neelima Aunty would be at work.

Nurse Jivika was regular in terms of looks. But there was something exquisitely neat about her appearance. Her long hair was neatly wound in a French roll and her dark skin was flawless. Robin's silky tresses had met their longer match. Jivika's spotlessly white skirt and crisply ironed shirt seemed ready for a detergent commercial. Jivika began on a good note with the Rahas. She admitted to being relatively new to the profession, with only a few prior assignments but proved to be highly efficient. Robin was stuck at home in the afternoons. So we took to playing cards in his room while Jivika attended to Prasoon Uncle, reading to him and administering medicines at proper intervals.

One day, Pluto arrived early and found that Robin was on the phone in his bedroom. He was trying to solve an educational puzzle with a classmate. Pluto slid down on the leather sofa and his eyes caught an old *Newsweek* sitting on the centre table. As he bent forward to browse through it, he noticed Jivika bending next to Prasoon Uncle's bed and searching for something. The sight of Jivika's perfectly shaped derrieres lured him like an invitation to the Cirque du Soleil. He walked into the room on the pretext of inquiring about her patient. When he saw that Prasoon Uncle was in deep sleep, he casually brushed his hand on Jivika's inviting bottom. Acting as if it was an accident, Pluto apologised. Whether he thought that it would just be a casual touch or if he was testing waters for greater sin, we would never know. But Jivika's response bowled him over. She stood up and without uttering a word, put her arms around Pluto's neck and kissed him. Pluto was rattled by the new face of the demure nurse. He muttered an insincere complaint about Robin being in the next room and suggested that it would be an arrant embarrassment if they were caught. Jivika did not back away and with her arms still around his sweating neck, she dauntlessly suggested that if he wanted to sleep with her, he should be frank with Robin and avail his bedroom.

Pluto emerged from the room, bravado heavily shaken and libido suitably stirred. He could not bring himself to lay the proposal to Robin right away for he knew that Jivika's job was not to dish casual sex while her raison d'être took an afternoon nap. We began to arrive one by one. As we were getting ready for our daily game of cards, Pluto brought up the subject.

We were stunned to hear what had happened. At first, Robin was unbending about giving consent to this ridiculous proposition, but Pluto pleaded for his support. This was a chance of a lifetime and he would miss it if he had no assistance from his friend. Robin was in a moral dilemma. He wanted to help his friend but the act, in his father's present condition was not palatable. A discussion was followed by another discussion and then another one.

Finally the debate ended. Robin was outvoted 4-1. He would not come in the way of his comrade and a prurient nurse. Rules were formulated and agreed upon. Jivika could surrender to her bodily demands only if it did not interfere with her job. Robin would leave his bed as a platform for an outlet to their concupiscence. The couple could not use the sofa. The cleaning lady, Lalu's Ma came around 3 p.m. everyday and Neelima Aunty returned around 4:30. So the only suitable time could be after 2:00 when Prasoon Uncle slept after downing his prescribed pills and 30 minutes before Lalu's Ma showed up.

'2:00 – 2:30 is too short,' Pluto protested feebly. 'Lalu's Ma doesn't come before 3 p.m.'

'You can't keep it that water tight,' I reasoned.

'Half an hour is enough time,' Kirit proclaimed.

'Safety first.' Sig admitted.

'Take it, or leave it,' Robin was direct.

'Done!' Pluto was on.

Although Pluto had not verbalised an appointment, he was ready for the next day. He arrived at 5D hoping to conquer the world when he was struck with a slice of bad news. Jivika had got her period. Disappointed, he had to continue with the card game for the next few days. Finally, his tarry ended and the young mariner was back. Generally Prasoon Uncle drifted into his routine afternoon nap easily, but that day, he was restless. Pluto and Robin anxiously waited for him to fall asleep but he was struggling. By the time he sailed into deep sleep, Lalu's Ma had arrived to do the dishes.

But Pluto Sen was not deterred by his misfortune. He was back again the next day.

The curtains in Robin's bedroom had been drawn to ensure privacy and a sandalwood scented joss stick was lit to accentuate the mood. The faint hum of the air conditioner cut through the palpable tension like a jackknife carving through butter. Jivika attended to Prasoon Uncle with usual dexterity and displayed no fear of being discovered. She put the patient off to sleep and stepped out. Pluto and Robin were anxiously waiting in the living room when she stood in front of them like a model on a ramp. Then she plucked off her hair clip and placed it between her sparkling teeth. The lustrous hair released from the constricting French roll and caressed her shapely back. Uncharacteristically, Jivika had already applied a pale lipstick and highlighted her angular eyebrows. Robin and Pluto were speechless. It was impossible to believe that the same Jivika could transform into her caregiver persona when cruel incontinence struck or debilitating stroke paralysed. Jivika had morphed into a woman of the world who knew exactly what she wanted and cared little about how she got it. She acted as if Robin did not exist and looked directly at Pluto. When she lifted her eyebrows quizzically, Pluto stood up.

As soon as they walked into Robin's bedroom, Pluto dived upon the seductive nurse like a starving cheetah on a sprinting gazelle. Jivika appeared to have encountered similar attacks in the past. Calmly she reminded Pluto that they had thirty minutes and he need not transform into a caveman from the pages of ancient history. Rather than enjoying the act, Pluto was fixated on getting the job done. Some others may have cherished the risk but the looming stress of being discovered had already taken a toll on him. In a flash, Pluto had undressed completely. Jivika warned him to leave his T-shirt on for quick recovery, in case they had to break the act. A hushed argument arose between them when she refused to take off all her clothes. It had to be her way or not at all. Pluto realised that losing the argument would mean losing his chance. Reluctantly, he consented.

When Jivika raised her skirt to accommodate Pluto, he realised that in the haste of the imminent kill, he had forgotten the prophylactic. In pulsating excitement, his victory flag got tangled in the bed sheet. But instead of disentangling from the abrupt, undesirable bondage, he plunged deep into her with all his might, encapsulated by the floral, cotton sheet. Irritated with Pluto's stupidity, a disgusted Jivika retracted, dampening the eager lover's spirit along with Robin's bed sheet.

In the living room, Robin was nervously sipping tea and visualising the action inside when Jivika stormed out and headed towards his parents' bedroom. Quickly, he entered his bedroom and discovered his crushed friend, wrapped in failure. In a matter of seconds, Robin unearthed the reason for Jivika's scorn and burst into a fit of laughter. After he recovered, fresh bed sheets were laid quickly and the soiled one dumped in the wash. Pluto left, dejected, never to return until after Jivika left a month later.

We coined a new slogan: 'If you don't have a condom, there's always a bed sheet.' Although the escapade was a disaster for Pluto, it had been established that Jivika was available. So the next hot topic was, who would be willing to try his luck? I bowed out, more concerned of scandal than moral restrictions. Robin would be in only if Kirit agreed to venture. Sig was seriously dating a classmate, Tina, and not in the running. Kirit took less than a minute to decide.

Two days after Pluto's disaster, Kirit walked into 5D in the afternoon. Jivika knew what was on his mind when she opened the door. She was seduced in less than five minutes. That evening, Kirit raved about Jivika. Pluto's face was sullen at the missed opportunity while the rest of us lapped up any detail Kirit threw our way. The next day it was Robin's turn. Brimming with confidence, he approached Jivika. But to his great surprise, Jivika wanted to have nothing to do with him. Stunned in disbelief and pride deeply bruised, Robin limped out. When he brought it up in the evening, Kirit offered him an instant solution. The next day, Robin gifted Jivika with the replica of a Swiss watch along with a phony French perfume. That cleared his way and Jivika opened up.

Kirit and Robin had a systematic approach. They began taking turns with Jivika, every alternate day. Saturdays and Sundays were days of rest because Neelima Aunty would be at home, attending to her husband. I was pushed by them a number of times, but did not succumb to the pressure.

Kirit and Robin's efforts went on uninterrupted for two weeks.

Then one evening, Robin got an alarming phone call. A young woman with a husky voice, who refused to reveal her identity, claimed that she knew of the erotic afternoons at the Raha residence. She added that she lived in the building but refused to disclose the source of her information. Robin protested that it was a malicious innuendo but froze in fear when the mystery woman said that she was curious to see how Robin would prove that to Neelima Raha. The anonymous caller wanted 50,000 rupees to remain silent.

Next day, when Jivika came in to work, four young men were waiting for her. Pluto was too embarrassed to join us. Jivika told us that we were stupid to think that she would have as much as breathed about her escapades. Wasn't it obvious to us that her job and reputation would be at stake? She was right. We asked her to watch out for an enemy who had got wind of the events at 5D.

We pooled our talents but were inept at handling blackmail. A brainstorming session followed. We had been scared out of our wits but knew from detective novels and mystery thrillers that the blackmailer wanted money and could not prosper by giving us away. We had to bide time.

The next evening the blackmailer called to ask Robin if he had started working on arranging the money. Robin tried to negotiate the amount to ten thousand. The suggestion fetched him a plethora of abuses and the stakes were raised. Now it was 60,000 rupees!

I had done nothing wrong but was intrinsically involved in the jam. The fling with Jivika was meant to be a freebie for Kirit and Robin and a vicarious thrill for Sig and me. It had turned into a nightmare for all of us. If the blackmailer talked, word would get around. How would I convince my parents that I had no part to play in all of this, other than participating in lewd jokes from the sidelines?

We could not lodge a formal complaint with the police. Our only hope was to get the blackmailer to talk as much as possible and accidentally reveal her identity. But it was unclear what we would do once we knew who she was.

Every young woman and every Aunty in the building became a suspect. Robin urged the blackmailer to be patient. He confirmed that he was doing his best to arrange the demanded sum. The blackmailer decided to up the ante for the delay. Now it was a whopping 70,000 rupees! She pointed out that since the five of us participated in the crime, the punishment should be shared in equal measure. Every evening she tracked progress. We would be present during the calls but Robin did the talking. How could we arrange this kind of money? Even little Vani would come up short if she fundraised for our sleazy venture. Plus there was no guarantee that the blackmailer would not ask for more after the payoff. In the messy event of a disclosure, it would be easier for Jivika to get off the hook. She could claim to have been the victim of lusting young men. Fear of discovery was taking a heavy toll on us. Kirit was afraid too, but his genius in displaying courage in times of great adversity stood him head and shoulders above the rest of us. Robin also stood his ground. The two main culprits were also the best stress managers. Pluto, Sig and I were the worst affected. Our studies suffered. Every conversation revolved around saving our hides.

Hopelessness was beginning to take over when we got our break. In the middle of what had become a routine argument with the blackmailer, she mocked Robin about Pluto's fiasco. Robin was much too observant to miss that. When the conversation was over for the day, he calmly replaced the receiver and high fived his assembled friends. Since none of us had leaked the story of Pluto's stupidity, it could only have been Jivika. We knew that it was not her speaking in a different voice because the blackmailer also called when she was at work. Clearly, it was the handiwork of someone she knew. She became our chief and only suspect.

The next day, we stampeded her as soon as Prasoon Uncle dozed off. But Jivika was a seasoned nut, very hard to crack. She called us delusional and stated that if she had to extract money from us, she would not seek the help of an accomplice. That way she would not have to share the loot. She had a point.

When we could get nothing out of her, we told her that we would give her the benefit of doubt. But for her own good and ours, she should leave the job without delay. She complained of losing her wages for the rest of her days, so we raised the remaining balance in less than an hour. Kirit asked her to call in sick at her nursing agency. They would arrange for a substitute. Jivika agreed at once, took the money, and left us confused about our so-called detection.

Later that evening, the blackmailer made her routine call without displaying any knowledge of Jivika's departure. We were somewhat relieved. If the blackmailer squealed, it would still be a nuisance, but to establish the truth would not be easy in Jivika's absence.

The next day, Robin had a huge shock in store. Promptly at ten in the morning, Jivika walked in to work, exactly as she had done for the previous eight weeks. Her face exuded a strange coldness that Robin had not witnessed earlier. Before he could ask for an explanation, she volunteered that after a long discussion with her husband the night before, she had reached the conclusion that she should not let any blackmailer scare her away. A discussion with her husband? All the while we had assumed that Jivika was single. Robin was completely thrown off-guard. He told her that she should leave quietly for no money would be paid to the blackmailer. Without her physical presence, no slanderous accusation would work. Jivika's true colour blobbed. She flew into a rage and flung a cushion at Robin, thereby startling him. Her exquisite face underwent a demonic transformation. In a whispering rage, she hissed at Robin to pay the blackmailer to avoid further trouble. Robin was terrified that if he disagreed, she could accuse him of raping her. In abject terror, he promised to work on assembling the compensation as soon as possible. Jivika warned Robin that if she saw any of us in the flat the next day, she would create a scene that he would remember all his life. Soon she cooled down and went back to work.

When the bell rang at 10 a.m. the next day, Robin was already shaking in apprehension. He opened the door to find Jivika accompanied by her husband, Bilal Majid. The sight of the puny man, dressed in spotless white shirt, white trousers and white sneakers gave him the quivers. Incessant chewing of betel leaves had stained Bilal's teeth and the red hue on his thick lips resembled cheap lipstick. The kohl eyeliner and gold studs gave him a sinister appearance.

Bilal shook Robin's tremulous hand while chewing a mouthful of betel leaves. In an unusually gentle tone, Bilal said that he knew how five boys in the building had taken advantage of Jivika's helplessness and it was time for justice.

When we met that evening, Robin was on the verge of losing his nerve. He suggested confessing to his mother. We were rattled by his decision and persuaded him to remain calm. Kirit's leadership acumen came in handy. He swung into action mode. Asking us to wait in the common room, he left.

Kirit was back in less than ten minutes. He had called Pop Mama. Before we could object, he stopped us. 'I know that it's a little embarrassing but we all know that he can deal with it like no one else.'

'I agree,' Pluto raised his hand in support.

'I won't be able to look him in the eye,' I croaked.

'You didn't even touch the nurse,' Sig reminded me.

'I'm not sure if it's the right thing to involve him,' Robin was not convinced.

'Trust me,' Kirit thumped his shoulder.

'What did you tell him?' Robin asked.

'Just that it's an emergency and we need a hand,' Kirit said casually.

'And?' I asked again.

'And he asked us to come over,' Kirit seemed relieved.

'When?' Sig inquired.

'It's an emergency. Get out of that seat. We're leaving in two minutes,' Kirit pushed Sig out of his chair.

We stepped out. Kirit and Robin slid the keys into the ignition of their slick Japanese motorcycles. The rest of us would ride pillion. Sig and I squeezed in with Kirit, while Pluto perched like a monkey on Robin's back. The year before, Pop Mama had bestowed a surprise upon his favourite nephew. He took him to an abandoned garage next to a shebeen near the Kolkata docks. There was a long line of expensive motorcycles resting on their stands. These were all foreign made smuggled motorcycles assembled after a police raid. Kirit was free to pick one of his choice. After high school, Kirit had a brand new car. But a trendy, brightly coloured blue and yellow Yamaha motorcycle would be a chick magnet.

Papers were arranged to make the vehicle legitimate. Kirit was ready to flaunt it the next day. Pop Mama suggested that the four of us should pick one from the smuggled collection while it lasted. Sig, Pluto and I declined because our parents would not allow it. But Robin helped himself to the expensive gift without hesitation.

Pop Mama listened to our problem. We were dreading an interrogation about the truth, but were relieved when he did not bother to check the veracity of the blackmailer's allegations. What we had imagined would be the first and most embarrassing question, never came up. Pop Mama, a true hero, had saved us from lying or being subjected to sordid confessions. Not only was he a panacea for all ailments, he treated us like adults and respected our privacy. He assured us that he would deal with the problem appropriately and relieved us of our worry.

Pop Mama took down the name and address of the nursing agency. Then he wrote down an address on a piece of paper. 'Tell the nurse that this flat belongs to Tiger's father and he has the keys.'

'Shit! Why me?' I almost screamed.

Pop Mama continued. 'Ask her to collect the money from there on Monday between five and six.'

'But she'll be working at Robin's place until four,' Sig pointed out.

'That's enough time for her to reach this place, even if she gets stuck in a traffic jam,' Pop Mama pointed out.

'So I would have to take her there?' Robin asked.

'Nope. You don't have to be there. Unless you wish to,' Pop Mama pointed out. Kirit frowned. 'What if she suspects that it's a trap?'

'Good point. She is likely to bring her husband and another accomplice for safety. I'll take care of them.'

'If she disagrees and wants the money at my place?' Robin was concerned that Pop Mama's idea would not work. Pop Mama was ready for this one. 'Tell her it'll have to be your way.'

'She can be stubborn,' Pluto came alive.

'There's a pattern out there, Pluto Sen. She knows she's close to the finishing line and will want to get it over with.'

'We're putting you in danger,' I said.

'I'm in far greater danger everyday,' Pop Mama laughed it off.

'If you arrest her, word might get around,' Sig conveyed his fear sheepishly.

'Who said I'll arrest her?' Pop Mama's confidence was nerve racking.

'But, what if...?' Robin began to raise another question.

'No ifs, no buts,' Pop Mama stumped him. 'Be brave, Robin. You have to be firm.' Pop Mama placed his hand on Robin's head the way Michael Jordan gripped a basketball. He promised Robin that when he sent out a note of warning to someone, it never went unheeded. Robin was enthused. 'I'll be tough, Pop Mama. I want this to end more than she does.'

'I'm sure,' Pop Mama winked at him and called out to his old faithful. 'Gaja!' Aladdin's lamp had been rubbed. The genie appeared from thin air. He had a tray filled with imported chocolates. We set aside our worries and dug in.

Robin followed the plan to the tee. When Jivika strutted in the next morning, he told her that three of us had chipped in 10,000 each, while between Kirit and him, they had raised 40,000 rupees. As she looked at the address, Robin expected an opposition. But she tucked the address chit inside her shirt without a debate. In the next few minutes, she announced that although Prasoon Uncle wanted her to be around for a few more days, Friday would be her last day.

Robin's parents were sad with her decision but bought her lie about other patients being in greater need of her services. Throughout effusive praises on the day of her departure, Jivika was her chameleonic self, coy and smiling. Even Aurobindo liked her and asked her to drop in whenever she was in the neighbourhood. She vehemently opposed the generous tip handed by Prasoon Uncle. She said that she had simply performed her duty. She touched the Rahas' feet for their blessings and left. Robin did not find her attractive anymore. Jivika had made it clear that if Robin failed to show up at the venue at the time mentioned, she would call Neelima Aunty right away and reveal the truth.

Who knows what might have happened if we did not have the right connection? You were a nobody without connections. From getting a cooking gas cylinder to admitting your children to a half decent school, from getting tickets of the newly released Bollywood film to receiving your university transcripts on time, you had a slim chance at life if you were not connected. You needed to know people. Or else, you got in queue. A queue that could suck the lifeblood out of you. A wait that could take a lifetime to end. This was a game where the perpetual winners were the kings and queens who ranked higher in life, thanks to their connections. We were blessed. We knew Pop Mama.

By then, Pluto's embarrassment had transformed into anger. Jivika's mistreatment of him led him to want to see her walloped. Sig and I were mortified at the thought of being present at the venue to support Pop Mama. Robin stayed home for he had had enough of Jivika. Kirit was ready for revenge.

The illegally occupied flat near the Dhakuria Lake belonged to Pop Mama. He had a similar abode in Jamir Lane. When he needed to take the law into his own hands, these flats proved to be valuable assets.

At the stroke of five, Jivika and Bilal arrived with a male accomplice to collect the money just as predicted by Pop Mama. Inside the flat, two men waited along with Pop Mama and us. They were Pehelwan Singh and Lanka Shome. Pehelwan Singh was a wrestler in the state of Uttar Pradesh and had won the state championship in his youth. A knee injury prevented him from competing at the nationals and he had to leave the sport he loved. Soon after, he fell in love with a Bengali tourist and married her. He moved to Kolkata, learnt Bengali and joined the police force. Legend had it that during a raid at a smuggler's den in the small by- lanes of North Kolkata, he was abandoned by the police force when goons outnumbered them. Half a dozen machete wielding men blocked both exits to the lane that could facilitate escape. His police revolver was lost in the skirmish. Undeterred, Pehelwan Singh warned the heavily armed men of dire consequences as his assailants crept towards him. Some gangsters also pounced upon him from the thatched rooftops. Pehelwan Singh fought them with his bare hands. Vicious machete blows did not deter him. He seized a machete from an attacker and launched a counter offensive so fierce that the street battle turned into a bloodbath of unprecedented horror. When the municipality came to clear up the mess, the cleaners either threw up or went into complete shock at the sight of the gore.

Eleven men had been hacked to death in as many minutes. When Pehelwan Singh emerged from the mangy lane drenched in blood, most of his attackers were lying face down in the open gutters on both sides. Their oozing blood was turning the water in the drains into a nauseating pink. Alarmed onlookers of the slum banged the feeble doors of their tumbledown hutments and held their bodies against them as added support. Pehelwan Singh stumbled out of the ghetto with a blood stained machete. Scared eyes gazed at him from all around the neighbourhood windows. He hailed cab after cab to no avail. No one wanted a bloodied machete wielding passenger with an arm almost cut open and dislocated from the wrist. Pehelwan Singh walked to a hospital. His recovery was remarkable. He was back on duty after five months in hospital. The presiding doctor, astonished by his comeback affectionately termed him the Rambo of India. The most surprising thing was that Pehelwan Singh could always crack a joke about the incident, which included how he felt when he received machete blows on his torso one after another. Generally the listener would freeze at the graphic account. He added fuel to the furnace by either taking off his shirt or lifting the leg of his trousers to reveal marks that the best make up artists would fail to create.

Pop Mama's second handyman, Lanka Shome had not progressed at his job as he was always under scrutiny for torturing suspects. The investigations would be a sham, more often than not. He invariably got away because the department loved him. They needed ruthless and dangerous men like him when the law was not enough to contain criminals. Equipped with inferior weapons and shackled in bureaucratic handcuffs, they realised the value of fearless men like Lanka Shome. He acquired the nickname, Lanka due to the lavish use of red chillies on miscreants. The police often dealt with criminals strong enough to break their interrogators. But with Lanka Shome on their team, it was always a win-win situation. Once, Lanka Shome was posted at a Central Kolkata cinema hall to shoo away black marketers. When a foolish racketeer abused him by calling him a government sanctioned pickpocket, Lanka Shome punched him in the chest. The recipient of the blow took off like an unmanned rocket and crashed into an aquarium. Some eyewitnesses said that his heart had instantly stopped beating while others swore that it had literally popped out of his mouth from the impact. No one knew the truth because Lanka Shome never spoke about the occasion. He had gathered the wiggling fishes from the street and forced them down the black marketer's throat. It was not certain if the blow had killed the man or his death resulted from the forcible insertion of fish down his gullet. In the inquiry that ensued, Lanka Shome was released due to a fudged report by the police department. It said that neither the blow, nor asphyxiation by gulping live fish was the cause for the unfortunate death. Being a hardcore vegetarian, the sheer distaste for fish had killed the man.

Whatever the truth, these men were legends. I had heard their stories from Kirit and it seemed surreal to see them at such close quarters. When I shook Lanka Shome's hand, my entire palm disappeared into his grip. Each of his thick fingers resembled a large plantain. Like Pehelwan Singh, he was gifted with brute strength and the friendly grip almost gave me an instant cure for my three-day old constipation for which I was taking psyllium husk at night. He saw through my fright and his eyes lit in amusement.

Jivika walked into the neighbourhood convenience store to stay out of sight. Bilal and his male accomplice, an equally short and unpleasant looking man with receding hairline, walked up to the flat on the third floor. We were chatting in the master bedroom. It had a king-sized bed and mirrors on all four walls and the ceiling, facilitating Pop Mama's co-curricular activities. When the bell rang, I nearly jumped out of my body. Pop Mama asked Kirit to open the door and raised a finger to his lips. We shut up at once.

Kirit walked out confidently to the living room while Pluto, Sig and I watched the proceedings from the crack in the bedroom door. He looked into the eyehole. Pop Mama's accomplices were already positioned in the kitchen and storeroom. Pop Mama had slumped into the sofa and lit a Dunhill. He was not in the least perturbed and appeared to be expecting old friends. Kirit showed a victory sign with his index and middle fingers. I wondered why. A month later, while pondering the events of that day, I realised that he had indicated the number of visitors.

As soon as the door opened, Bilal and his accomplice stepped in forcefully, almost pushing over Kirit. Bilal saw Pop Mama and rudely inquired his identity. Kirit said that Pop Mama was his uncle and was present to pay on behalf of the boys. Pop Mama smiled at them, happy that they had joined the party. He told the aggressive men that he wanted to be certain that there were indeed recipients of the loot and that his nephew was not swindling him. From the distance, we could read the amusement on Kirit's face. 'Where is the money?' Bilal demanded as he walked up to Pop Mama, the accomplice by his side. Pop Mama asked the men to enjoy a cup of tea before business.

Bilal Majid had had enough. He zipped out a long razor from his hip pocket and unsheathed it with the hope of scaring Pop Mama. Pop Mama laughed out aloud as Pehelwan Singh casually walked out of the storeroom. Lanka Shome emerged from the kitchen with a large, raw plantain hanging from his belt like a loaded gun. It was smeared with red ground chillies. Bilal's accomplice sensed danger. He jumped over the couch and dashed towards the door. But Pehelwan Singh had already blocked the exit.

Bilal's accomplice knew Pehelwan Singh. He fell at his feet. He pleaded that he did not know that the boys were under his protection. A gun had appeared in Pop Mama's hand and Bilal stood quietly in his tracks, his mind racing to find an escape route. Before Pop Mama could ask, Pehelwan Singh said that Bilal's accomplice, Kaalia, was a former pickpocket. Kaalia kept holding Pehelwan Singh's feet and revealed that he was Bilal's neighbour and only helping him to collect the blackmail money. He would be paid rupees 2000 for his efforts. He confessed that his wife, Shakila made the threatening phone calls to the household where Jivika was employed.

Watching the events unfold from the bedroom, I was surprised how quickly Kaalia came out with the story that kept us intrigued for weeks. We were pushing each other by now to get a better view of the living room. I was glad that we had sought Pop Mama's assistance. This was too complicated for us to handle on our own. Pehelwan Singh asked Kaalia if he should beat him up. Kaalia let out a yowling cry and promised that he had stopped picking pockets. He added that he was working in a tannery in Tangra now, the city's Chinatown district. He profusely apologised for succumbing to the temptation of picking up some easy money. Pehelwan Singh said that he would let him go, but if any of the boys of Vanilla Apartments fell down the stairs in their own home, he would blame Kaalia and pick him up for the hiding of a lifetime. Kaalia knew who was in charge and ran towards Pop Mama. He held his feet and pitifully begged Pop Mama to sanction his release. He blurted out that Jivika was hiding in the neighbourhood convenience store.

Pop Mama instructed him to bring Jivika to the flat. Inside the room, we thought this was foolish, for the minute he stepped out, he would scram. But we were wrong.

Obviously Kaalia knew Pehelwan Singh well and visualised his plight if he scooted or tipped off Jivika. He had started towards the door to fetch Jivika when Pop Mama asked him to stop. Kaalia froze in his tracks. Pop Mama asked him to empty his wallet. Leaving him with only the bus fare, Pop Mama added that if Shakila ever called anyone in Vanilla Apartments, no one would ever see her again. Kaalia promised that would never happen and blurted out his address for everyone to hear. He said that Pop Mama could check on them whenever he wished. Kaalia thanked the policemen for the new lifeline and left in a hurry.

Deserted by his ally, Bilal was not sure how to react. Pop Mama asked him to start talking. That was the power of the police. Bilal said that he was a tailor by profession. The cloth factory that employed him had recently locked out for which he could not feed his three children and undertook the seedy venture.

'Will they be happy when they find out how you financed their education?' Pop Mama was too gentle with the criminal. Realising he was trapped, Bilal played the smart card. He admitted that he had made a mistake and should also be given a chance to reform. Pop Mama stubbed out his cigarette in the crystal ashtray while Bilal eyed the classy Omega on his wrist. Pop Mama said that he was considering it, but he would have to speak with Jivika before coming to a decision.

There was a knock on the door and Lanka Shome whisked it

open. Jivika stood there with Kaalia. At the sight of Lanka Shome, she knew something was wrong. Recovering quickly, she turned and attempted to make a run for it. But Lanka Shome had been in this business for too long. He grabbed her long flowing hair and pulled her back into the room. Jivika was lucky that her head did not snap from the force of the whisk. The door was shut and Kaalia left the premise as quickly as possible. Lanka Shome kept holding Jivika's hair and did not let go. Jivika squealed that she would call the police. Lanka Shome and Pehelwan Singh laughed heartily. Jivika was shocked to learn that the police had already heard her call. 'Madam, we are here to serve,' Lanka Shome laughed. 'And protect,' added Pehelwan Singh.

Jivika shut up at once, realising that she had been led into a trap. She glanced at Kirit, now seated next to Pop Mama. Her eyes glowed with hate. Without preamble, Pop Mama asked Jivika how many children she had. Breathlessly, she replied that she was not a mother. At her sudden confession, Bilal headed for the door. But Pehelwan Singh caught his arm and twisted it violently behind his back. Bilal's face was contorted beyond recognition and he yelped like a puppy that had been run over by a careless toddler's tricycle. Pehelwan Singh applied a little more pressure causing Bilal to go on his toes. 'He wants to grow taller. Here, let me help him a little,' he laughed. By then, Bilal was standing so high on his toes that he resembled a ballet dancer practicing for a recital. I thought he might faint.

Lanka Shome still held on to Jivika's hair. Knowing the strength of his grip, I was afraid that Jivika could lose all her lustrous hair that evening. Pluto whispered to us, 'I just thought of the most apt slogan for the 'Happy Hair' commercial.'

'What?' I was not sure what he meant.

'Breaking news for breaking hair! Stop breakage with Happy Hair shampoo and conditioner,' Pluto giggled as he added a new dimension to the shampoo commercial we saw everyday on TV. We experienced mixed feelings. On one hand, we were happy that justice was being meted out; on another hand, it was shocking to see two adults being humiliated like this. Lanka Shome asked Jivika to answer all questions truthfully and completely, unless she wished to be lifted off her feet by her hair.

Under duress, Jivika confessed that Bilal was not her husband. He was a pimp who guided her to frame people. They had been working together for nearly two years. She was a registered nurse who seduced the men in the homes where she worked as a caregiver. He blackmailed them and received a commission. Bilal countered the claim by saying that Jivika was his wife.

Pop Mama smiled, 'We can sort it out, can't we, Lanka?' Lanka Shome, still holding Jivika by her hair, pinned her face down on the teakwood centre table and gagged her mouth with a handkerchief. She was handcuffed. We were trembling inside the room in anticipation of the fearful unknown when Pop Mama asked Kirit to leave the living room. Kirit joined us in the bedroom and jostled for a prime position near the crack of the door. Pop Mama knew we were watching and stood up. He walked briskly towards the bedroom and pulled the door shut.

Jivika and Bilal's muted howls were deafening. My knees began to tremble in apprehension. Sig rushed to the bathroom and threw up. Pluto wasn't blinking. Kirit was the most stable amongst us, but even he looked slightly shaken. I considered walking out and requesting Pop Mama to let them go but could not bring myself to do it. My head was throbbing when we emerged from the bedroom after Jivika and Bilal had left. We thanked Pop Mama and his police thugs for their support. Jivika's admission of the truth had been swift. She was a habitual blackmailer and Bilal was indeed her lawfully wedded husband. We had no way of knowing what happened in the living room that led to her quick confession. Jivika and Bilal decamped from our lives forever. We were free.

# CHAPTER ELEVEN

# *Lifelines*

$\mathcal{C}$heap labour has never been in short supply in India. Complicated city existence is bearable due to a willing and able stream of cooks, maids, drivers, guards and cleaners from surrounding villages. They work for long hours and without their contribution, life comes to a screeching halt.

The wealthy can afford to employ an army of servants, chauffeurs and gardeners. However, a standard upwardly mobile middle-class family can also boast of a full-timer who works all day and stays in the same household to slave again the next day without losing time in travel. They can also keep a part-timer for other household errands. Often, duties expected of domestic servants are not very clearly defined. Their responsibilities vary from one household to the other, depending on the need and set up.

In the mid-eighties and throughout the nineties, full-timers were common in Vanilla Apartments and all the other high-rise buildings in the area. No family survived without domestic help. Villagers inadept and unsure of the ways of the city came without any recommendation but were hired simply based on trust. Prior experience was not an imperative and no proof of identity was required. They stayed with the family either inside the same flat or had a room in the staff quarters housed in the rear portion of the building, almost hidden from the residents' view. They only went to their quarters to sleep at night or for an afternoon nap as they spent majority of their waking hours with their employers.

Part-timers arrived in the morning to wash buckets full of dirty clothes, scrub utensils sticky from morsels of food left from the previous night, and sweep and swab the floors carelessly stamped by their employers' expensive shoes. They were quick on their feet for they had no time to waste, hopping from one house to another. The more reliable and efficient ones completed several assignments a day and were in high demand. Their rates were higher and whims more varied than their lesser counterparts.

The *presswalas* ironed clothes back to their old glory after maids gave them a vicious manual beating to take all the dirt and grime out. Dukhi, our *presswala* was stationed in front of Vanilla Apartments. Rickety like a rotting bamboo stick, he stood behind his ironing cart and pressed hundreds of clothes every day with the aid of his son, Sukhi. Although his main clientele was from Vanilla Apartments, on slower days, he serviced other households in the neighbourhood. No receipt was ever required by a customer nor was any paperwork necessary to keep track of bills. Mistakes were rare. The restored wardrobe would be delivered neatly bundled in thick khaki paper.

Some chauffeurs, distinguished from plain 'drivers' by their uniforms, suffered long and boring days after driving their employers to work. They sat in the heat and dust of noisy parking lots waiting for their employers to emerge from their air-conditioned offices late in the evening. They did or did not wash the cars they drove depending upon their contract but Vanilla Apartments had its very own car washer, Safai. When the building was new, the young man had entered the administration office in search of work. He kept pitching that he could *safai* (clean) everything in the building. In his display of zeal, he repeated the word so many times that Jhola began to call him Safai. The name stuck. Jhola was particularly impressed with Safai's stainless steel muscles that could surely send Hulk Hogan scampering for cover.

Safai was perhaps the most hard-working man I ever knew. He began work exactly at four in the morning and washed eight cars every hour. By the time he took his first break at 10 a.m. he would finish doing nearly fifty cars. He kept track of the owners' fluctuating schedules and planned his work in such a way that cars were ready to go when needed. When he was done, the cars glistened like fine metal. During his break, he chatted with the drivers and chauffeurs who still hung around. His breakfast comprised no less than a dozen bread slices dipped in tea. After the starchy meal he walked into his friend, Kishlu's room in the staff quarters for a power nap. Kishlu, the faithful help at Pluto's would be at work. Safai had no vices. All the money he made went to his wife and son in a nearby village. By noon he would be ready to work again. He picked up some young children from morning school and dropped others off to afternoon school. Later in the evening, he brought back a bunch of kids after cricket and tennis coaching and music and dance lessons. By the time he retrieved all the tired boys and girls back from their daily routines, it would be eight in the evening. Before he rested, he ate a hearty meal. His plate contained a mountain of rice that was hard for a cat to clear with a jump.

Vanilla Apartments had provision for twenty-five rooms in the staff quarters. They were never vacant. The boxy rooms were cramped and there was a perpetual dampness in the walls. Small beds, ceiling fans, mini stoves and earthen water pitchers completed the furnishings. Full-timers were entitled to meals at their employers' homes but some found occasional use of the mini stoves.

These rooms served as lovers' nests too as there were several trysts between the servants and the maids. Although meant to be clandestine, privacy was never practically possible, given the shortage of space and the Nosy Parkers of the buildings. But as long as work was not disrupted and they were not caught doing anything outrageous, most residents stayed away from intruding in the private lives of their employees. These domestic wheel greasers worked in homes for years together and knew each and every friend and relative of their employers. Often, they acted as guardians of the young in the absence of their parents. Employers also treated them as part of their own families. Children never addressed them by their names, as a mark of respect. They would invariably acquire a suffix of a kaka (uncle), dada (brother) or didi (sister) to their names.

Kishlu, the full-timer at the Sen household had been with the family even before Pluto was born. Nirmal and Urmi Sen travelled frequently leaving Kishlu in-charge of Pluto. Kishlu was in his mid thirties when he first arrived from the Birbhum district near West Bengal. He had come to Nirmal Uncle's office to find work as a peon but Nirmal Uncle had nothing to offer him. Kishlu had studied only up to Grade X. Not knowing how to drive a car limited his options. Nirmal Uncle, being a kind and generous man brought him to his ancestral home. He asked Kishlu to help in his father's passionate hobby, gardening. But he insisted that Kishlu would have to study further in his spare time and learn how to drive.

Kishlu was intelligent and understood that few employers

would want him to progress. He accepted the condition gracefully. When Nirmal Uncle and Urmi Aunty moved to Vanilla Apartments with Pluto, he came along with them. Occasionally, he would go back to help out the old man with his gardening, but Nirmal Uncle's prosperous father already had too much help. Kishlu moved into the staff quarters below. Unlike others who took leave once or twice a year to visit their families during the Durga Puja or other festivals, Kishlu had nowhere to go. His parents had passed away and he had strayed from his village.

Kishlu was very popular for his eveready nature to assist and neighbours would often come to the Sens to enlist his help. Since the couple was always on business tours, they did not object to him making some money on the side. Kishlu never made any financial demands. He kept to himself. Pluto referred to him as Kishluda.

Kishlu had attended an evening school for adults and cleared his Grade XII exams with good scores. He had no fear of ridicule or the uncertainty of being in a class where most others were young enough to be his son. Later, when he completed his graduation from technical school, Nirmal Uncle asked Kishlu to move on, now that he was qualified to enjoy a better future. Kishlu was offered a Quality Control job at a nearby factory where most of the skills learnt in school could be put to good use. But he decided to join only on a part-time basis. Nirmal Uncle was disappointed that after all the efforts, Kishlu was not ready to get ahead in life. He was too tied to the Sens and did not wish to move away from them.

Technically the staff quarters could only be availed by a full-timer working in one of the flats. It was not a hostel. Kishlu, now a part-timer at the Sens, did not qualify for the housing. But since everyone had use for him in the building, Nirmal Uncle sought and received special permission for Kishlu to be housed even as a part-timer.

When Urmi Aunty asked him if he wished to get married and start a family of his own, Kishlu revealed that he had been married once. His wife had delivered a stillborn and died during childbirth. She encouraged him to remarry and not be so morose about his earlier loss. But Kishlu was not interested.

Kishlu bought gifts for everyone in the family with his first salary from the factory job. Nirmal Uncle and Urmi Aunty scolded him for spending his entire pay on them. When the month was over and it was time for Kishlu to get paid, Nirmal Uncle gave him his old full-time wages, like he had been doing for many years. But Kishlu's honesty was an example to follow. He said that he could not accept it because he was now a part-time worker at the Sens. On top of that, he pointed out that he virtually did no work because their new part-timer completed everything before he could even get to it. Nirmal Uncle had to force him to carry on with his old salary.

The Sen family's love for Kishlu had grown by the day. But the human mind is a trajectory of thoughts and ideas, good and evil. Who knows what went on in Kishlu's mind? After twenty-five years of being with the Sens, one day Kishlu left without a word.

The Sens had stepped out of town as a family for the first time. They flew to Toronto to attend the silver jubilee wedding celebrations of Urmi Aunty's older brother. Everyone was aware of the rift between Nirmal Uncle and Urmi Aunty but this was a special occasion and the family went to attend the weeklong function. Since there was ample space in their sprawling Oakville home for friends and relatives outside Canada, the Sens decided to extend their stay and spend an extra week there.

Pluto had the trip of his life. His parents were together and that was a rare treat by itself. When the family was ready to return, they spoke with Kishlu over the phone and announced the details of their flight. Kishlu would pick them up from the airport. This was routine when they were out of town for work. In all the years he was with the Sens, Kishlu had never turned up late. Be it the train station or the airport, Kishlu would be waiting with a smile. His hair had turned grey and he had gained some weight over the years but the bright smile made him look much younger.

When the Sens reached Dumdum airport and did not see him there, they tried to call him. Strangely, the phone line seemed disconnected. They brushed it off as some glitch by Kolkata Telephones and knew that Kishlu must be on his way. But when there was no sign of him until almost an hour later, Pluto called me to check if Kishlu had fallen asleep. They were not annoyed with his absence. They were more concerned for their faithful help.

When I walked to Pluto's flat, I saw an incredible sight. The door was open and there was no furniture in sight. There were some people talking in loud tones. 'What's going on here?' I asked the assembled men. 'A new occupant is moving in,' someone replied casually. I was speechless. When Pluto called me back in ten minutes, he had the same reaction. The Sens raced back in a prepaid taxi. By then, I had informed Jhola. When Pluto came in with his parents, Kirit and I were waiting for them at the entrance. Robin and Sig were not around.

Jhola had stopped a stocky, middle-aged man from moving into 4G. A heated argument had broken out. The agitated gentleman,

Manas Palit claimed that he had purchased Flat 4G and was all set to move in. Jhola explained to him that when a flat was sold in the building, it was mandatory for the seller to formally notify the administration office. The office knew nothing of the transaction. The movers waited patiently. They had never faced a problem of this nature and did not know how to deal with the opposition.

But where was Kishlu? A crowd had assembled by that time. It had still not occurred to anyone that Kishlu was the mastermind of this foul play. When Bheem Bahadur checked the staff quarters, he found that Kishlu's room was empty. The door to the room had been left open and all his belongings were gone.

Slowly everyone began to emerge from the haze. Manas Palit had been duped out of eighty thousand rupees in cash, the seemingly throwaway sum he had paid for the flat. Kishlu had forged the property papers and they looked legitimate enough to fool the man's lawyer. He was so convincing that when Manas Palit had come to inspect the place, he never suspected for a moment that Kishlu was not Nirmal Sen, but the family servant.

Kishlu had told him that he was emigrating to Canada with his wife, to be with his son, Aapluto Sen. Although this was not a panic sale, he wanted to make the deal quickly and get on with his new life. Wonder of wonders, Manas Palit claimed to have met Urmi Sen. A woman? With Kishlu? Every new revelation seemed so unbelievable. What had happened to all the furniture? No one knew. Manas Palit said that Kishlu had offered to sell the flat furnished but when he said that he wanted to retain his own items, Kishlu had agreed at once.

Two sofas, three TV sets, refrigerator, aquarium, kitchen appliances, everything was gone. Either he had started selling the

items one by one from the time the Sens had left for Canada or he
may have taken everything with him. Bheem Bahadur said that he
saw the beds were being removed a couple of days ago at night and
even gave a helping hand to the movers. Since Kishlu was such an
old timer, Bheem Bahadur did not bother to ask him any question.
Of all people, Baba had also seen Kishlu the week before, guiding
two men who were carrying away a fridge. Upon being asked, he
had said that the fridge required servicing.

More stories surfaced about Kishlu meeting people along the
way while removing every single item from Flat 4G. Their faces
covered by their hands, Nirmal, Urmi and Pluto Sen sat in the
administration office. Each time he was asked, he would glibly lie
that the Sens were renovating. No one suspected him of any
misdoing because he was always in charge of the affairs of the Sens.

Suddenly Nirmal Sen jumped up from his seat. It was a Sunday
and the bank were closed. But he desperately wanted to check if
Kishlu had polished money off his bank accounts. Urmi Aunty also
sprung back to life. 'The cars?' she remembered. Kirit and I ran to
the basement to check. The two parking spots allotted to 4G
were empty.

Kishlu cheated the Sens? How could that be possible? They
were his benefactor and he was their caretaker. The family had
done so much for him. Everyone knew that he could die for the
Sens. There must have been some mistake.

Baba informed Sudip Uncle and requested him to consult Pop
Mama but he was holidaying in Milan and could not be reached.
Manas Palit realised that he had been swindled. He did not own
the flat. What was worse, he could not file a complaint with the
police. He had succumbed to greed and paid the entire sum in

cash, the source of which he had not disclosed to the income tax authorities. In the event of a police inquiry, he would be in greater trouble.

He resigned to it as a bad debt and vowed to find the swindler by his own means. Finally, Pluto's home was safe but they had lost all their belongings. Left with only the suitcases they had carried to Canada, the Sens walked into their home like zombies high on cocaine. The massive swindle by their most trusted lieutenant left them mute and clouded by grief.

Kishlu had not bought a train or plane ticket using any form of identity, so where could he have disappeared? He had a head start but how far could he have gone in that short time? Kishlu did not have an identity card. When the police took his picture and went to investigate in his village in Birbhum, it transpired that no one there had ever seen him or known anyone by that name! He had lied about his identity from the very beginning. Who knows if he ever had a wife and a stillborn? The police also tried his factory and found out that Kishlu had quit the job weeks ago. No one had any personal information about him.

The most intriguing matter in all of this was the mysterious woman who had posed as Urmi Aunty. No one had ever seen Kishlu with any woman. Never had he spoken about any girlfriend to any of his friends in the building or at the factory. Then Pluto remembered something. When Urmi Aunty had asked him to marry and make a home for himself, Kishlu had shied away. But later, in private he had told Pluto that one day he would leave without a trace along with his wife and then, everyone would miss him. Not fathoming his true intent, Pluto had jokingly asked him for the exact date of such action. Kishlu had laughed and carried on with his work. Pluto also remembered the sight of Kishlu hiding from Danger Baba. 'Was that also an act?' he wondered.

It became clear that Kishlu had been planning this deceit for many years. The financial loss was not so difficult for the Sens to bear. Kishlu could not take anything from their banks as the Sens knew their bankers personally. But he had fled with 80,000 rupees belonging to Manas Palit along with the proceeds of the cars and appliances. The Sens retracted their police complaint. Sudip Uncle opposed this move, 'You're making a big mistake, Mr. Sen. The scoundrel must be caught.'

'Kishlu, or whatever his name was, made a mistake; a very big mistake,' Nirmal Uncle shook his head. 'But he had been a part of the family.' He had only one question to ask his loyal servant of so many years. 'Why?'

'We will let him be in peace,' consented Urmi Aunty. The Sens had taken a trip together as a family for the first time and now agreed upon something after many years. By swinging a Houdini Act, Kishlu had inadvertently brought the distant couple closer.

For several weeks, residents of Vanilla Apartments discussed Kishlu's betrayal. If Kishlu could do this to the Sens, no one could be safe from any domestic help. When it came to servants, tales of both unflinching loyalty and devious betrayals were heard. We have had the same part-timer for over two decades. Lalu's Ma lived in a slum an hour away from Vanilla Apartments. The same month we moved in, Ma had hired her without an interview. When she started working for us, she was the mother of three young children. Lalu was the oldest child and she was referred to as Lalu's mother. 'Lalu's Ma, what did they call you before Lalu was born?' I had asked her shortly after she started with us. Surely she had a name before the advent of her son. But she giggled and looked away and I could not infer the title of her earlier avatar from the twitter. Each time I tried, I came up with the same result. The actual identities of Lalu's Ma and other maids like Monty's Ma or Ghonta's Ma still remain buried like a treasure chest in the deep seas.

Lalu's Ma is now a young grandmother. She still comes in every day and enjoys the benefits of long-term employment such as annual bonuses, extra tips and saris on special occasions. But she has moved on with the times. Her quality of work has taken a back seat. She rushes through cleaning the floor, doing the dishes and washing the clothes in less than an hour. Baba jokes that the speed with which she uses the broom on the floor, she could easily solidify her position in the Indian Women's Hockey Team at the next Olympics. Ma also laments her lax attitude and expects her to grow back her old dedication. But she is supremely confident of Lalu's Ma's unflinching loyalty to the Bose household.

Lalu's Ma works for fewer households now than she did as a younger woman. She had started working at 8G the same day she began with us. Mira Das of 8G was a respected actress in regional cinema. She worked with all the renowned Bengali directors in art films and was much more than just a known face. Although she was never mobbed, she had enough low-key stardom to be recognised and acknowledged everywhere in the city. Lalu's Ma was her part-timer but a constant chaperone when she went to buy her favourite *hilsas* and prawns from the famous fish market of Gariahat. Lalu's Ma's expertise at understanding the texture of fish and papayas, Mira Das' favourite fruit, always saw her accompanying the film actress to the market on Sunday mornings.

Mira Das lived in an ivory tower. To the outside world, she was a cold and heartless woman who had banished her husband from her life and home because they could not agree upon anything. Her husband, Bakul Das was a failed movie director who struggled throughout his life to create path-breaking films. No path was broken by his efforts but he successfully managed to ruin his marriage. He was a brilliant man with progressive ideas way anachronistic for local cinema to adopt and there were no takers for his directorial style. On the other hand, Mira Das lent a Midas touch to every project. Average cinema turned into gold if she chose to take a part. Although she was never the highest paid actress of her time, she was never out of work. While big stars commanded exorbitant fees, Mira Das preferred longevity and charged reasonably. She wanted producers to return even when her films failed.

Mira Das' son, Pranabesh was around the same age as Vick Kundu and Mukul. Pran, as he was popularly known, barely knew his father for Bakul Das was not allowed to step into Vanilla Apartments. He grew up without seeing his father and led a stiflingly sheltered life. Mira Das wanted him to become a film actor. She forbade him from playing with us in the sun for if he grew dark, he would become unsuitable to play lead roles. Pran could not step out in the rain along with teenagers like him to enjoy the first burst of a monsoon shower. Mira Das could not let her son catch a cold. There were some protective shackles for all of us but we broke free and enjoyed a few things outside the rulebook. Pran could not. He lived an unusually quiet life for a teenager, mingled with few people and devoured books. It was a curse to be born into that loneliness. Mira Das chose his friends. When Pran rebelled, he was told that they were special and he could not be seen mixing with the *hoi polloi*. Pran wanted out. He did not enjoy watching

Bengali films, let alone considering having to play a part in them.

Movie sets and dubbing studios were Mira Das' life. She cared deeply for her son but Pran needed to grow up with his lungs full of fresh air. Imported video games lay strewn all around his bedroom. But what he really needed was friends. In moments of loneliness, Pran played the piano. He was a natural and his music teacher was confident that one day he could play his favourite instrument professionally with some major philharmonic orchestra in the world.

It was excruciating to see Pran's barriers. Some kids thought how lucky Pran was to be born as Mira Das' son. But they failed to see that he paid a very heavy price: freedom. Pran was well groomed and so polite that in spite of the distance he maintained with the rest of the world, no one disliked him.

One day, as I walked down Gariahat Road towards Ballygunge Phanri, Mira Das' car slowed down beside me and honked me into attention. The shining silver Mercedes was the only one of its kind in our parking garage and a source of both collective pride and envy for the residents. Pran was driving. Their old chauffeur, Rustom was seated next to him while Mira Das sat in the rear. I hopped in next to Mira Das. The dark windows and heavy air conditioning cut them off from the grim realities of the road. It was a ten-minute ride to my destination. Mira Das was nice to me. She inquired about Baba and Ma and how my studies were proceeding while she kept a close vigilance on Pran. Although he maneuvered the fine vehicle through the easy traffic he was unnecessarily rebuked on several occasions for shoddy handling. I got a first hand glimpse of the overbearing film star.

Mira Das hired a new chauffeur when Rustom passed away.

Rustom had been with Mira Das since she began her acti.ig career. She attended his funeral with Pran and tears trickled down her cheeks from beneath the dark glasses. Pran wept bitterly and Mira Das did not implore him to display restraint. Pran had grown up with Rustom around and the old chauffeur looked after him like his own son when his mother went away on long outdoors.

Vir, a young man with a crew cut and long, sharp-edged sideburns was hired only because of a solid reference from a well-known Director. Mira Das was rightfully possessive of her car and would not let a novice touch it. It was always a joy to see it gliding in and out of the basement garage. Sometimes when we played cricket in front of Tulip Montessori, we would stop the game and watch it move on the road like smooth mayonnaise on rugged toast. We were exempt from the world inside but knew that Mira Das was sitting there, hiding behind her dark glasses and watching us gape at the beauty of the road-glider wafting past. Perhaps she was a tad sad that her son could not play like everyone else on the street. But she was too strong to let her heart rule over her head.

Mira Das was lost in the very world that embraced her with such grace. She was a queen of hearts but her own chambers were filled with a vacuum and she longed for love and acceptance outside her professional life. However, she had an impeccable reputation. She was an attractive film actress exposed to the debauchery of all kinds of men surrounding her. But her integrity was above reproach. She was a no-nonsense person, an intellectual who intimidated the unintelligent with her sharp wit bullets and vast knowledge, both of the arts and the sciences. Most of her spare time was spent watching her own films and critiquing them with the mission to improve her craft. Her only vice was reading cheesy Mills and Boon romantic novels. Flat 8G housed a small library and she never tired of adding to her collection. Books were kept so neatly, it seemed that they had not been touched at all. But she read everything that she owned, at times more than once.

In a short while, Vir gained the confidence of his employer. Although his John Travolta walk from Grease irritated her, he had proved himself worthy by treating her car well. Around the same time, Mira Das' secretary, Kamal was diagnosed with pancreatic cancer and quit his job. The post needed to be filled but Mira Das was in no hurry. She wanted to wait for the right person. Vir took the opportunity to step in. He wanted a shot at the job. After all, he had worked with his referee, the movie director and knew some people in the studio, Mira Das was hesitant at first but agreed to place him on trial. If he failed to identify good projects for her, she would seek a substitute.

Mira Das admired the young man's enthusiasm. Soon Vir was reading proposed scripts and offering his opinion on whether she should undertake the projects. He was blessed with beginners' luck. The films, which he asked Mira Das not to consider, began to fail one after another. Mira Das grew more and more dependant on his amateur advice, which she mistakenly read as wisdom and foresight. Vir was no clairvoyant. Nor did he understand the complex craft of filmmaking. He gave the scripts a cursory glance and passed a layman's opinion. But the successful fluke recommendations rendered him trustworthy in the eyes of Mira Das. And he took full advantage of that.

Pran sat for the SAT test and America called. It was the obvious choice of a good student with great resources. When he left, we knew that he was gone for good. As expected, he did well, got his green card and settled in Boston. During his earlier years in the US, he visited Kolkata once a year but gradually that got pushed to two years and then the trips stopped altogether. Mira Das was still busy and found it difficult to travel to be with her son for an extended period of time.

When Pran moved to California from the East Coast, her trips grew even less frequent. Long flights did not agree with her anymore and her days there were extremely lonely. With her son at work for long hours at a stretch, her holiday would comprise waiting for him to return home. When he did, he was too exhausted and unable to make meaningful conversation. She felt like an intruder in his life and said goodbye to America. She asked Pran to fly to India to see her from then onward. Once when I bumped into her waiting for the lift, she smiled sadly and stated how lucky my parents were to have me with them. I believed that the American sun shone brighter than our own. I told her that I'd rather be basking in the California sun. Mira Das quickly corrected me, 'Remember something Tiger. The fragrance of your own soil comes back to haunt the man who has left his home for another land.'

Mira Das conferred total trust on Vir and he had gradually begun to control her life. Pran had noticed the shift during a short visit and resented it. Vir read the opposition and tightened his grip on Mira Das. Slowly but relentlessly he began the uphill task of pitching mother against son.

When Pran decided to marry an Italian American colleague, Mira Das was keen on breaking her vow and wanted to travel to America to oversee the wedding. But Vir was adamant, 'Pran should come to Kolkata to get married.' When Mira Das tried to reason that the bride's side should get to choose the wedding venue, Vir erupted, scaring Mira Das, 'But this is his homeland.' Vir added that Pran should first fly to Kolkata with his fiancée to seek formal approval from Mira Das.

Reluctantly, Mira Das asked Pran to fly all the way to seek a formal approval. Pran thought that was ridiculous for she had no objection to the alliance and had met the bride on an earlier trip. He could not manage to take any more days off from his busy schedule. Pran did not come and Mira Das refused to travel. The wedding took place without the presence of the groom's nearest and dearest relative: his mother.

Vir had succeeded in creating the first big rift in the small family. Things took a nastier turn when he began to systematically siphon off money. It was easy as he was already in charge of her finances. He had become volatile and Mira Das increasingly grew scared of her chauffeur-turned-secretary. Mira Das had a very comfortable life. But she was not unreasonably extravagant. But Vir's lifestyle underwent a radical change. Mira Das' old Mercedes was gone. Now, she owned a Japanese model of Vir's preference. Officially, it was still Mira Das' car but in reality, she used it only when it was kept free by Vir. The notorious aberrant who wrote his last essay before dropping out of school in Grade VIII, had developed a penchant for Mont Blanc pens. His wife and two boys along with a spinster sister had moved into Flat 8G. Backed by Mira Das' resources and recommendations, the boys started attending Pran's prestigious alma mater. But they were big misfits in their classes.

Signs of grave danger had been spotted by Mira Das' acquaintances. Some among them suggested that she was allowing Vir too much autonomy in every aspect of her life. But Mira Das was trusting to a fault. She failed to see the inherent danger of such unbridled conferment of faith. Vir was going over the top. He had begun to decide the roles she should play without seeking her opinion. And for the first time in all her life, Mira Das tasted failure in her profession. Gradually roles began to dry up. Producers were fed up with Vir's tantrums. The more rejections came, the more aggressive he grew. His boorishness increased no end and he took charge of Mira Das' entire existence. He would not let her take Pran's calls and began to destroy all letters from California.

Pran suspected that something was not right. Whenever he called, Vir said that his hyperactive mother was asleep. In the meantime, word leaked out that Mira Das slept for most part of the day. Vir attributed such uncharacteristic behaviour to her failing health, but inside sources revealed that Vir was feeding her generous doses of opium. Mira Das was so hooked to opium that she was at his mercy.

A major blow landed on the family when Vir got Mira Das to sign the beautiful flat to him. The deal ensured that Mira Das could live there until her death. But Vir would get possession of the flat as its sole owner after she passed away. The callous son who had abandoned his mother to settle in America would have no claim in the property. When Mira Das legalised this absurdity, things became worse for Pran. Pran heard about it through some members of the film fraternity. The docile young man felt helpless. He called home to verify the truth from his mother.

When he accosted Vir of mistreating his mother, Vir promptly handed over the phone to Mira Das. She confirmed that Vir looked after her very well and whatever he had heard were rumours. Pran said that he was coming to Kolkata and Mira Das paused for a while. She blocked the mouthpiece and consulted with Vir. Then she came back on the line and asked him not to bother. Where was Pran when she had asked him to bring his fiancée to Kolkata? Where was he when she needed him? All through the ranting, Pran realised that the words were not her own. She was being prompted. The terror that Pran heard in his mother's voice broke his heart. He realised that Vir's subterfuge had to be exposed without further delay. Feigning frustration, Pran yelled back that he would never come to Kolkata. But he made up his mind to jump the culprit with a sudden visit.

After the call ended, Mira Das went into depression. The thought of being stuck with no one but a crooked secretary and an opium habit hit her hard. Neighbours heard her crying while Vir yelled abuses at her. On the rare occasions she stepped out, her face would be covered with huge sunglasses. Dull bluish marks on her swollen face indicated that Vir's mistreatment of his employer had graduated to corporal. Vir had removed Lalu's Ma from service after she protested the injustice. Lalu's Ma shed tears as she narrated Mira Das' plight to Baba and Ma.

The tactical error of not associating with any neighbour and remaining on a pedestal proved to be a major setback for Mira Das. No one wanted to interfere when she needed them the most. Usually neighbours would step in, complain, protest, call the police or even take the law into their own hands. But in this particular case, no one wanted to get involved. However, the local police station received a tip from an anonymous caller about the happenings at the famous household.

Alerted by the call, Officer-in-Charge, Tej Thakur strolled into Vanilla Apartments unofficially to check on the faded film star. Mira

Das was mortified by his sudden appearance. Vir sat with them, eager to participate in the conversation when Thakur asked him to leave the room. He stood up reluctantly with his fists clenched. But before he left the room, Vir glared at Mira Das. The unspoken threat in his eyes was evident. His controlling manner clearly pointed towards the truth.

After Vir had left the room, Thakur told Mira Das that he knew what was going on in her household. Sweat beads appeared on her forehead. To save herself from another hiding, she showered effusive praises on her confidant and his family. Her over-reaction displayed the crisis at hand. Vir was eavesdropping. He walked in and confronted Thakur, 'I know why you have come here.'

Thakur knew that unless a formal complaint was lodged by Mira Das, Vir would remain cloaked in her immunity. Her support for the miscreant had not only sealed her own fate but also rendered him invincible. 'If there's nothing going on, why do you think people complained?' Thakur asked. Vir shook in rage, 'Malicious neighbours,' he said, 'They spread these stories because they can't tolerate that I stay here with my family.'

'Why does your family have to live here?' Thakur inquired.

'I have long work hours. That's why they moved in.'

'So Mrs. Das doesn't have a problem with that?' He directed the question towards Mira Das. She shook her head but her pupils were frozen in fear.

'I can give my life for this household,' Vir claimed dramatically.

'I hope that day doesn't come soon,' the threat in Thakur's voice was evident. He stood up, gave a short bow to Mira Das and left.

The day Vir's family moved into 8G, Lalu's Ma had come running to our flat. To her horror, she found that Mira Das had been relocated to the floor of the living room while Vir and his wife had occupied the master bedroom. No mattress was laid for her and the greying, hapless film star of yesteryears had to use the folds of her sari as a makeshift bed. On days she dared to raise a feeble protest, Vir rationed her food and opium. Vir's sons shared Pran's room and his sister occupied the guest room.

On a Sunday morning after Thakur had come to check on Mira Das, the doorbell rang at 8G. Vir's sister opened the door and let out a shriek. Pran had come from America! He walked past the confused woman into the living room. The flat did not remotely resemble the home he grew up in. Mira Das' memorabilia and pictures were gone. The frames were all intact but they contained pictures of Vir and his family. The tastefully decorated home had turned into a swine sty. The furniture was the same but the sofa covers were tacky. There was a liquor cabinet filled with expensive whisky. Mira Das never drank alcohol or entertained with any. Pran was swept with an overwhelming sense of sadness. He kept his cool and walked towards his room when Vir stepped out of the master bedroom and blocked his way. He said that his boys were asleep and it was not Pran's room any more. When Mira Das emerged from the bathroom, Pran took several seconds to recognise her. At the sight of her son, she shook like a lone leaf in the face of a hurricane. Pran thought that she was in the middle of a stroke. When he dropped his handbag and jumped towards her to prevent her from slumping to the ground, he realised that it was not a fatal call. Mira Das had either shaken out of fear or it was a withdrawal symptom of the rationed opium. Pran was devastated. He asked his mother to pack right away and come to America on the next available flight. But she had no desire to go anywhere.

Pran was literally pushed out of his own home. He lodged a complaint with the police. But Mira Das continued to protect Vir and the law could not touch him. The fear of being beaten up by Vir and his family and the thought of being denied her daily dosage of opiates led Mira Das to disown her son. Helpless and exhausted of options, Pran spoke to a lawyer. Mira Das continued to protect Vir and nothing could get her out of the misery. Her fate was sealed. She had become a prisoner in her own home.

Pran lost hope. He went back to America. Public interest in Mira Das weaned. Today she lives only in name, a ghost of her glorious past and an opium addict, quietly waiting for death to claim her as its own.

# CHAPTER TWELVE

## First Day First Show

$J$adavpur University was an important seat of learning in Kolkata known for its academic excellence. I did well in the Higher Secondary Exam and Sig excelled in the Joint Entrance Exam that paved our entry there. He joined Engineering while I opted for Humanities. The day I was interviewed by the Department of English, Sig joined me to offer moral support. An erudite Professor judged my half-mast English and asked my view on the controversy surrounding the State Board of Education. For weeks, the city newspapers had been abuzz with criticisms of the Board's grading methodology. An investigative journalist had discovered that in a school in the outskirts of Kolkata, question papers had been leaked the day before the final English exam. Stray reports of several below-average students acing the exam was a hot topic. In another incident, a Board Examiner had forgotten a stack of uncorrected papers in a tramcar. Some had flown off and there was no way to trace them. In that lot, everyone received exactly the same scores, which was perhaps good for those sure to fail but not so for students hoping to score big.

Shortly after, I was delighted to see my name on the admission list. I had sneaked in like a castie, a term we used for slimy gatecrashers, the word originating from castor oil. Those who were admitted to Jadavpur University generally stayed on for five long years to complete their Masters program. But that was perhaps more due to the scarcity of good jobs than an innate inclination to pursue higher learning.

Sig had always been the best student in our group. But while preparing for the tough Joint Entrance Exam, he had improved greatly by sheer application. By the time he was in his second year of Computer Science and Engineering, everyone who knew him was confident that he was poised to shine. Although I whiled away creative energy on philosophical nothings in the long corridors of the English department, I was not faring badly either. Blessed with the speed necessary for verbatim note taking, I did not have to work too hard in the reference libraries outside the classrooms.

Five days a week for four years, Sig and I left together for university. We walked leisurely towards the three-wheeled auto rickshaw stand between Gariahat market and Golpark and hopped in for a hair-raising ride to the university. My haircutter at 'Mona Lisa' salon had once cracked wise, 'When my customers walk in after an auto ride, I don't need a comb to raise their hair for the cut.' The auto rickshaw, colloquially known as autos, could accommodate three grown-ups on the rear seat. But invariably they would carry five passengers, plus the driver. Two passengers would be precariously seated on both sides of the driver. These passengers were weaker in reflexes or simply late arrivals who failed to grab the three legitimate thrones at the back.

The space next to the driver could comfortably seat only a supermodel's posterior. The rest of humanity's derrieres would be out in the open, exposed to the dangers of reaming by neighbouring vehicles. It was rare to find women perched next to the driver. At the sight of the young and beautiful, knights in crisp cotton and sweaty polyester would chivalrously vacate their rear seats and move up next to the driver.

Typically Sig and I sat on both sides of the driver, our arms uncomfortably entwined to prevent a rollover on to the busy streets. We were free to board the next vehicle in the queue, but there was an unsaid protocol to accept what you got. On one occasion, we were seated next to the driver when all three passengers hopped off from the rear. But before we could claim the vacant seats, three menacing eunuchs in garishly coloured saris barged in. As we sheepishly returned back to our tight spaces, they clapped and sang the latest Bollywood songs, all the while mouthing the musical accompaniments. We were certain that we would be extorted out of the cash resting comfortably in our wallets, way before we reached our destination. But the eunuchs were so involved in their singing, they left us alone and we survived the ride.

I would hop off at the Bengal Lamp bus stand in front of the main gate for the Arts sections and Sig would proceed for a few more minutes to the 8B bus stand for access to his department. As a routine, Sig would meet his vivacious girlfriend, Tina there and they would walk together to their classroom. Sig Sanyal and Tina Dutt had been an item for four years. Their romance began when they found themselves seated next to each other on the first day of their class in Grade XI at South Point High School. The school was a knowledge factory that churned out graduates by the thousands. With that many students, it was not possible for all of them to know each other. When Tina wondered why she had not seen Sig around, he reasoned that perhaps she had but there was nothing special about him to remember. She thought he was funny and the first class began in a few minutes. During the class, Sig assisted Tina with a mathematical problem and their friendship was sealed.

That evening when he recounted the story of befriending Tina to all of us, we cheered for him. Sig had found a girlfriend, 'first-day-first-show.' It was a matter of honour to proclaim that we had been present for a new Bollywood release on the very 'first-day-first-show.' The second show, even on the first day would never have the same cache. So also in every thing else in life, 'first-day-first-show' had a special significance.

It took only a few days for their friendship to blossom into romance. Sig was totally devoted to Tina during their four year courtship. They were a normal, steadfast couple with no mushiness or melodrama of new lovers. They had no fights and never made unreasonable demands from each other. They were friends first, a couple later.

Sig would hold Tina's hand to assist her through the treacherous traffic in front of the congested university gates but that was the extent of the physicality of their relationship. Kirit brought to Sig's notice that if he continued in this celibate manner, Tina would surely walk in a matter of time. 'Not touching her is a sign of great disrespect,' Kirit tried to incite Sig. Robin and Pluto agreed instantly, 'Great disrespect.' I decided to keep my opinion to myself. Sig came up with a sincere justification, 'She is worthy of more respect.' Wolf-whistles and lewd gestures followed but did not bother him. He brushed us aside like buzzing flies attacking his delicious fruit custard. Soon, the world's interest in the boring couple diminished into a comfortable simmer. Ever so often, there would be speculation of an imminent wedding. But both Sig and Tina smiled and evaded the topic whenever it surfaced in a public forum.

I liked Tina from the beginning. She lived near Priya Cinema Hall opposite Deshapriya Park. During big banner releases, she never failed to fetch tickets for us using her connections in the neighbourhood. Tickets would be booked in advance many days before a Friday opening and while many aspirants returned in disappointment, we would walk into the theatre on the very first day.

The jerky hand of the large, black and white wall clock in the third floor corridor of the Department of History was set to welcome a lethargic band of world-weary students. Aaina, a close friend of Tina walked towards an open classroom, clutching a tattered notebook across her breasts like a mug of coffee filled to the brim. Classmates dragged themselves alongside her, bored expressions dimming the light off their faces. 'Aaina, I need your help!' a voice begged from behind. She turned around to find an unkempt Sig gazing at her.

'You startled me,' she complained.

'Sorry. I didn't mean to.' Sig was apologetic.

'That's okay. What's wrong? Why're you going around looking like this?' She asked. Sig's world had fallen apart. He looked around and whispered, 'Tina left me.' Aaina was surprised, 'What? Why?'

'She thinks I'm having an affair with you,' Sig muttered.

'What? Since when?' Aaina frowned. Sig could not meet her stare, 'For some time now.' Aaina demanded to know more. 'What does sometime mean? Two days, twenty days, two hundred days?' Sig looked around again to make sure that there were no eavesdroppers, 'A month or so.' Aaina was annoyed, 'That's not good. Why didn't you tell me before?'

'I should've done that,' Sig admitted his mistake.

'Most of the time when we meet, isn't she also around?' Aaina frowned.

'But I spent a lot of time at your place when she went to Bangalore for vacation.' Sig was apologetic. Aaina nodded in agreement, 'That's true. But look, this is really weird. You also visit other female friends of Tina. Why single me out?'

'Absolutely. That's exactly what I asked her. Tina was never the suspicious type. That was one of her great strengths. I don't know what's got into her lately.' Sig wondered. A bigger frown disfigured Aaina's face, 'It's strange that she didn't mention anything to me even though we see each other so often. The two of you have been fighting wars over me and I had no clue?'

'Tina is sure that you're clean. She thinks that I strayed,' Sig blinked repeatedly.

'Well then, just convince her that it's not true. Don't come whining to me,' Aaina was stern. 'I've been trying to, Aaina. Believe me. But it's not working. She doesn't want to see me anymore,' Sig was exasperated.

'Are you sure that she's not seeing anyone else? Maybe she wants to get rid of you? Perhaps this is an excuse? She may have met someone in Bangalore.' Aaina disrupted an already disoriented Sig.

'No, no, no. I know that's not true,' Sig vehemently opposed her idea.

'How can you be so sure? And if you are sure, how sure are you? 40 percent? 60 percent? 80 percent….?' Aaina continued to quiz him.

'100 percent!' Sig interrupted her.

'Stop acting like a high school kid, Sig. No one can be a

100 percent sure about anything or anyone. You're a student of Science and you should know that by now,' Aaina was sarcastic. But Sig was adamant, 'I'm a 100 percent sure.'

Their conversation was interrupted. A group of girls entering the classroom pulled Aaina along with them and she almost lost her balance. She smiled at their prank and promised to join them in a minute. Then she addressed Sig in a hushed tone, 'What am I supposed to do?'

Sig moved closer to her and croaked, 'Please convince her that none of this is true. She'll believe you.' Aaina rolled her eyes, 'Oh come on Sig, grow up now. I'm a close second to the prime suspect, even if she hasn't said it to me.' Sig was desperate, 'I know she will believe you. But she needs to hear it from you. She trusts you.'

'Doesn't look like it,' Aaina made a face and glanced at her watch. 'Look, I'm getting late for class.' Sig begged, 'Please?' Aaina's irritation was mounting, 'I don't think that is the best thing to do under the circumstances.' Sig looked as if he would fall at her feet. Aaina sensed that Sig may do something silly and played it safe. She continued, 'But if you insist, I'll have a word with her.' Sig looked relieved like he had just exited from a prison. 'Thanks, Aaina. You're the best. When will you call her?' Aaina shrugged, 'I don't know. Sometime.' Sig gave her a defeated look again. Finally, Aaina took pity on him, 'Okay, tonight. Happy now?' Sig's eyes lit up like a signal, 'And then you'll call me?'

'Umm.hmm,' Aaina agreed.

At that moment, Professor Ghosh entered the classroom and the students greeted him with a loud good morning wish. Sig knew that it was time for Aaina to leave. He thanked her for her support to get through a difficult time. Aaina turned and walked into the classroom. By the time she settled down on the front bench, the class was about to commence. Sig was still staring at her from outside. Aaina did not want to draw any more attention from her over-observant classmates than she already had. A student from the Computer Science department with a steady girlfriend had walked across to the other end of the campus in a state of disarray for a hushed tête-à-tête with a sexy, disreputable student in the History Department. That would make interesting fodder for the gossip mongrels. Aaina gave Sig a thumbs-up and her assurance lit him up. Sig departed quickly, in better condition than he had arrived.

The name Aaina had an element of strangeness to it, for literally it meant mirror. She lived near the Lake Market and within walking distance of Tina's home on Lake View Road. They hung out together and shared their joys and woes of life. Many a time she would walk up to Tina's place in the morning. A sumptuous breakfast prepared by Tina's grandmother would follow. Fed to their necks, they would take an auto rickshaw from the intersection of Lake View Road and the long and busy Rashbehari Avenue to Gariahat junction for a bumpy connecting ride towards the university.

Aaina was a daredevil who dexterously juggled a string of boyfriends and successfully maintained a longer waiting list of suitors. Rumour had it that she had seduced her uncle when she was still in high school and blackmailed him thereafter. She had also got a schoolteacher, Upen Jalan into deep trouble. Upen's part-time maid had chanced upon them in a compromising position and demanded money to keep her mouth shut. When the poor educator refused, the enraged maid leaked the news at a neighbour's house where she also worked.

The neighbour, Nelo Nandi was delighted to find out that Aaina visited the schoolteacher more for Biology drills than for assistance with the other life sciences. It only helped that he was a muscleman for a political party in the neighbourhood. Nelo swooped in at the opportunity. He promised to get the political party involved to expose the molester. The press would be called in to add insult to the injury. Fear overtook the errant academic and he sold off his house to meet Nelo's demand. Paupered, Upen went to live with a kind aunt in the outskirts of the city. All was well for a few months before trouble came knocking at his door all over again. Nelo arrived at Upen's school while he was conducting a class and demanded more money. When Upen pleaded that he now lived from pay cheque to pay cheque, Nelo said that he should have thought of that before exploiting his juvenile student. The threat was clear. If he failed to cough up the mentioned sum within the next couple of days, the press would love to hear the salacious tale of exploitation. Upen begged for mercy but Nelo's demand was unalterable. The next day, the harassed and distraught teacher flung himself out of a local train. He was crushed under its wheels.

There was some gossip about Aaina's ostensible collaboration with Nelo and sharing the money from Upen's house sale. Later, she was the one who let Nelo loose to exert pressure on Upen all over again. No one knew the whole truth but the buzz was loud and clear.

Sex was Aaina's weapon of choice. Although there were prettier girls all around, Aaina attracted the most suitors for her magnetic personality and easy reputation. I knew her quite well as a college mate. She was always nice to me. I was neither suave, nor especially intelligent. I was not talented in music, art or any sport. The paltry pocket money handed down by my honest father was no help in wooing the ladies. Unlike other students, I was safe around Aaina because I had nothing that she could ever desire.

Aaina's father, Ranjan Roy was a corporate heavyweight. On weekends he played bridge with industry heads at the Calcutta Club, a domain of corporate honchos. He was known for his marketing acumen and adorned the boards of several organisations, corporate and charitable. It was no secret that he exploited the wives of junior employees for hedonistic pleasures. If they looked away or assisted in 'fixing' their wives with the boss, a promotion would be imminent. Aaina's mother, Roshni Roy was a former actress in the Bengali film industry and a ravishing beauty in her heyday. But a raging alcohol problem had cost her dearly. She had lost her looks and her teeth were perpetually stained from the incessant chewing of tobacco. She could not find solid employment in the industry any longer. As a survival strategy, she slept around with the nouveau rich producers and financiers of the day. From time to time she landed small and insignificant roles due to the services rendered but no one offered her lead rolls anymore. Roshni Roy and Ranjan Roy were not on talking terms for many years and lived in separate wings of their palatial house. Their hatred for one another was so profound that she would take a shower if she accidentally stepped on his shadow. To counter her move, Ranjan would forcibly retch to display his disgust whenever he spotted his wife in the house. Such a venomous home environment had robbed Aaina of any sense of propriety. She grew up virtually on her own but whenever she got into any controversy, her parents absorbed the blame for creating this young succubus. Aaina was trouble and avoided by many. But due to her generous availability she always had more friends than anyone of us could ever hope for.

That evening, Aaina lay in bed in a black T-shirt and white cotton panties. She was on her tummy and her underwear had slid into her callipygian crevasse. She dialed into a cordless phone, legs crossed and heels nearly touching the base of her spine. At Vanilla Apartments, Sig was in his own kitchen. A brand new cordless phone from Fancy Market dangled from his belt exactly like the raw plantain hanging from Lanka Shome's belt. Sig liked his phone that way. Narrowing his eyes without reason, he whistled the signature tune of *For a Few Dollars More* under his breath. His day was usually made when we addressed him as Squint Eastwood.

As soon as the phone rang, Sig announced that it was for him. Preeti Aunty grumbled that Sig's constant chatting with Tina over the phone had adversely impacted his studies. Sig ignored his mother and walked out of the kitchen. When Aaina's voice came through the line, he concentrated like a neurosurgeon hunched over an operation table, 'What took you so long?'

'Guess what? I was on the phone with Tina all evening.'

'Give me the good news.'

'She admitted to suspecting us. Actually not us, just you. That's good news, isn't it?'

'This is no time for jokes.'

'I'm sorry, Sig. But she wants to say bye bye to you.'

'Didn't you explain…?' Sig began when Aaina interrupted him. 'I did what I could do and she's fine with me. But she thinks that you're a slime ball with the hots for me.'

'There has to be a way,' Sig was crestfallen.

'Actually, there is a way,' Aaina agreed.

'Tell me,' Sig said hastily.

'Tina said that there's a way to test your love. But I'm not sure you want to go there. It's unreasonable,' Aaina stated.

'Don't be so mysterious. You know I'll do anything to get her back,' Sig was eager to know.

'Okay, then listen…'

When Sig confided in me, I was agape in disbelief. 'It's suicide,' I warned Sig. But Sig's mind had been made up. 'Are you with me, or not?' He had put me in a spot. I wanted to help him but his plan was demented. He read my hesitation and his shoulders drooped. 'I thought you were my best friend.' Sig's dramatic mood had overpowered my common sense. I was doomed. I agreed. 'Tomorrow then,' Sig smiled and shook my hand with great vigour.

The next morning Kolkata was humming, as usual. Horns blared on every street. The busy intersection of Lake View Road and Rashbehari Avenue was vibrant with the rush of commuters. Sugarcane carts were in motion. Fruit vendors yelled the price of the prized *haapoos* mango. An umbrella repairman tried hard to grab the attention of anyone with damaged umbrellas. Buses were overloaded with commuters who hung on to protruding steel rods and their dear lives like bats slinging from a tree. People were on the verge of popping out of the fragile, overcrowded trams like tuna trying to escape the bondage of cans. The security guard in a recently robbed sweet shop yawned like a lion after a heavy bison meal. A rickshaw puller offloaded passengers. It was an everyday scene in the area. But that day would not remain ordinary much longer. My foolish friend was on a mission. I would witness it and the memories would be emblasoned in my psyche forever.

Sig and I anxiously waited on the footpath across Tina's house. After every ten seconds, Sig glanced at his watch. I urged him to back out. There was still time. No damage had been done yet. But he was determined to tread on burning charcoal. He was convinced that if he followed Aaina's advice and did the impossible, he could win back Tina's love.

Aaina had already entered Tina's home and we expected them to walk out together to undertake the journey to the university. Both of us were sweating profusely in feverish anticipation.

Finally, after what seemed like a lifetime, Tina stepped out with Aaina. I almost lost my nerve. As I braced myself to run for cover, Sig began to take off all his clothes. He was going ahead with the plan! In a flash, he was naked. He waved to the girls, 'Tina, I love you. Tina, I love you!'

The world around us suddenly muted. The bustling street came to a standstill. A man returning from the fish market, a little boy walking towards his school bus, the security guard with the lion's yawn, Tina's grandmother who had stepped out on the balcony to wave the girls goodbye, the rickshaw puller now in the middle of a testicle scratch, a milkman and his rusted bicycle – every activity on the street was frozen in time. In my mind, those few seconds played out like a slow motion sequence in a classic Bollywood flick.

Sig continued, 'Tina, I love you.' People around us began to recover. They stared at this unbelievable spectacle in utter disbelief. Tina noticed Sig right away. Like every other soul on the street, she was too shocked to react for the first few moments. In the middle of all this, did I spot an all-knowing wicked smile on Aaina's lips? I could not be sure as we were on the opposite footpath. Sig was completely naked but had slipped his sneakers back on. He also sported a red and white Allwyn Trendy wristwatch. Sig, the sanest among us all had lost his mind. He shamelessly kept waving out to Tina.

I had been assigned to pick up Sig's discarded clothes but his act had completely overwhelmed me. I completely forgot the purpose of my presence. Tina exclaimed, 'Oh, my God, Aaina! What's he doing?'

A six-year-old girl was carrying a schoolbag heavier than her own weight when she saw Sig. She pointed out the unbecoming sight to her mother, 'Look, look Ma! That man there is naked.' Her mother noticed Sig and panicked. 'Don't look at him, Sulekha. Don't look!' Sulekha giggled, 'But he's naked.' The tormented mother forcibly turned Sulekha's face away from Sig's direction, took her daughter's hand firmly in her own and walked away briskly. Sulekha kept looking back, giggling all the way. Sig had moved away from his clothes that lay in a heap on the ground and I went along with him in a trance. He yelled again loud for everyone on the street to hear, 'Do you believe me now, Tina? I love you and only you. See, I can do anything for you.'

Tina increased her speed when she saw that all eyes on the street were now fixed on her. Aaina sped up to keep pace. Tina walked so fast that she was panting. She could not conceal her surprise and asked Aaina, 'What's he talking about?' A slyness lit Aaina's face as she shrugged, feigning ignorance, 'I don't know.'

A wandering tramp stepped on Sig's clothes and picked them up. 'It's my lucky day,' he exclaimed. Sig yelled louder, 'I love you Tina. I love youuuuuu.' At his histrionics, a skinny cyclist got distracted and bumped hard into a parked Fiat, making a visible dent on its pristine body. The burly driver jumped out and grabbed the disoriented cyclist. He shook the biker like a coconut tree in the midst of a Florida hurricane, 'I'll kill you, you little ant. I'll melt your bicycle and pour it in your ears.' The trembling cyclist took the threat seriously. To save his functional ears, he pointed towards Sig, 'It's his fault. He distracted me and I bumped into your car.'

The burly driver turned to Sig and fumed in anger. Sig was still calling out to Tina. Frustrated, the burly driver shook the cyclist like ridding a potato sack of lizards and rumbled in his ear, 'Get that puppy dog for me.'

'But…', the cyclist began to protest.

'Now!' the burly man growled. The cyclist's resistance evaporated. He was left with no choice, 'Yes Sir. Sure Sir.'

'Go before I melt your bicycle,' bellowed the burly man. The cyclist broke into a run. He began to head fast towards Sig. I saw him coming and yelled out a warning, 'Sig, run. Run, Sig.'

Sig had already moved away from me. He was walking parallel to Tina and Aaina on the opposite footpath. He heard my cry of warning and noticed the reed thin cyclist running towards him. The sight of the advancing cyclist triggered a panic in him and he broke into a run. The much slower, burly driver ran after the cyclist and urged him on, 'Faster donkey, faster!' The complying cyclist increased his speed, 'Yes, Sir. Thank you, Sir.' Not sure how to help Sig in his hour of need, I began to follow them. Sig gave a final wave to Tina as she stepped into an auto rickshaw. As the vehicle weaved its way through the dense traffic, tumbledown buses almost sandwiched it from both sides, their dirty grey smoke engulfing the beings of the nonchalant passengers. Least perturbed by its puny size and not succumbing to the intimidation by bigger, menacing vehicles, the auto rickshaw sped away like a hare in the middle of a hippopotamus stampede. A middle-aged man with gold-rimmed glasses was examining a pair of khakis at a clothes store that had just opened for business. Although it was early for a clothing store to be open for customers, it turned out to be a blessing for my barren buddy. The middle-aged man saw a strange sight through the glass window of the store. A young man, completely naked but for sneakers and a wristwatch was running on the footpath next to the busy main street. A skinny man, a burly man and another youth were in hot pursuit. Instinctively, he grabbed some clothes off a rack and ran out of the store. A conscientious saleswoman noticed the mini larceny. She tightened the loose ends of her sari and began to chase him.

Rashbehari Avenue was agog with excitement unbeknownst to it. The saleswoman ran hard. 'Get back here,' she ordered the petty thief.

'Can't you see that the poor guy has lost his clothes?' he responded.

'That's his problem,' came the heartless retort.

'You don't have to help. I'll do what's necessary,' he assured her.

'After you pay for the clothes,' she was exasperated.

'Look missy, get back to your store. I'll pay later. I promise,' panted the middle-aged man with the heart of gold.

'Don't you missy me, mister. I have a name.' She yelled at the top of her voice.

'What is it?' he inquired.

'Shimana,' panted the overzealous saleswoman.

'I'm Piyush,' the middle aged man introduced himself.

'I don't care. Get back here,' she screamed as if he had stolen her frontal lobe.

'Stop being hysterical, woman,' Piyush tried to drive sense into her.

'This is daylight robbery. I'll call the police,' an unfit Shimana was slowing down. She croaked, 'I want my clothes back.'

'I haven't taken your clothes. They belong to the store,' Piyush found humour in such a crucial moment.

Sig reached a sleepy executive, formally clad in a tie and dress shoes. He held a rexin briefcase with his employer's logo engraved upon it. His name tag read: Badal Seal. Badal moved out of Sig's trajectory and asked him, 'Hey, do you have the time?' Still running, Sig quickly glanced at his watch. Badal began to run next to him. 'It's 8:50,' Sig told him. Badal panicked, 'Shit man, I'm late again.'

The two way tramcar tracks on Rashbehari Avenue played the role of a street divider. Many people waiting at the tram stops noticed the runners. From the ground floor window of a house, a young woman removed the curtains and looked out to check the commotion. A lascivious smile lit her face as she saw the road-side spectacle. Suddenly a tall man appeared next to her and angrily pulled the curtain over her face, creating a rude interval in her morning delight. The flimsy fabric entered her mouth and she spat it out in disgust.

Sig crossed over to the opposite footpath. Badal Seal, the cyclist, the car driver, Piyush, Shimana and I crossed the street along with him. A bored mendicant was plucking at the lone string of an *ektara* when he saw us approaching. His melancholy switched at the sight of the Pied Piper of Kolkata. Rejuvenated, he joined the run, strumming vigourously. Sig was surprised, 'Why're you running?' The mendicant was happy, 'You're an inspiration dude. Keep going.'

Sig was passing by Triangular Park. A Japanese tourist was busy shooting everything in sight with his movie camera. His female companion saw the runners approaching them, 'Hiro! See, naked man! Shoot him!' Hiro spun around like a top that had just been released. 'I shoot him. Yumi, follow me.' Hiro joined the run, followed by Yumi. Sig continued to run for his life, followed by the mendicant with the string instrument, Badal Seal, skinny cyclist, burly car driver, Piyush, Shimana and new entrants in the race, Hiro and Yumi. His faithful friend, Tiger Bose was yet to quit the race.

Everyone laughed aloud on the street. Two teenaged girls were in splits. Curiosity got the better of a blind man standing next to them, 'What's going on? Will somebody tell me? Why is everyone laughing?'

The young ladies were embarrassed for a brief moment. But one among them gathered the courage to inform him, 'A man's running completely naked and some people are chasing him.' In the true spirit of the moment, the blind man also burst out laughing. At his mirth, the teenagers nearly choked with laughter.

Sig passed a gaudily dressed eunuch gently licking a peeled banana. The eunuch dumped the banana, lifted his sari all the way up to the chest and started running next to Sig, 'Running for our rights, sweet leaf?' Sig was shaken by the new entrant. He always feared eunuchs and believed them to be nothing more than aggressive extortionists. 'I don't have any money,' he cried. The supportive eunuch was offended, 'I don't want your money, rosemary.' Still running, Sig continued, 'My girlfriend said that she'd take me back if I ran naked on Rashbehari Avenue in rush hours. Why're you running?' The eunuch had a twinkle in his eyes, 'For you, sweetass,' and squeezed his bottom. The pinch instantly left a dull red mark on my good friend's fair bottom. Sig cried out from the sting and apprehending further molestation, increased his speed. The eunuch struggled to keep up, 'Wait! Not so fast. Slow down, sweetass. Go easy, tightass. Can't keep up with you, round ass,' and finally ended with, 'fuck you, jackass.' Sig ran and ran and ran. The sequence of his followers had altered. Now he was closely followed by Hiro, who had already begun filming the run, Yumi, who urged her gladiator, Badal the executive, Piyush from the clothes store, the mendicant with the musical accompaniment, Shimana the saleswoman, the skinny cyclist and the burly driver, who was slipping back with every step, and of course, me, the old faithful.

As Sig turned into Dover Lane, I realised that he was heading home on instinct. Panic gripped me. What would the neighbours think if they saw him running naked into the building? If anyone saw us from the balconies what would be our excuse for such outrageous behaviour? How would Bheem Bahadur react? Would the liftman recognise Sig? All these questions were racing through my mind when Sig came face to face with two elderly women. They glared at him with diaphanous distaste. Lily, the taller of the two, twitched her nose as if she had been forced to smell panther dung, 'What is this world coming to? This city is not worth living in anymore.' Her shorter companion realised that Lily's knees had given way. She supported her from dropping to the ground and shouted for assistance, 'Help! Smelling salts. Help! Water.'

Ramesh Bagchi, a distinguished looking man in his late fifties, spotted Sig and the galloping entourage from a distance. He rubbed his eyes and blinked vigourously to make sure he was not hallucinating. Without wasting a minute, he walked up to a public phone booth by the side of the street and dialed a familiar number from memory, 'Hello, Alok? It's Ramesh. Your son is running naked on Dover Lane.' Sig was almost out of breath. He turned another corner into Garcha Road and bumped into the stomach of a uniformed policeman. It was like a springboard but before he could be flung back from the impact, the cop nabbed him.

One by one, Sig's pursuers reached him. They surrounded him and tried to talk at once. But they were all out of breath and it was hard to understand what anyone was saying. Sig struggled to free himself from the law enforcer's clutch. 'Let me go! Let me go!' But the policeman was delighted with his catch, 'You're coming with me to the police station. There, you can tell me who stole your clothes.' The skinny cyclist got back his breath, 'He ruined my bicycle! He'll have to pay for the damage.' The burly car driver roared, 'He destroyed my car. I want compensation.' The mendicant strummed, 'He's my inspiration.' Badal realised that instead of heading for work, he had blindly followed the runners, 'Shit! What am I doing here? What time is it?' he asked again. Instinctively, Sig glanced at his watch and responded, '9:10.' Badal was on the verge of tears, 'I'm dead.' Piyush handed over the clothes to Sig, 'Put these on.' The eunuch was furious and his eyes spat venom at Piyush, 'Brute!' But Piyush was adamant, 'Come on, don't lose your dignity. Wear these.' Shimana objected, 'No, he won't. You haven't paid.' Yumi was so excited she could barely stand still. 'Did you get him, Hiro?' Hiro dripped saliva from his mouth like a dog after a game of catch and fetch. But he was triumphant, 'Yes, yes. Good film, good pictures. Now we go to the newspapers.' We all heard that. If Hiro played out his fantasy, Sig would be displayed in the buff for the viewing delight of the entire city. He had to be stopped. By now a small crowd had gathered and amidst the chaos, Sig called out to me in desperation. 'Stop the tourists, Tiger! Get their camera. Don't let them get to the press.' But Hiro and Yumi had disappeared. Piyush saved the day for us. Sig put on the ill-fitting clothes that he provided so generously. Sig was taken to the Gariahat police station, a few minutes away from the turbulence. Nearly fifty curious and unemployed bystanders joined the expedition.

When we reached the premises, Officer-in-Charge, Tej Thakur demanded an explanation. Abashedly, Sig and I narrated what had transpired. We were afraid to be booked for public indecency or disrupting peace but Thakur and the sub-inspectors broke down into a maniacal laughter. They were sympathetic towards Sig. We were not booked. Instead, we were served tea and sweets. The skinny cyclist had fled; the burly man was pushed out of the police station when he demanded indemnity from Sig. Shimana was paid by Piyush and I emptied my pockets to compensate him.

We fell sixty rupees short of the entire price of the clothing. Sig and I promised to mail the remaining balance to him the same day if he gave us his address. But Piyush was a gentleman. He refused the money and told us not to be this foolish in the future.

Thakur was no less magnanimous. He called up a few major newspapers and TV stations and requested them not to carry Sig's nude pictures to save him and his family further indignity. Alok Sanyal was in office when he received a call from his friend, Ramesh Bagchi claiming to have witnessed an asinine sight involving his son. He returned home early from work and confronted his son. I provided the reliable alibi and assured Alok Uncle that we had been to university together and had returned by the same bus.

Ramesh Bagchi must have seen someone else who looked like Sig. It was Sig's big secret and he made me promise that the events of the day must remain only between the two of us. Kirit, Robin and Pluto never got to know about the momentous episode in their friends' lives. The next morning, Sig bought each and every newspaper. No one had carried any of the pictures we feared might appear in print.

For the first time, Aaina had made a serious miscalculation. She believed that after the livewire action from Sig, Tina would never get back with him. Initially, Tina refused to take Sig's calls and left him confused. Hadn't he done the impossible to win her back? Then why was she behaving like this? He asked me to meet Tina and find out why she had changed her mind. I was reluctant to visit her without an invitation, more because I would now be just as unwelcome as Sig. But Sig was a nag and cajoled me into it.

Aaina had not anticipated this move. My timing had been perfect. Tina was in the shower when I went over to her place. Her grandmother let me in and asked me to wait. She was reluctant to talk to me at first but since I was already there, she did not have the heart to throw me out. After her preliminary ranting subsided and I finally got a chance to speak, I asked her a simple question. 'Why did you ask him to run naked?'

'What?' she was surprised.

'What purpose would that serve? You could have just talked it out,' I suggested.

'Are you also a nutcase like your friend?' she asked. I had touched a raw nerve. She continued, 'Why the hell would I do such a thing?'

'What?' Now it was my turn to be surprised.

In the next few minutes we had worked out that Aaina had instigated Sig's action. Tina had never suggested the nasty punishment for Sig. Aaina was angry with Tina for not trusting her and had taken sweet revenge.

Time does take care of everything. After a few days, the incident was forgotten. Tina fell out with Aaina and was back with Sig. It was evident that Aaina had schemed the embarrassing episode so that Sig and Tina would grow apart. Sig never spoke with Aaina ever again. Aaina's loss was far more than her cheap revenge. She had lost two valuable friendships. I was a casual acquaintance but after the incident, even I crossed the street every time I saw her approaching. What purpose did her vendetta serve? The word was bound to get out at some point. In the privacy of Sig's home, I wondered aloud, 'What a fool she is. Why did she risk telling such a stupid lie?' when Sig replied casually, 'Elementary, my dear Tiger. We "were" having an affair.'

# CHAPTER THIRTEEN

# Sweet Dreams

*I*n the two years since Mukul had left, he wrote only a handful of letters. I had never received an exclusive letter from him although I wrote to him three times in his first year in America. Baba urged him to respond to my letters but he wrote back saying that he was too time-strapped for individual replies. His phone calls had become less frequent. Gradually letters were not fully formed sentences anymore: they were bullet points stating facts. We brushed it all off. After all, he was busy in America.

Along with one of his first letters came pictures of his new life. In one snap, we saw him hanging out with Ishaaq in their kitchen. 'I wonder what they are cooking,' I teased Ma. 'Chicken, not beef or pork,' Ma said without batting an eyelid. Baba released a quick guffaw, something which I had seen only a few times since my birth. It meant that he was amused beyond words. The pictures had a profound effect on my growing desire to take off for America. Mukul's description of the skies and clouds of Nevada increased my yearning to see the American firmament. 'The blue is like denim. The clouds feel like floating scoops of vanilla ice cream,' he went on and on, spellbound with the astounding beauty he had been fortunate to behold.

With a few months left to finish his studies, Mukul came under tremendous stress. He had to find a job and change his student status. If he failed, he would have to return to India. Mukul's industriousness paid off in the end. He landed a job in the same town. We were ecstatic. Two years of hard work had come to fruition. We went to all the temples where Ma had offered special prayers for Mukul. Baba and Ma were not just thankful but now doubly enthused that Mukul would soon be in a position to assist me.

My time was fast approaching. I was studying hard for the GRE. Robin, Sig and Pluto were also studying for the same exam. All our conversations revolved around Barron's guidebook and how much we scored in each practice test session. We pleaded Kirit to apply along with us. But he was not interested. He had already traveled twice to the United States. He had also visited Sudip Uncle's brother many times in England. He had all the financial resources he could ever need, and yet he was not interested in studying in America? We could not understand him.

Kirit Banerjee was constructed from a different alloy. He loved India more than anything else. If anyone criticised our slums, he objected by presenting our rich heritage and prized culture. When others spoke of rampant corruption and crippling bureaucracy, he pointed out our democratic nature and secular ways. At the mention of the population mess, Kirit recognised growing opportunities in our masses. As cars drove too close to us and emitted their smoke to overwork our lachrymals and bursting lungs, he asked us to enjoy the thrill. When there was talk of using seat belts as a safety measure, he called us cowards who aped the west.

Kirit was not applying to a single university abroad but he had great interest in all our applications. He constantly encouraged us to go for our hearts' calling. He was getting ready to join Sudip

Uncle's flourishing export business. He had recently joined his father on a trading trip to Australia and New Zealand. Upon his return, he described these heavens which we had only glimpsed during international cricket. Sig was the most confident and scored more than all of us in the logical and analytical sections. Pluto and Robin went neck to neck. My scores were respectable enough and I believed that I had more than a fighting chance.

Baba had written to Mukul in great detail about my plan to study Creative Writing in his college. He also asked how much money Mukul was making and saddened when his son evaded the question. When Ma probed, Mukul confirmed that he would help me in my effort. To everyone's surprise, Mukul asked me to post my application directly to him. He had connections at the admissions office. He was going to take care of the $75 application fee and push my application not only for an admission but also for a decent scholarship. He would hand it over to them personally and follow up on my behalf.

It was a tremendous boost for us. By this small gesture, Mukul had made us all proud. He advised me to refrain from applying anywhere else. If my mind had been set for his school, what would be the point in wasting valuable money on other applications? 'Every cent matters when it comes to the crunch,' he convinced me.

My application was ready. My references were solid. My GRE and TOEFL scores were sent directly to Henderson. *Magic,* a children's monthly and *News This Week,* a popular weekly had been carrying my articles for some time now. I had grown quite popular as the writer with the strange nom de plume, Tiger Bose. These articles were certain to assist in my admission in the Creative Writing program. I was in my last year of the M.A. program in English.

Physically, I was still in town but mentally, I was ready to soar high in the clear skies of America. I had started to experience the high Mukul had felt a few years ago.

Sig's papers were ready too. He had the best scholarship among all of us. But no matter who fared better, we all stood next to each other. There was no rivalry whatsoever. Kirit faced the potential of losing all his most loved friends to America in the same year. But he was a lion heart. Nothing negative could ruffle him. In fact, he joked that he would have to widen his business base in the United States now that we would all be there. He added that he would have to travel to America frequently because we would not be able to return home for years. Kirit Banerjee came with love in his heart and our victory was far more important than his personal loss.

Pluto's visa would not be a problem. Nirmal Uncle and Urmi Aunty were solvent. In addition to that, Pluto had taken his first visit to America before starting college. He visited an uncle who was a supremely successful businessman in New Jersey. There, he had had the taste of their good life and wanted a piece of it. But what appealed to him mostly about America was the sense of freedom. Freedom to speak, freedom to breathe, freedom to dream. Anyone could joke about 'The President.' To top that, anyone could become 'The President.' In four weeks, he had developed a slight American accent, beating Vick Kundu, who had to stay in Canada for a year before his speech altered. After the trip, his mind was completely made up. He applied to three universities but his first choice was Rutgers because of its proximity to New York City and the successful relatives in New Jersey. Sig and Robin did not care. They just wanted out. And I was all set to join my brother in faraway Henderson, Nevada.

The day Sig's letter of acceptance came from Boston University, we drank so much beer on the terrace that we could not walk back home without each other's help. Luckily for us, Nirmal Uncle and Urmi Aunty were travelling and we stayed over at Pluto's. Chinese food was delivered from Kim Wah restaurant on Garcha Road and we called our homes to say that we were celebrating Sig's acceptance by staying over at Pluto's. Preeti Aunty grumbled to her husband, 'Either it's Tina on the phone or he's staying over at Pluto's.' Alok Uncle was also not too happy that Sig would want to spend the eventful day with his friends instead of the family. But he consented. Tina joined us and drank a lot of beer with us. She had applied to the same universities as Sig and was all set to head off hand-in-hand with her beau. But I knew that someday Sig would move on. When it was time to drop her home, Kirit brought out his old Datsun and we all crammed in to see her off. We sang Elvis, we sang Pink Floyd, we sang Morrison and then we sang Michael Jackson's songs throughout the ride. The excitement of travelling to a new world was simply unbearable.

Within a few days, Robin received his acceptance letter from the University of Syracuse and Pluto was admitted to his first choice, Rutgers. We drank to our hearts' content again. I was not tense for Mukul had confirmed the receipt of my application and I had a letter from the school that they had received my GRE scores. But when a few more days passed without event, the gang urged me to push Mukul to find out the reason for the delay. If he did have such a good rapport with the international admissions office, he should at least save us the anxiety of the extra wait for the postal confirmation. When I brought this idea home to Baba and Ma, they asked me to place a quick call to him. In all these years, we had never called him from India. It seemed strange to be calling up my own brother. My call went to an answering machine. Although I walked back from the phone booth disappointed, my wait ended soon.

When I returned home, I found Baba sitting on his favourite easy chair which had astonishingly stood the test of time. Ma was unusually quiet. Their mood reminded me of the day we had discovered our winning ticket. But something was wrong this time. I just felt it. 'What's the matter?' I asked.

'Mukul had called,' Ma said softly.

'And?' I asked her.

'He said that the school rejected your application.'

'What are you saying?' I stood there stunned in disbelief. I had been denied admission? How could that be? Couldn't Mukul convince them? There was no back up. I had not applied anywhere else. Like a fool, I had completely relied on his advice not to apply anywhere else. I had not even sent my GRE scores to other universities where they were prepared to post even without an extra charge. How could I have been so stupid? My world came crashing down. What would I do now? I had to sit down. Baba did not utter a word but sat with a frown on his face. Ma sat next to me and placed her hand on my shoulder. But nothing could comfort me. The whole nightmare seemed so improbable. With my GRE score, I may not have landed a top scholarship, but not being offered admission to a mediocre college just seemed wrong. What about my recommendations? What about my articles? What about Mukul being an alumni? Nothing counted?

Baba and Ma did not know how to console me. 'What about his great rapport with the admissions office?' I kept on. But with my repeated queries to which they had no answers, I simply accentuated their misery. Their hearts cried for me. Ma began to weep. I held her in my arms and promised that I would make it next year. GRE scores would still be valid, so I could easily use my scores to get admission somewhere else. But as I made the claim, I knew how hard it would be. Mukul's college was average. If I had been rejected there, what hope would I have anywhere else?

I took the failure in my stride, all the while cursing myself for sticking with a single application. Baba and Ma knew that I may have lost a valuable year due to Mukul's misjudgement. They were riddled with cyclopean guilt for they had convinced me to trust Mukul's personal experience instead of applying to several schools, as any sane person in my position would have done.

When I broke the news to my friends, they were shocked. I would not be joining them in America. We would not board the same flight into a new world. Their time had come while mine stood still.

I was slowly recovering from the trauma when I received a letter from Mukul's college. I saw the envelope and thought that finally they had sent me a formal note of regret. Without opening it, I tossed it into the paper bin under my desk.

Two days later, when it was time to clean out the bin, I noticed the letter all over again. My heart throbbing in disappointment, I tore the envelope open for a quick glance before throwing the failure out of my life forever. I could not believe the content. The college had not received my completed application! It was indeed a letter of regret. But they regretted that I had missed the deadline for the Fall semester and urged me to apply for the Spring session next year. Clearly there must have been some mistake. My head was spinning.

When I read out the letter to Ma she asked me to calm down and wait for Baba to return. Then I could discuss it with him. But what would Baba know about America and American universities? I went straight to Sig's place. He was not home. Frustrated, I ran to Pluto's. He was also not around. Damn. Robin was the next option. Thank God he was home. Neelima Aunty opened the door and knew that something was up, 'Is everything alright at home, Tiger?' she asked, genuinely concerned. 'Yes, yes. I'm just excited about something,' I barely managed to smile.

'I can see that,' she relaxed.

'I wanted to discuss something with Robin. About my admission,' I said.

'You gave me a fright, Tiger,' she walked into the kitchen.

My nickname was so popular that almost everyone I knew had started calling me Tiger. Quite often, I reacted late to my real name: Chinmoy.

Robin was surprised to see me at an odd hour. But he knew something important had come up. 'Tiger?' he asked. I passed on the letter to him. He read it quickly and frowned, 'That doesn't make sense.'

'Do you think they made a mistake?' I asked feebly.

'That's ridiculous. This is America,' he shook the letter with all his might and continued, 'They don't make mistakes like this. Mukul didn't submit your application at all.'

'You think so?' I was half-embarrassed and part fuming.

'I'm ready to consider a second opinion,' Robin was enraged.

'Sig and Pluto aren't home,' I declared.

'Kirit is,' Robin was already slipping on his sandals. He called out to Neelima Aunty in the kitchen, 'I'll be back in ten minutes.' We heard Neelima Aunty's voice, 'Where are you off to now? You just came in an hour ago.'

'Yeah, I know. But this is important, okay? I'll be back soon.'

'Don't be late,' we heard her faint reply as we stepped out.

Kirit was watching a moronic sitcom when we walked in. Dolly jumped all over us, ecstatic at the sight of our sudden appearance. But it was time for her weekly bath and Sumita Aunty grabbed her and took her away. Kirit read the letter and exclaimed at the top of his voice, 'Bastard!' Sumita Aunty heard him from the bathroom and hurled across a scathing reprimand, 'Kirit! No swearing in your father's house.'

'Okay, okay, I take it back,' he responded and whispered, 'I'll break his arm next time I see him.'

'So you also think he played a dirty game with me?' I asked. Kirit put a muscular arm on my shoulder, 'I know it's hard for you. But I'll change my name to Bovine Banerjee if I find out that Mukul hasn't tricked you.' I broke down in silent tears. Someone had opened up a well of emotions concealed inside me. My cheeks were glistening and slippery within a few seconds. Kirit and Robin pushed me into the bedroom and shut the door. I had been humiliated enough. They did not want Sumita Aunty to inquire more and add to my agony. They held me and prevented me from slumping to the floor. My mind was too cramped and exhausted at the thought of being betrayed by my own blood. My entire career, my entire life was on the line due to his colossal deception. All this time, my own brother was lying to me? But why did he need to do such a thing? He could have said that he did not wish to help me and that would be the end of it. The family would never force him to do anything for us. Maybe he thought we'd never know.

When I had recovered somewhat, Kirit and Robin walked me down to our flat. Baba was back and had heard the preliminaries from Ma. But he was not sure what she was talking about. My friends stood next to me while I read out the letter to him. He let me read without any interruption. Then he took it from my hand and read it and re-read it two more times. When he was done, he barely managed to say, 'There must have been some mistake.'

'Call him right away and find out,' Ma suggested.

'He must be getting ready to leave for work. It's early in the morning there,' I observed.

'Don't delay. Talk to him before he steps out,' urged Ma. Kirit agreed with her, 'It'll take you a good ten minutes to walk to the phone booth and he may head out by then. Come upstairs and call from my place.'

We had no international calling facility at home for there were often horror stories of subscribers receiving huge bills for calls they had not made. Line tapping by crooked elements was not uncommon. Kirit always asked me to make international calls from his home. Naturally there would be no question of paying him back. But I never misused the option. The money was nothing for him but I hesitated. Baba and Ma asked me to go with Kirit.

Within the next few minutes, Mukul's phone was ringing in another world. A sleepy voice took the call. 'Hello?' It wasn't him.

'Can I speak with Mukul?' I asked as I clenched the letter in my free hand.

'Who's calling?' The voice was polite.

'I'm his brother from India.'

'Oh, hi Tiger, this is Ishaaq, Mukul's friend. Is everything okay at home?' The polite voice had turned friendly.

'Yeah, everything's fine, Ishaaq. Is Mukul around?'

'No, he left for work. I had a night shift and had just gone to bed.'

'Sorry to wake you up, Ishaaq. But I was calling Mukul to find out about my application.'

'Application?'

'Yeah, I had applied to the Creative Writing program at your college.'

'Really? Wow, that's great. Mukul didn't mention anything,' Ishaaq was surprised.

'Maybe he forgot,' I was still trying to protect Mukul.

'Mukul's not the type who forgets. Maybe he wanted to surprise me,' Ishaaq laughed.

'Maybe,' I was at a loss for words.

'Good, now we'll have you here with us. When are you coming? This Fall?' he asked sincerely.

'I don't know. That's what I was calling to find out.'

'I'll leave a note for him to call you back ASAP,' he volunteered.

'Thanks man,' I said when I read the genuineness in his voice.

'How are your parents doing?' Ishaaq was in a mood to chat.

'They're fine. They talk of about you quite often. Could you please add in the note that I had called about my admission?'

'Of course I will. Don't you worry, Tiger. We're here for you.'

'Thanks, Ishaaq. Take care.'

'You too, brother. Bye now.'

'Bye.'

Kirit and Robin had heard the conversation through the speaker. 'His best friend had no clue? What a swine!' Robin was ready to punch Mukul from 8000 miles away.

'He was always secretive,' I did not know what else to say. Kirit patted me on the back, 'Let Rani Aunty and Tanmoy Uncle talk to him when he calls back. You keep your cool.'

'What if he doesn't call back?' I expressed my concern.

'He'll call at some point,' Robin was certain.

'You start the application process for Spring on your own. You don't need his help,' Kirit was charged.

'He's right. Don't let petty squabbles take you away from your goal,' Robin made sense too. But it was hard to ignore this agonising fraud. Kirit thought for a moment and said, 'Everything points out to Mukul being a traitor. But before we crucify him, let's make a call to the admissions office.'

'To be sure?' I asked. Kirit nodded.

'Good idea,' Robin was excited. 'Let's ask them if they had received your application at all and the truth will come out.'

I hesitated to make another long distance call at Kirit's expense. Kirit had spent thousands of rupees to entertain his friends all these years. Why was I reluctant to make a phone call from his line? It did not make sense. He knew what I was thinking and lightened the mood, 'When I visit you in America and call Kolkata from there, don't charge me then.' Robin laughed. I tried to smile. Before I could say anything else, Kirit had snatched the letter from my hand and started dialling the admissions office. The next few minutes established Mukul's treachery. The college had not received an application from a Chinmoy Bose.

When Baba and Ma heard about my phone calls, they were devastated. They believed that the Gods would take care of my applications from then on. Mukul returned the call after a few days. Baba did not bring up the subject. But Ma did. Initially Mukul denied the allegation and claimed to have submitted my application. But when Ma told him about my phone call to the admissions office, he did not have a plausible excuse to offer. He said that due to enormous workload, it had slipped his mind and he had missed the deadline. To cover up his mistake, he had lied. I did not wish to speak with him. Ma promised him that I would apply to the same college on my own now and make it there by spring. Mukul obstinately maintained his weak stand of stress and forgetfulness.

With Robin, Pluto and Sig gone, Vanilla Apartments was not the same. Kirit and I had dropped them off at the airport. Robin and Pluto had taken the same flight while Sig went a week later. But he joined us at the airport to drop them off. In their absence, Kirit and I made it a point to check on their parents from time to time. Aurobindo had moved into Robin's larger room and Pluto and Sig's parents were left alone.

Mukul had stopped writing letters completely after the incident. However, he called once a month barely for a few minutes. Had my parents forgiven him? Who knows? We never brought up the subject. They spoke with him about insignificant things and did not ask much about his life in America anymore.

A few months had gone by. Luckily for me, the school offered the program in spring and I was granted admission. I was writing for *Magic* and *New This Week* as a freelancer and patiently awaiting the day. Pluto was already in New Jersey and Robin was in Syracuse. Sig was in Boston but Tina's visa had been refused. She had broken into pieces. After the misfortune, it was all over for them. There was no formal break up but the long distance between them could not sustain their love. They drifted away with the passage of time.

Finally, my turn had come. When I received the letter of admission, Baba decided to test Mukul one last time. 'It's time for us to ask him to help Tiger with the expenses,' he said. Ma did not cherish the idea but reluctantly agreed. The thought of my parents being cornered to beg for his support revolted me to the core. If he refused, I could not bear their humiliation. Since the lottery, they had never bought anything for themselves. Their lives revolved around their sons and everything had been set aside for Mukul and my future. They had depleted all their resources to maintain Mukul's expenses in America. Now, without his financial assistance, I would be found wanting. When I revealed my thoughts candidly, Ma asked me not to worry about them. They were willing to swallow their pride for me.

Baba must have felt miserable to make the all-important phone call. Ma and I joined him at the phone booth. Mukul claimed to be barely managing his own expenses and was non committal. But Baba did not give up. The conversation was not leading anywhere. Mukul kept providing evasive replies and Baba's frustration was growing with every passing minute. Quite uncharacteristically, Ma snatched the receiver away from Baba's hand. She asked Mukul to reply with a simple 'yes' or 'no.' Could he help Tiger or not? Mukul tried to slither his way around Ma's question but she had tolerated his tomfoolery for too long. The dam had burst and Ma snubbed him royally. Finally, Mukul's answer was a decisive but clear 'no.'

In all the sadness, we came back cleansed with the knowledge that we had been deceived throughout. All the doubts were gone. In a way the phone call brought closure to the incident that had rocked my faith. But along with the knowledge came great apprehension. Ma was eternally optimistic but I knew the uphill task I faced. We could barely prove financial stability for a year. Baba said that he would not let me fail this time. A patient man who never wanted to take a step forward all his life without a cattle prod from my mother had turned activist overnight. Tanmoy Bose, the most unambitious man I had ever known was ready to mortgage his sole possession to fulfill his son's dreams.

I put my foot down. I knew what the flat meant to Ma. She wanted her own home more than anything else. How could I allow them to mortgage it for my unreasonable whim? I could never flourish by accepting this unfair gift. They would be left with nothing. I made it clear that I appreciated their love and sacrifices, but I would not enjoy a single day in America knowing that our home was mortgaged.

I went ahead with the visa interview with whatever little resources we could pool. Baba, Ma and Kirit waited outside. They had accepted my stand and knew that my chances were slim. But they joined me on this life-altering journey. When I walked out after the interview, Baba and Ma were anxiously awaiting my return. Kirit ran towards me. I shook my head but Ma was smiling. She thought that I was repeating the stunt Mukul had pulled at the same spot a few years ago. But Baba understood that it was over. Kirit placed his ever supportive hand on my shoulder. My application for a visa had been rejected! By thumping an unambiguous stamp on my virgin passport, an unknown visa officer had unilaterally decided the course of my life.

Slowly, the enormity of the decision began to sink in. The street beneath my feet had turned into jelly and I was sinking into the quagmire. The skies were closing in, ready to drown me in a nameless darkness. Ma broke down in agonising tears and her face was haunting to watch. I could not look into Baba's eyes. He was completely broken, a dead man. It was numbing to see my parents that day. To lose one's dream is to die. But to see the pain of parents who witness the loss of their child's dream is worse.

Kirit wiped off a quick tear with the back of his hand, a first for him. A crowd had begun to gather around us. Sometimes they cheered with the winner and at other times they closed in on the loser. 'What happened, boss?' 'You didn't get it?' 'There's always a next time.' The comments started coming. Nothing had changed on the ruthless street. Dreams were made and shattered daily. But the drama went on. Kirit ushered us into his car before the crowd swelled any further. No one spoke during the ride back home.

My American dream had ended. When dreams end, does life end too? 'Everything good or bad must pass,' Baba concluded from this nightmare. Mukul called after a gap of three months. He must have checked with the admissions office to see if one Chinmoy Bose from Kolkata was on his way. How relieved he must have felt at my no-show.

A year later, Kirit had the opportunity to travel to Los Angeles for ten days. Sudip Uncle had begun to establish a strong client base in the United States and Kirit would be his representative this time. Before he left, Kirit asked Ma if she wanted him to check on Mukul, who was not far away. His magnanimity was unquestioned. Although he disliked Mukul, he was ready to waste his valuable time over a hard-boiled son who did not care to drop a line to his aging parents. Ma was slightly reluctant. 'But you're not going to the same city,' she tried to reason.

'Henderson is not that far from Los Angeles. I'll be stopping in Las Vegas anyway,' he revealed his plan.

'How long will it take you to get there?' Baba inquired.

'It's less than an hour's drive from Vegas.'

'Go only if it's not inconvenient for you,' Ma gave him Mukul's address. Baba reluctantly approved.

Kirit finished work in Los Angeles and rented a convertible. He drove to Vegas and checked into a hotel. After playing at a casino all night he was ready to drive to Mukul's the next morning. He knew that if he called before showing up, Mukul would find some excuse or the other to avoid him.

When he reached Mukul's working class neighbourhood, he found the address without trouble. There was no doorbell and he knocked on the door. A man covered in grime opened the door and asked him to walk in, 'Come on in Morgan,' he said in a husky voice. 'Morgan?' Kirit was surprised.

'You're the plumber, right?' Kirit smiled, 'No Sir. I'm looking for the tenant, Mukul.'

'Oh, you mean, the Indian guy?' he frowned.

'Yeah,' Kirit was all set to meet Mukul.

'They moved to number 1325. Same street. Here, let me show you.' The unkempt man leaned out of his porch. He directed Kirit a few houses away on the same sidewalk and said, 'Then where's Morgan? He said he's five minutes away.'

'He must be on his way,' Kirit stated the obvious when Morgan's Plumbing Services' vehicle pulled up. Kirit thanked the helpful man and left.

He reached number 1325 and saw a Korean woman hand washing a battered Pontiac. She gazed at the young Indian man in his shining convertible. As he approached her, she turned off the hose.

'Hi there, I'm looking for Mukul Bose. Does he live here?'

'He lives here alright. Who're you?' she inquired.

'Do you know if he's in?' Kirit asked.

'I'll tell you when you tell me where you're from and what do you want to see him for?' she acted stubborn. Kirit did not offer any resistance. Displaying his most charming smile, he said, 'I'm an old friend from India.'

'You're from his hometown in India? But your English is great,' she was surprised.

'So is yours,' Kirit's charm was working. The Korean woman smiled and let him into the small living room. The cheap furniture did not impress Kirit Banerjee, a man with a taste for the finer things in life. 'Are you the landlady?' he asked as he looked around the room like a police dog ready to search for evidence. The Korean woman laughed in amusement, 'You could say that. I'm his wife.' Kirit was jolted out of his relaxed bearing. He had least expected to hear that, 'You're kidding me, right?' The Korean woman frowned, 'Why would I do that?' She asked him to take a seat as she disappeared into a room.

Kirit's mind was working furiously when a sleepy Mukul walked out of the room in shorts and an oversized T-shirt. When he saw Kirit sitting in front of him, he looked as if he had seen a ghost. 'What the hell are-you-doing-here?' he stammered.

'I was in Vegas. So Rani Aunty asked me to drop by and see how you're doing.'

'Oh yeah?' he was taken aback.

'Oh yeah,' Kirit retorted. 'So, how are you doing?' Kirit asked.

'Pretty good. Kirit, I appreciate your stopping by, but I gotta get back to bed. I had a long night.'

'I'll leave in a few minutes. But I've come a long way. Won't you offer me a cup of coffee?' Kirit was deliberately being a nuisance.

'We don't keep coffee in the house,' Mukul said shamelessly.

'How about some tea then?' Kirit Banerjee was hard to shake off. Mukul hesitated. Then he shrugged and addressed the Korean woman who was observing the exchange with great interest, 'Bong-cha, could you please make a cuppa tea for my friend?' Bong-cha did not seem to mind, which suited Kirit.

As soon as she slipped away, Kirit got to work, 'What's going on Mukul?'

'What do you mean?' Mukul tried to act innocent.

'She said she's your wife.'

Mukul joined Kirit on his couch like lightning and grabbed his hand. 'Kirit, you're like my brother.'

'Yeah, I know. But is she your wife?'

'Yes,' Mukul admitted and looked towards the kitchen to make sure that Bong-cha was safely tucked away. Then he continued in a whisper, 'But it doesn't mean a thing.'

'Oh? So this drama is for...'

'My Green Card.'

'I see.'

'But I'll divorce her as soon as I get my GC,' Mukul promised.

'Does she know that?' Kirit asked.

'Are you nuts?' Mukul was afraid Kirit would give him away.

'How long have you been married?'

'Six months,' Mukul confessed.

'Why didn't you tell Rani Aunty that you've moved? They don't even know where you live.'

'Well, I was going to, but...', Mukul was groping for a suitable response but he was no match for Kirit's interrogation skills.

'If you hadn't moved just a few homes down the same street, I wouldn't have found you. What would I say to your folks then? That their son had left without a trace?' Kirit was turning up the heat.

'Please Kirit, try to understand,' Mukul begged.

'Is this how you repay their sacrifice? Don't you think they deserve to know a little more about their son's life?' he asked earnestly.

'No.' Mukul was firm. 'They won't understand. This is America.'

Mukul was right. How could the doting Boses fathom an alliance of this nature? Kirit's Rani Aunty had never eaten a single meal without her husband by her side since 1965, and his Tanmoy Uncle was as befuddled about his good fortune today as he was on the day when Rani Aunty had uttered the 'Y' word.

Bong-cha served tea. Mukul did not utter another word. His eyes pleaded with Kirit not to divulge his secret plan for his unsuspecting wife. Kirit gulped down the tea, thanked Bong-cha and left.

When he returned home he asked me to come up to his place. I walked in and Dolly began to run around in her usual frenzy. Tongue hanging out and saliva dripping on her chest, she settled down next to me to hear Kirit's narration of Mukul's sordid world. When he was through, he sought my opinion on how much he should reveal to my parents. 'Skip the Bong-cha part of the story,' I recommended. 'Mukul has punished them enough.' Kirit congratulated me by thumping my back with a violent pat, 'Spoken like a true Royal Bengal tiger.'

Kirit came home with gifts for all of us, a ritual after every foreign trip. He passed on Mukul's new address to us and confirmed that he was doing well. Baba inquired if Mukul had offered him to stay for the day or taken him out for a meal. Kirit lied point blank. 'He did. But I was in a hurry and had to get back to my hotel.' My parents knew that Kirit was not going to complain. They could tell that he had not been received well but would never have guessed that their son had been married unless Mukul made the fatal blunder of calling up the very next day. The minute Ma said that Kirit had visited us, Mukul assumed that his secret was out. He said that Kirit had thought that his Korean landlady was his wife. When Mukul tried to correct the mistake, Kirit had threatened to malign him by telling his parents that he had clandestinely married her for a green card. Mukul's frantic rambling gave him away. Ma absorbed the story and said quietly, 'But Kirit did not mention any woman.' Mukul was caught in his own trap. When Ma put down the phone, she looked at Baba. He had heard the conversation on the speaker. They knew.

They also knew that Kirit must have told me. And they knew that I had kept this piece of news from them. I saw pride in their eyes. Pride for Kirit. Pride for me.

Mukul had won his heart's desire. He was in America. He was living his dream. But what a price he had paid. He had lost much more than he had gained. He betrayed us, the only three people in the world who would stand up for him. I had missed the American dream, but I was better off. My parents were proud of me. My friends always stood by my side.

The next day, as I walked towards Vanilla Apartments from Gariahat Market, I felt someone staring at me. It was Pandey, the watchman of Tulip Montessori and the devout spectator of our street cricket. He was beaming. As I wondered why, he pointed out three freshly coloured wickets drawn at the same spot that held our cricketing legacy. New young cricketers had moved into the area. They had marked their territory the way we had done many years ago. The street would come alive all over again.